Francis reached into his pocket and brought out a bracelet that she recognized immediately. Surely he was not going to offer her something so valuable!

"No, no," she whispered.

"But it is yours," he insisted, reaching for her hand.

"No," Dia said more loudly, recoiling. "I cannot accept anything so valuable."

Francis, to whom fifty pounds was a trifling sum, made another mistake, saying, "Only fifty pounds. I never missed it."

"You will not miss the bracelet either, for I will not take it back," she retorted sharply. "What sort of 'lady' do you think I am? You cannot buy me with words or money, sir!"

"Indeed," he protested, "I mean this for a gift. There are no—er—strings attached."

"No," she croaked because of a lump that had risen in her throat. "No strings, because I will not accept such a gift. I had thought you were a gentleman, my lord, but it is now obvious that you think me—"

"Adorable," he supplied.

"Something to be purchased?" She dashed a hand across her eyes.

"You do not understand—"

"Oh, yes, I do. It is very plain that you do not consider me to be—"

"Something to be cherished? My dear, I do."

The bracelet, dangling loosely from his hand, created flashes of gold light to reach her tear-filled eyes. "Everyone warned me," she lamented, and ran through the garden to reach the kitchen door.

Stunned, his lordship slumped upon the garden bench. . . .

BOOK YOUR PLACE ON OUR WEBSITE AND MAKE THE READING CONNECTION!

We've created a customized website just for our very special readers, where you can get the inside scoop on everything that's going on with Zebra, Pinnacle and Kensington books.

When you come online, you'll have the exciting opportunity to:

- View covers of upcoming books
- Read sample chapters
- Learn about our future publishing schedule (listed by publication month *and author*)
- Find out when your favorite authors will be visiting a city near you
- Search for and order backlist books from our online catalog
- Check out author bios and background information
- Send e-mail to your favorite authors
- Meet the Kensington staff online
- Join us in weekly chats with authors, readers and other guests
- Get writing guidelines
- AND MUCH MORE!

**Visit our website at
http://www.zebrabooks.com**

A
DOUBTING
LADY

Dorothea Donley

Zebra Books
Kensington Publishing Corp.
http://www.zebrabooks.com

ZEBRA BOOKS are published by

Kensington Publishing Corp.
850 Third Avenue
New York, NY 10022

Copyright © 1999 by Dorothea Donley

Zebra and the Z logo Reg. U.S. Pat. & TM Off.

First Printing: June, 1999
10 9 8 7 6 5 4 3 2 1

Printed in the United States of America

One

"Dia! Dia!" The voice was feeble and plaintive.

"Coming, Mama."

Turning from the window where she had been looking into the cul-de-sac in which they lived, Dia Carlisle entered the room adjoining and threw back a curtain to let sunshine spill indoors. "It is a beautiful day, Mama," she said bracingly.

"I cannot believe it," replied the lady in the bed, though she had turned her head and could see sunlight splashing upon her coverlet. "It has rained for *weeks*."

"Well, Mama, it could not continue forever, else we would be washed away down into the Thames." Dia shoved back another curtain so that sunshine reached her mother's face. "You must rise this morning and have your breakfast in our parlor, where you can look out into the street. All is sparkling."

There was no view from the bedchamber except of a grey neighboring wall, and not much more from the front windows of their home, but the house in which they rented rooms stood in the center of three within the cul-de-sac and at least faced toward the cul-de-sac's entryway, which people could be seen crossing as they walked briskly along Langham Street.

Mrs. Carlisle allowed her daughter to draw her upright, insert her feet into fleecy slippers, drag her to a standing position, and drape a robe about her. With no help from the fragile lady, who seemed stable enough if obliged to exert no effort, Dia propelled her mother inch by inch toward the adjoining room, snatching a hairbrush from a dresser as they passed it.

It was slow progress across their parlor, which was a large ground floor room that had once been the dining salon of this house in the days when it was a private home. The parlor comfortably held all the furniture and shabby treasures of life when Mr. Carlisle had led the family, though Mrs. Carlisle's chamber (once a breakfast room) was small, and Dia's room behind that was even smaller with one narrow window, a single bed, and drab pantry presses put to work as wardrobes.

But the ladies were thankful to be snug, convenient to their church, and generally pampered by the owner's maiden sister, who was kindhearted if not especially bright.

Dia had scarcely settled her mama before a front window and started to brush her hair when Miss Docking tapped and came in with a bowl of gruel.

"Oh see, Mama, what Miss Docking has brought for you," cried Dia, as if this did not happen most mornings.

Her mother accepted the bowl, screwing up her face as though to see it clearly (or to avoid seeing it), and allowed her daughter to tuck a napkin under her chin.

"You are so kind, Miss Docking," Dia said, with double volume as if her words came from two of them.

The landlady, whose hair and garb were dispirited grey, made a growling noise and went out again. As this occurred several times a week, neither Carlisle lady thought much about it. When Papa was living, they had been permitted the use of a cubbyhole by the rear stair as a sort of pantry-kitchen, where they could fix simple meals. Now Dia took her meals belowstairs with other boarders and carried food to her mama, who ate less than a sparrow.

"Has Mr. Whipple gone out?" asked Mrs. Carlisle.

"Yes. I heard him go. That is what awakened me, Mama."

"Like a clock, he is," mentioned her mother, as she did almost every day.

Mr. Whipple was too old for Dia and too young for Mrs.

Carlisle, so neither gave him much thought except to wonder where he went.

When her mother had finished swallowing what Dia spooned into her mouth, the girl took away the napkin and bowl and went belowstairs for her own meal. She would bring Mrs. Carlisle tea when she returned. This would save steps; it was their custom.

The first floor front above them was the domain of Mr. Pond, a civil man of pudgy shape, who was often away as he traveled with "fabrics" or some such thing. Behind him were two young women clerks, who could be heard giggling on the stairs, but who bothered no one as they did not presume to entertain gentlemen callers.

Above Mr. Pond was Mr. Whipple. Miss Docking had her room behind his, and three servants shivered in the attics.

Number 2, Langham Court, was a respectable house, wholly without interest for thieves, peddlers, beaux on the strut, or constables.

Mr. Carlisle had managed tolerably as a single gentlemen on a small patrimony. When, in a weak moment, he had made a match with a pretty, fluffy little lady with only one hundred pounds to her name, and soon thereafter acquired a daughter to gladden his heart, he moved his little family into Number 2 and began to give lessons in English history and literature, Latin, and classical arts to students needing to cram for the upper forms of Harrow or Eton. Mrs. Carlisle, having no ambitions, was content, while Dia, who was as beautiful as was to be expected for a daughter of Zeus and Hera, grew by the age of fourteen into custodian of her parents. She had more common sense than the two of them combined and no personal vanity at all.

After her papa's death, Dia and her mother had continued their placid life, although Mr. Carlisle's students faded away, and now—more than a year and a half later—Dia was beginning to worry about the meeting of expenses. Mrs. Carlisle's doctor had to be paid, the Poor Box at All Souls could not be neglected, and Miss Docking's kinsman would certainly expect to receive his rent!

Dia had no one to consult but herself. Papa had schooled her well in the subjects he knew best, but what parents would pay *her* to teach their hopeful sons? Her mirror told her plainly that she scarcely looked fourteen though actually she was past eighteen.

During the afternoon of that sunny day, when Mrs. Carlisle had been settled for a nap, Dia pored over her papa's account book, knowing their money was sadly low, but hoping to find an error that would favor her. Once, she remembered, Mr. Whipple had sighed that he would surely have to pawn his gold-headed cane. He had not done so, for she saw him carry it from time to time. The memory stayed with her, however, and she wondered now whether there was something she could sell or pawn. A scan of their sitting room was not helpful. She could not carry a piece of furniture to a dealer by herself, and to have a dealer come here would be distressing to her mama.

The sole possibility that came into her mind was the gold bracelet that had belonged to the grandmother she never knew. It was Dia's only piece of jewelry, and the thought of parting with it was painful, yet something must be done. Thirty-five pounds? Fifty? That much money would last them quite some time . . . months. After that, she would have to think of something else.

Perhaps employment of some sort. As a secretary? She wrote neatly. Or a seamstress in the back room of a dress shop? It would mean long hours with poor pay . . . and *who* would watch over her mama while she was away?

Somehow the sunshine seemed to fade outside Number 2.

The bracelet would have to go.

Fifty pounds would carry them for months, and perhaps in that time she could find children to tend . . . or another elderly person she could care for, along with her mama.

Once the decision was made, Dia felt better, more sure, even stronger. Miss Docking agreed for the tweeny to accompany her to Oxford Street, and Dia set off down Great Portland Street, wearing a cloak, a grey bonnet that partially concealed her face, and the gold bracelet on one wrist, hidden by a glove.

At busy Oxford Street she hesitated, wanting to stay in respectable areas, yet shunning expensive ones. The tweeny, delighted to escape an hour of drudgery, followed willingly when Dia turned east.

It was a good choice, for in less than two blocks she had found not one but two jewelers' establishments, and she selected Hendrick's, which seemed cleaner, more genteel, smaller than the other shop. Only one customer was ahead of her, an elderly gentleman talking with Mr. Hendrick himself, whom she easily identified by the jeweler's loupe suspended from a cord about his neck.

Dia could hear movements in a room behind the counter, though no one was in sight. This might mean she would have a chance for private discussion with the jeweler, so she stood aside quietly with her servant, waiting for the other client to leave.

Meanwhile another person came into the shop and waited silently behind her, which was unfortunate, for she wished to be private on such an errand as hers. She avoided looking at the newcomer's face, having only the impression of a large gentleman of some elegance.

"Yes, miss?" The jeweler beckoned her forward as the elderly man was leaving the shop.

Dia was obliged to move to the counter, blushing with embarrassment as she stripped off a glove and extended the wrist with her cherished gold bracelet upon it.

"I would like to sell this," she whispered.

Mr. Hendrick was no stranger to ladies short of funds, so he said gently, "Very pretty, miss, but I do not purchase items—I *make* them."

"Oh!" said Dia, dashed. "I see. Would you be so kind as to give me an estimate of its value and advise where I might go to sell it?" Mortified to be overheard, she colored deeply.

"If you will let me take it in hand to examine it—?" he suggested.

"Oh. Yes," she said, unfastening the bracelet from her arm and handing it to him.

Mr. Hendrick turned it about, counting the hexagonal links and testing the clasp. "Quite old, I think?"

"Yes—my grandmama's."

Mr. Hendrick scanned her youthful face. "Older than that, I expect."

She admitted she did not know. "Papa did not say—just that it belonged to Grandmother Car—" She broke off awkwardly, not wanting to reveal anything that might identify her. "Can you tell me where to take it—and give me some idea of its value?"

The jeweler, having had long experience with ladies in pinched circumstances, and realizing this was no servant girl stealing her mistress's jewelry, said, "Thirty pounds, miss. I can suggest a dealer."

"Thirty? Oh." Dashed still lower, she held out her hand to take back the bauble. "I see. If you will tell me . . ."

At this point a deep, pleasantly resonant voice said, "May I see the bracelet, Mr. Hendrick? It might be just what I want for my—er—sister."

"Certainly, my lord," Mr. Hendrick replied, passing him the bracelet.

Dia stole a look at the gentleman as he, too, counted the links and examined the small, etched loops connecting them. "No name or date, I see," he murmured. "Seems in very good condition. Thirty pounds is not much. Surely nearer to forty, I would think."

Astonished at this help from a stranger, Dia held her breath.

Mr. Hendrick murmured he was thinking of net value, after a dealer's commission.

"Ah," said the stranger, dangling the bracelet across his own wrist, presumably admiring the sheen. He shot a glance at Dia and caught her anxious expression. "Fifty pounds, considering its antiquity. Will you sell it to me, madam?"

She stammered, "Why—yes."

The bracelet disappeared into the gentleman's pocket, and from another pocket he drew a roll of notes, off which he peeled fifty pounds.

"You have solved my problem, madam," he said, looking into an upturned face framed with golden waves and a grey bonnet.

"I am glad," she responded, thinking mostly of her own problem. Tossing the jeweler a half smile, she fled from the store, followed by the wide-eyed servant girl, to whom she whispered, "Say nothing, please!" and so she did not hear the gentleman ask, "Who is she?"

Mr. Hendrick was sorry but he did not know.

So the gentleman nodded briefly and strode out to the kerb, where his curricle waited. He took the reins from his groom with a jerk of head said, "See that grey bonnet, Adam? I want to know where it goes. I'll stay here as long as necessary."

Two carriages with friends passed while he waited, the gentleman in one saying, "Ho, Francis! Shopping for your lady-bird?"

Lord Francis Knollton retorted, "Pawning my watch."

"More likely buying the shop," the friend said, laughing as he drove on.

The second passing friend called, "Team winded?" as he wheeled smartly by.

His lordship ignored this sally. The teasing was good-humored. Ahead, his groom turned north into Great Portland Street behind Grey Bonnet and her little servant. His curiosity was aroused . . . what a modest girl, for such a beauty. The beauties with whom he was accustomed to dance and flirt were spoiled by attention, sometimes haughty, other times too coy, always aware of their own charms. Oh, there were dazzling girls by the score hoping to lure him into matrimony, but he had no illusions about them. He realized, in fact, that his title and fortune meant more to them than the person that was himself.

Nor was he seeking a *chère amie* when he'd sent his groom after Grey Bonnet. One did not often see such modest charm and honest eyes in the shops of London. He was assailed by the conviction that she might need protection from fashionable rakes.

Adam was not long in returning. "Langham Court, m'lord. I was close behind her at that point and almost ran into her when she stopped suddenly. I dodged past, m'lord, and when I looked back they had gone into that court—Langham Court, m'lord. So I turned back, quick like, but I could not tell to which of three houses they went, for they weren't to be seen."

"Never mind," said his lordship. "You did well. She was carrying a sum of money, yet she seems to have reached home safely. Step up."

Adam joined him and was highly gratified to receive the reins.

"Home, please," directed Lord Knollton, pondering to himself, *Carew? Carteret? Carnegie? She started to say Car— something.* He turned his head to Adam. "You say there are three houses in the court? Do you think they have rear doors?"

Adam replied that he would scout and see. "Can't say, m'lord. I'll take a look behind them."

"But she has seen *you.* I had better send the boot boy," Lord Knollton decided. "He's a sharp lad—cannot stay polishing boots for the rest of his life." He fished a coin from his pocket and passed it to the groom. "Keep mum," he warned.

"Certainly, m'lord." All Adam had seen was a grey bonnet. It was ver-ry interesting that his lordship should be concerned about a strange female whose name and address he did not know. But Adam surely knew when to keep his mouth shut.

Lord Knollton was set down at his residence in Upper Brook Street and he went in asking for his youthful stepmother, Lady Lydia Knollton, who called to him fondly from the upper landing.

"Sara is asking for you, Francis. Do come up to see her before you dress. You are taking me to Lady Sefton's dinner, are you not?"

"Indeed I am. And the envy of all the gentlemen I will be," he replied. By this time he had reached Lydia's side and they went together to a family parlor behind the drawing room, where Lady Sara was splashing in her pudding under the benign eye of her besotted nurse.

"Fwancie!" cried her wee ladyship, extending her spoon like a scepter.

Francis at once knelt beside his half sister to take the spoon and scoop pudding into her mouth.

When Francis's father had presented him with a beautiful stepmother no older than himself, the polite world had watched with interest for an explosion that never came. Lydia won everyone. The anticipated intrigue never materialized. Francis and his exquisite stepmother never became romantically involved, only devoted, and by now the *ton* had ceased to whisper or speculate. The old lord's death had changed nothing. Knollton House remained a happy place for all within it. The scandalous idea of a marriage between a stepmother and her stepson had never occurred to those two. Lydia lived mostly in London, Francis mostly at his estate in Gloucestershire, coming to town for main and lesser Seasons. Each pursued an independent life when inside the same walls. With an elderly cousin to lend unshakable propriety to the household, they remained devoted friends.

But not quite close enough for Francis to admit his folly in tracking a young girl he had seen only for a few minutes.

Two

Mrs. Carlisle was stirring when Dia returned, richer by fifty pounds. There was just time to stuff the precious pounds into her bodice and hang up her cloak. Her mama need never know she had been gone, nor for what reason.

There was one tense moment for Dia when Miss Docking knocked to say the post had come belatedly, but there was nothing for anyone except something that appeared to be a business letter for Mr. Pond. "Who else but a merchant could expect letters?" Miss Docking asked. Always being sparing of words, she luckily did not mention Dia's visit to Oxford Street.

"Will Mr. Pond be coming soon?" Dia asked.

Miss Docking shook her head. "Who knows? He is gone more than he's here, but he pays monthly. Business must be good."

Dia nodded. "I hope so. He is a kind man."

Everyone in Number 2 had felt Mr. Pond's benevolence one time or another when he offered ends of bolts. Even Mr. Whipple had been favored with a length of russet wool, which Dia had hemmed into a scarf for him.

Mr. Docking, owner of Number 2, had other properties to manage. He seldom showed his face to them. But Miss Docking always seemed to have time to natter a bit, between counting potatoes and scones. "Enjoy the sunshine this morning, ma'am?" she asked Dia's mother.

Mrs. Carlisle twitched her shoulders. "Well, I *did,* but all the water is not gone. I saw quite a puddle in the court."

"Oh, Mama," protested Dia, "that is only where a cobble has sagged and holds a wee pool. It is not where anyone walks."

Certainly not a hazard for Mrs. Carlisle, who did not even venture into the hall! She was only in her middle forties, with a full head of hair, which was only slightly grey. Strangely, she seemed to have given up on life (if she had ever enjoyed it) and was sinking into a bare sort of existence that both distressed and aggravated her daughter.

Through a front window Dia could see Mr. Whipple turning into Langham Court from the street. He wavered a bit and she hoped he had not been wasting his slim funds on cheap spirits again. Presently they heard him at the front door, fumbling with the latch.

Miss Docking raised her brows and clicked her tongue.

Then Mr. Whipple was safely within the house, and seeing the Carlisles' open door, labeled A, he shuffled over to greet them. Dia was relieved to find that he was not cup shot.

"So delightful to come home to lovely ladies," he declared smoothly enough, doffing his hat.

Miss Docking rolled her eyes and headed for the cellar stairs and her duties.

Dia asked, "Have you enjoyed the sunshine, Mr. Whipple? I hope you walked about in it."

"So I did, so I did, pretty miss."

"I hope you missed the puddle in the court," Mrs. Carlisle said, having nothing else on her mind. "A distressing pool!"

"Puddle? Pool?" He pointed and scrutinized first one foot and then the other. "Dry shod like the Israelites, ma'am. Safe ashore."

Dia twinkled at him. "You are a Tease, sir! I think you have spent the day securely at some coffeehouse or museum."

"Close enough," he replied, drawing a mauled tablet from his pocket. "A bookshop. Making notes for a little essay that I have in mind to submit to the journals."

She had heard talk of journals before and held no confidence in his breaking into print, but was glad for Mr. Whipple to find harmless amusement. He needed a project to fill his time. "Something new?" she asked.

"That's it! A little prod to the city fathers that streets could be cleaner."

"Should fix our sagging cobbles," Mrs. Carlisle inserted single-mindedly.

Dia said, "It is only one cobble, Mama, and—anyway—it is in a private court. I do not know who should be responsible for that."

"Just my point, missy. *Someone* should be accountable to the citizenry," Mr. Whipple declared.

"Should you not complain to Mr. Docking?"

"Oh, no, no, my dear girl. Why, he might raise my rent!"

The young ladies of Room C arrived home then and, seeing the door of Room A standing open, peeped in, said, "G'day," and skittered up the staircase to rearrange their faces before it was time for supper in the cellar.

"It does one good to see pretty faces," said Mr. Whipple with a bow in Dia's direction.

Her mama received a double bow, though she only said, "I hope they did not get their feet wet in the puddle."

The invisible Mr. Docking evidently believed that maintaining his property in good condition was a way of keeping respectable tenants. Though it was necessary to use a cellar room for dining purposes, the whole lower level was neatly whitewashed, and an ancient, but serviceable, carpet lay upon the dining chamber's stone floor. Two raised windows at the front not only admitted light but also gave an excellent view of knees and feet approaching through the courtyard. The oak chairs, set around the table, actually matched, and a large, dim painting of London Pool hung above the grate.

To help her, Miss Docking had three servants: the tweeny who had accompanied Dia to Oxford Street, a cook and part-time duster, and a gangling youth to carry out slops and tend fires. All in all, the tenants were comfortable, and they did not begrudge Mr. Docking his rents.

Dia had known no other home. Her papa's gentility had rubbed off on her, and although her mama's helpless femininity was not *her* style, she was a proper little lady. Poor Papa! He had been reared to something better than a lodging house, but he had accepted his lot gracefully, being without fail both kind and courteous to the lady who had taken his name. Material things had mattered little to him.

To those who knew the small family it was no surprise that Dia was a beautiful girl, since Mr. Carlisle had been a well-proportioned gentleman with no excesses of ears, Adam's apple, or nose, and Mrs. Carlisle—though faded—still wore a clear complexion and sweet face.

Presently, Miss Docking struck her dinner gong, and the two girls could be heard skipping down from above. Others met them in the hall. Like a large, concerted appetite all descended to the cellar, except, that is, Mrs. Carlisle, who preferred to keep her watch upon the courtyard in case other cobbles succumbed to water in some mysterious fashion.

All this time Dia had been extremely conscious of the pound notes secreted in her bosom. She did not *think* they could drop out, but hastily retied her sash more tightly so as to prevent their slipping to the floor. It would have been mortifying to attempt an explanation!

Fortunately, everyone's interest was in food, not in the slight rustle that Dia made when she moved. She, like the rest, was too engrossed to hear furtive footsteps in the hall above.

Lord Knollton had chosen his agent well, for young Harry the boot boy, looking upon his master's odd request as a step to greater things, had smeared his face with a bit of dirt and substituted his own clothes for Knollton livery. Then he'd loped through intervening streets to Langham Court. He soon discovered three houses, none of which had rear doors; they abutted a fence that he was not anxious to scale. Passing it would not provide any ingress to the buildings, but only expose him to view from other places. So he considered the fronts, hopping about the cobblestones on one leg, as if idly playing a game.

Number 1 showed no lights, though darkness was coming on, and the knocker was absent from Number 3, leading him to guess that its occupants had gone from town. He chose to test Number 2.

Approaching from the right, luckily out of Mrs. Carlisle's line of sight, and skipping up five or six steps, he tried the latch carefully; the door opened with a small squeak of protest to a deserted ground floor hall.

"Look for names on doors," Lord Knollton had said.

There was one here. "Carlisle."

He heard nothing from Dia's mama, nor did she hear him. He fixed the name Carlisle in his mind. This being the only name card on the ground floor, and clinks of silverware and china mingled with casual conversation coming from the cellar stairs, he deemed it safe to glide up the stairs to the next level. One door here read *Pond.* Farther back there was another door marked *Misses Froam.* And on the second floor he found *Whipple.* One other door at that level was locked and bore no name.

Harry thought rather astutely that Lord Knollton would have no interest in persons who slept in attics, so he climbed no higher, but glided like a whisper down the stairs again and slipped out into the court, unseen, unheard, and unsuspected.

Lord Knollton received his report without facial expression, though he did reward Harry sufficiently to send the boy whistling as he went to wash his face and resume his livery. Oh, Harry would keep mum for sure!

His lordship, meanwhile, fingered the bracelet in his pocket and debated where to put it. Astonishing the lack of privacy one had! His valet was sure to find the bracelet, and although the man would ask no questions, he would wonder at it's not being mentioned. Damnation! A man should have privacy! Francis spurned lies and wished to make no explanations, so the only solution was to keep the bracelet in hand.

Already his evening clothes were laid out. Before ringing for

Shooker, Francis transferred Miss Carlisle's bracelet to a vase upon the mantel. Then he began to shed his buckskins, and he was just ready to hand them to Shooker when the valet entered. Shooker was followed by a boy with hot water. His lordship continued to strip and hand the valet his clothes before stepping into his bath. He never lolled in hot water. In no time Lord Francis had washed and dried and donned clean underclothes and his black evening breeches. When Shooker went out with the soiled garments, Francis retrieved the bracelet from the vase and slid it into a pocket. The bracelet, temporarily, thus remained hidden upon his lordship's person.

If Francis had left Miss Carlisle's bracelet casually cast upon his dresser, perhaps Shooker would have attached no importance to it. But to mention it casually himself might have caused his valet to mention it, also casually, belowstairs. This meant Lady Lydia's maid might also speak of it to her mistress, and *this* he did not want, although he was not sure why.

Even so, twice during Lady Sefton's evening party, his stepmother had occasion to ask, "What are you jiggling in your pocket, Francis?"

"Oh—my snuffbox," he said.

"Nasty stuff!" she retorted. "I hope you are not overindulging in that!"

"No, no. Do not worry. I am beginning to collect the *boxes*."

Lady Lydia laughed and said she supposed every gentleman must collect something.

Lord Francis said, "Just so." He turned away to friends, realizing he would have to buy several small boxes to make an honest man of himself.

During the course of the evening he noticed, as he had done many times, that what Lydia collected was a circle of admirers. It was reasonable that she should do so, for she had pretty, smiling, kissable lips and an endearing warmth of manner that drew approval. As often before, he rather wondered that she had not contracted another marriage. Then he remembered that her marriage to his father had seemed one of mutual and genuine affection, although there had been such a difference between their ages.

He was loath to step into Parson's Mousetrap, and Lydia seemed to feel the same, though perhaps for different reasons. At least she never tried to press him into a permanent relationship with any debutante of any season.

Meanwhile, at Langham Court, Dia Carlisle was not thinking—or trying not to think—of the gentleman who had bought her bracelet. She kept telling herself that it was the *bracelet* that mattered, not its purchaser. She hoped his sister would wear it and enjoy it—even though it was a simple thing, perhaps less grand than things with which a titled lady customarily adorned herself.

Sunday came, balmy, with gentle breezes to toss a lady's bonnet ribbons. Although Mrs. Carlisle sighed over "dear Mr. Lloyd" at All Souls Church nearby and wondered what his message would be that day, no persuasions stirred her from the parlor with its memories of "dear Papa."

All Souls was a short walk away, and Dia did feel it was perfectly proper for her to venture there alone, yet she also felt some guilt about leaving her mama . . . perhaps now and then, but not every week. So she did not attend the service that day.

Some squares away Lord Knollton was preparing to escort Lady Knollton to St. George's. It was one of the things that she liked about him: He did not spurn a church service. She did not, of course, suspect that his mind was less on hymns and invitations to eternal life than on how to have another look at Miss Carlisle. It had occurred to him that All Souls was the nearest sanctuary to Langham Court. Presumably Dia could walk there if she wished to do it. So he surprised his stepmother, as they went out to their carriage, by asking why they never visited All Souls, the new church of Nash's design.

"Habit, I suppose," she said. "Would you like to go there today? Let us do so by all means."

"What an amiable mama you are!" he teased.

"No. I mean it. The round portico is so unusual. I would like to see inside."

So see it they did, though standing or sitting, coming or going, Francis scanned the congregation without a glimpse of the pretty little creature he sought.

What was there about the girl that had caught his eye? He could not decide. By the age of twenty-five he had met hundreds of young women, all puffed off by anxious mamas. Many were charming, some even prettier than this one (at least as he remembered her), some actually intimidating because of their poise and jewels.

Perhaps . . . perhaps it had been the gratitude in her hazel eyes—and the lightness of her step as she had fled the jeweler's shop.

If he could just think of a plausible reason to call at Number 2 of Langham Court he would do so. But he could not.

Twice he had actually driven his curricle slowly along Langham Street so as to catch a glimpse of the court with Number 2 at its center, though no excuse for calling there occurred to him. "I am something of a fool," he admitted to himself, wondering why.

Lady Lydia, had she known his inner turmoil, would have said, "Spring in the air."

At least Spring had brought Mr. Pond home from his circuit of southern shires, and the whole of Number 2 welcomed him, for his unfailing good humor revitalized the house. Dia actually thought of confessing her money problems to him and asking what sort of employment she might seek when the fifty pounds ran out. Then mortification tied her tongue.

"I see your dear mama is still housebound," Mr. Pond said to Dia. "Needs a tonic, I daresay. Has her doctor seen her?"

"Yes," Dia answered, looking troubled. "She has a tonic and

I make sure that she takes it, but she—well—withdraws more and more."

Mr. Pond declared that would never do. "We must get her out into fresh air, now that Spring has decided to stay."

"Oh, she will never walk outside the door," Dia said despairingly.

"Then we must drag her!"

She had to smile, for she could not imagine even a dray horse succeeding at that.

"I will think of something," Mr. Pond said affirmatively. He had an optimistic nature, which was a large part of his success as a merchant of yard goods. He was not called upon to create a miracle, however, for Lord Francis Knollton acted first.

Lord Francis was sure that the suite marked *Carlisle* was the one he sought. How many of that name lived inside it he did not know, could not guess, and only surmised that little Miss Carlisle had pressing needs for which he might supply assistance. Of course he was acquainted with females of questionable gentility who were only too ready to accept a gentleman's "help." This one, he sensed (and hoped) might be different.

So, leaving Adam and his curricle out of sight in Langham Street, Lord Francis walked into the court, mounted the steps of Number 2, and rapped upon the door marked *Carlisle*.

His angelic quarry opened it and stared at him in astonishment.

"Good day," he said quickly. "I'm Knollton. Remember?"

Of course she remembered him, but she had not known his name, and she was too flustered to admit so.

Across the room, near a window, was seated a lady who looked only mildly surprised at his intrusion. There was enough resemblance for him to know he was confronting Miss Carlisle's mother.

Easing past the girl, who left the door ajar, he went directly across to Mrs. Carlisle. "How do you do, madam. I'm Knollton." He drew a chair to her side and sat down, ignoring the uncertainty of Mrs. Carlisle's daughter. "I already feel that I know you, for I think that I must have seen you at All Souls Church. You do seem familiar. Am I right, madam?"

"Well, yes, Mr. Knollton—"

"*Lord* Knollton, Mama," Dia corrected somewhat breathlessly.

Unfazed, her mama amended, "My lord. All Souls is where we are accustomed to worship—a pleasant walk if the weather is nice, but until now it has been so blustery."

"Oh, no one would wish you to battle storms for the sake of a brief service, although my mother—my stepmother, that is—attended with me last Sunday, and an uplifting service it was! Why did I not see you and Miss Carlisle?"

Mrs. Carlisle shifted a bit in her chair. "The puddles, you see. I should not like to wet my feet."

"My dear lady, the rain is over!"

Mrs. Carlisle shook her head. "How can one be sure? Langham Court still has puddles."

"Does it?" he glanced at Dia, who rolled her eyes.

"Well, one that I can see from here." Mrs. Carlisle gestured to her right and his lordship stretched out his neck to look.

"Only one little dab of a puddle, Mama," Dia reminded, "and it's shrinking fast."

"But England, you know—it can rain anytime, and then there would be no saying how many puddles."

Seeing the subject of puddles might never be exhausted, Dia asked if she could give the gentleman a glass of sherry. Of course she was hoping (although she was glad to have a perfect view of this splendid person) that he would soon go away, for the whole situation was embarrassing. Perversely, he said sherry sounded delightful, so she went across the room to pour a glass for him from her father's amber-colored decanter, one of their few elegant possessions.

Evidently his lordship cared nothing about elegance, for he kept his attention on her mother. "Such a charming young lady, Mrs. Carlisle. I do believe she gets her pretty face from you!"

Mrs. Carlisle by now was swelling with pride. "A very dear

daughter, my lord. I will assure you that her beauty comes from her father—such a pleasing countenance he had!"

Dia's hands were shaking a bit as she filled a glass for the visitor and brought it to him. Having done this, she chose a chair somewhat behind him, where she was not directly in his view and where she could feel more at ease.

"You must not stay closed up like this," he said, shaking a finger at the elder lady. "Next Sunday—yes, I have a plan—I will transport you to All Souls myself!"

Thereupon, he went first to one window and then to the other, where the daylight shone on his sleekly combed brown hair, turning it sorrel. "We can squeeze into my curricle, do you not think? Only two horses, of course, for I should not like to turn four in this court."

Mrs. Carlisle looked interested, but made a feeble protest that it might rain.

"No, no!" he laughed. "I shall not allow that! Besides, if it should dare to rain, Adam—my groom—will hold an umbrella over you."

How could the Carlisle ladies decline? He made it all sound easy and pleasant . . . and besides, they'd have the added delight of arriving in front of the Sunday crowd in such high style.

Before they could accept or refuse, footsteps sounded, a sharp rap came against the half-open door, and Mr. Pond, round as an orange, strode in with a stern eye upon the ladies' visitor.

"Lord Knollton," said Dia hastily, "this is our excellent neighbor, Mr. Pond."

Three

Unconscious of undercurrents, Mrs. Carlisle chirped pleasantly, "Lord Knollton comes to us from All Souls Church."

In a sense he had done so, though his lordship had never expected to be accredited by his connection with any church. He inclined his head politely, and Mr. Pond was obliged to return the bow, if stiffly.

Mr. Pond could recognize a spirited young blood when he saw one, yet circumstances forced him to mind his own manners and be civil in the presence of ladies. He glanced at Dia, noting the pink in her cheeks, and said, "Ah. Yes. Our ladies have not attended services at All Souls in recent weeks due to the weather."

"Nor have I often done so," admitted Lord Knollton somewhat obliquely.

"But we are to go next Sunday," Mrs. Carlisle announced happily. "His lordship will send his curricle for us."

"I will bring it myself," he corrected graciously, which only served to raise Mr. Pond's hackles.

Then Dia, sensing inexplicable friction without understanding it, said, "We are having sherry, Mr. Pond. May I give you some?" And Mr. Pond, who did not trust young bucks around inexperienced girls, and who intended to outstay this one, replied that, yes, she could.

Puzzled by her neighbor's strange attitude, she returned to the amber decanter and poured a second glass.

She could see a certain difference between the two men: the one so splendid in impeccable blue coat with artful neckcloth and biscuit-tan breeches upon muscular legs; the other in black, respectably cut and unobtrusive. She knew Mr. Pond to be both kind and gentlemanly; she *trusted* him. As for the young lord— were not his manners to her mother most civil and had he not done them both a secret and expensive service?

Having given Mr. Pond his glass, she poured a half one and took it to her mother, who began to sip it, almost unaware of doing so, while giving Lord Knollton her opinion of the physical benefits that could be attributed to wine.

At this point, the door still standing open, their conversation attracted the notice of Mr. Whipple, who had come downstairs. He entered, asking, "Is this a party?"

Though the Carlisle ladies never held parties, Dia immediately said, yes, it seemed to be one. She presented him to Lord Knollton and went to pour a fourth glass of sherry.

Meanwhile, Lord Francis was not slow to notice that the attitude of Dia's neighbors was a protective one, and this pleased him, for it told what he had already assumed—that Miss Carlisle was respectable. In fact, a gently bred lady. *How odd,* he thought, *to find a lady in these circumstances!*

And how odd, Dia was thinking, *for a noble to be visiting in Langham Court!*

Mrs. Carlisle, exhilarated by attention and sherry, had quite come out of herself, so to speak, and she was rambling on about rainy spells and church services, her doctor's approval of sherry, Dia's tender care (no mother had better!), puddles, and the imminent advent of Spring.

Fortunately, three men and Dia's mama were sufficient to keep conversation flowing. Dia was able to listen and look pleasant, although puzzled she certainly was by the faintly hostile manner of kind Mr. Pond and gentle Mr. Whipple. They conversed civilly, yet she felt somehow they were unlike themselves—oddly stiff, uncordial.

About Lord Francis Knollton she was even more unsure, but

perhaps that was because she did not know his true nature. In Hendrick's Jewelry Shop he had been decisive; here he was no less sure, yet now seemed to flow with the general conversation. When he addressed her mama he was no less firm—but somehow gentle? Yes, gentle—or at least deferential.

Very likely everyone, with the possible exception of Mrs. Carlisle, was relieved when his lordship set aside his sherry glass and rose to bid Mrs. Carlisle farewell.

"Servant, Pond. Servant, Whipple. I expect we shall meet again. And Miss Carlisle"—he turned the full force of a mesmerizing smile upon her—"of course we will see one another next Sunday."

Dia ventured a curtsy, abbreviated because of Mr. Pond's scowl and Mr. Whipple's nervous agitation.

His lordship returned a slight bow and went from the room, closing the door behind him with scarcely a thump.

They heard the outer door latch.

Dia sat down, releasing a pent-up breath, of which she had not been conscious. Mr. Pond of Room B and Mr. Whipple of Room D exchanged glances.

"My dear," began Pond, as Whipple nodded, "you have been honored by attention from a highly placed gentleman. I hope you will not count this as serious interest in yourself."

Mr. Whipple added, *"We* know you are a fine young lady, too sensible to suppose—"

"Not for the likes of him," finished Mr. Pond.

"No, of course not," she agreed promptly, if with a colorless voice.

Her mama was not prepared for aspersions to be cast upon one who was to drive her to church in a stylish curricle. "It is obvious," she declared flatly, "that Mr. Lloyd was missing us at services and asked him to fetch us there."

Their friends and fellow borders had no answer for that. They hesitated to spoil Mrs. Carlisle's pleasure. Indeed, there was a possibility she was right. So, not wishing to pain Dia with further Home Truths, the men shuffled their feet and said, "Yes. Well."

"Let us wait and see," suggested Dia with a fair assumption of tranquillity.

"Yes," agreed her mama. "If he sends his carriage, or comes himself, it will be an act of kindness, and one should not discourage courtesies like that."

"Aye," admitted Mr. Pond. "Might offset a record of drink or gambling."

"Atone, so to speak," contributed Mr. Whipple with a sigh.

Dia thought her fellow lodgers were rather ridiculous to hint that Lord Knollton had designs upon her virtue—for of course that was what they attempted to say without forming such words—but she had a particular reason to judge him more kindly. Besides, for all she knew, he might have a wife—or *fiancée*—or long-standing affection for some creature of the *demimonde*.

Fortunately Mrs. Carlisle, who had conceived the notion that his lordship had come to visit herself, paid no heed to the hints and warnings advanced by their fellow boarders. She would not have recognized an innuendo if it had sunk its fangs in her. Had not his lordship paid her flattering attention? Very likely because Mr. Lloyd hinted him her way! And she could not suppose Mr. Lloyd would be party to any impropriety.

As Mrs. Carlisle was congenitally transparent, Dia guessed her thoughts and reinforced them by pointing out that their noble visitor had directed his attention and conversation to her mother. Neither lady took Mr. Pond and Mr. Whipple seriously, though Dia thought they were sweet to defend the reputation of a girl not even known in fashionable circles. Lord Knollton had already assisted her to the extent of fifty pounds. What better evidence of his good nature could she find?

When Mr. Pond and Mr. Whipple had gone away, shutting the door to leave the Carlisles private, Dia reminded her mama that her stark black widow's bonnet was no longer needed— Papa had been gone nearly two years. They must sew on fresh ribbons of pink or yellow to welcome the arrival of Spring. Fortunately, new ribbons did not need to be purchased, for colored ones had been laid carefully away in tissue to be restored to bonnets when mourning ribbons were no longer needed.

"Well, yes, dear," agreed Mrs. Carlisle happily. "You are right. When his lordship was so kind as to call upon me, the least I can do is look my best when I ride in his carriage."

Had Lord Knollton called upon Mrs. Carlisle? The more Dia thought about it, the more she had to admit to herself that it could not be true, for how was he to know that her mama even existed? And how could he have discovered where they lived? Mr. Pond and Mr. Whipple clearly suspected him of pursuing a new *chère amie*. There was no other way to interpret their strange behavior, and she thought they were sweet to care about her, but Lord Knollton's courtesy and attention to her mother did not indicate a character that would debase her mother's daughter.

It was so pleasant to have something to enliven their monotonous old days—a carriage ride in a stylish curricle promised to be delightful, and if his lordship had any base ideas—why, there would be her mama beside her for protection!

Perhaps her mama, all unknowing, was right about Mr. Lloyd's sending Knollton to them. It could have come about that way.

As for Dia's own bonnet and dress, she had few to consider. Fortunately, her garments had been tastefully chosen and tidily kept. Lord Knollton did not need to be embarrassed at her appearance. She and Mama would not disgrace him. Besides, he was so splendid that people would be looking at *him*, not them.

If Dia thought her good knights, Pond and Whipple, had said their last word on Lord Knollton, she soon learned better. The very next day Mr. Whipple got her aside after breakfast to mumble that she must know he looked upon her as a daughter. Then he humphed a little and finally got out the words, "Count on me anytime."

"Dear Mr. Whipple," she responded, "Mama and I already know what a true friend you are. If you are thinking about Lord Knollton, he seems a real gentleman, and we cannot think Mr. Lloyd would have sent any other sort to call on us." She was not at all sure Mr. Lloyd had sent anyone, but if he had not, she could not imagine how his lordship had found them.

Mr. Whipple made some hemming noises and dabbed a handkerchief to his damp forehead. "Dear girl," he mumbled. "Must take care of you. Wouldn't want you to be deluded by—"

"But I am not!" she interrupted. "How could his lordship have found us, if the Reverend Mr. Lloyd had not sent him? And really, you know, the offer of his carriage is truly kind. Why, Mama has not stirred outside these walls for weeks! It will do her so much good to attend church again."

"Well, All Souls is near—an easy walk from here—and I would be glad to escort you."

"Oh, thank you! But first I must persuade Mama to venture out the door, which she has not done for so long. Lord Knollton's curricle seems just the thing to accomplish that."

"Yus, yus. But what will it lead to?" he fretted.

"Surely not to an abduction of the two of us," Dia said, laughing a little. "Shall we make a bargain? If this visit to All Souls Church is a success, we will be happy to walk with you the next Sunday."

Mollified, Mr. Whipple said he would count upon that.

Not only Mr. Whipple, but also Mr. Pond had found a time to approach Dia privately with further words of warning.

"I know you will not have your head turned by *me*," he said. "I can say you are a charming young lady, if I please—for you are that and we are old friends."

She nodded and smiled.

"This young buck, Knollton, is another matter."

Dia's smile having dimmed, he continued earnestly. "This chap is the sort to turn a girl's head—so handsome—with fine, approving eyes! Yes, and with an ingratiating manner. But, my dear, he's a *peer* and not likely to be serious about you. I do not want you hurt."

"Oh, Mr. Pond," she interrupted, "no one could be more of a realist than I!"

"Yes, you have coddled your papa and now your mama, but you have not wrestled with a splendid male who thinks only of his immediate pleasure. You must beware."

No longer smiling, Dia said, "Princes do not marry pauper maids. I do know that. But what possible harm can there be in my riding to church with my mother in any vehicle—except possibly a tumbril?"

Taken aback, Mr. Pond said hastily, "Now, now. I have made you cross when I am only trying to protect you."

Dia twisted her fingers together agitatedly.

"My dear girl! You have been a wonder and deserve the best of fortune," he said. "You must not think I am critical when I am only warning you against self-centered and rich young males, however charming. *Their* pleasures are all that concern them. Certainly you and your mama can drive to church with Lord Knollton. What you will have to watch is what comes next."

Next as yet had no meaning for her. If Mr. Pond could be right and Knollton's aims were only for his own—well, amusement, she would be sadly disappointed, although what her own hopes were she had not fully determined. A ride in a curricle was a pleasurable thing to anticipate, and Mama's taking an interest in something was such a relief that she did feel wonderfully hopeful, which was a new sensation for her.

And still the inhabitants of Number 2 were not finished with their advice. The shop girls of the second floor and the servants, however much interest they took in Miss Carlisle, would not presume to address one they considered above them. Yet Miss Docking, who was not a verbal person, evidently determined that Mrs. Carlisle could not be counted upon to look farther than immediate pleasure and would not caution her daughter as she ought.

"Miss Dia," Miss Docking said, meeting the girl on the cellar steps on Friday, "I hope you have a fine morning, come Sunday, but I beg you'll not be misled by his lordship. They say the Devil's busiest just outside a church!"

Not knowing whether to laugh or cry, but recognizing true concern, Dia clasped the woman's hand and said, "Thank you. I appreciate your caring. Where would Mama and I be without the friends here? We have no others."

"No kin anyplace?"

"Not that I know of. Wasn't Papa wise to place us here? But, really, a simple ride to church has been puffed out of proportion. Perhaps Lord Knollton is wishing he had never suggested it. I am just glad of something to stir Mama from the house. It is only for one Sunday, you know. Mr. Whipple is to walk with us the next week and we can truly trust him. How much better for Mama to have an interest other than puddles in the court!"

Miss Docking could not argue with that.

"Everyone wishes you well," she said.

Dia declared, "Nothing could be kinder!"

The whole situation had become an embarrassment to the girl. Neither her father nor mother had ever put themselves forward in any way. This was also true of inhabitants of Number 2. If Mr. Pond in his business travels had to assume some attitude of aggression, no one saw it here. He was clever about coming directly to the point of any issue, yet never manipulated those issues to his personal advantage. It was as if the Almighty, in designing Mr. Pond with the shape of a top had also assigned him good sense and winning ways. And Dia's fondness for fuzzy Mr. Whipple led her to be more reassuring to him than he was to her.

Sometimes she wondered what in the world would become of this household. She wished the girls in Room C would return to whatever town from which they came; there was no future for them in London. Were they perhaps Londoners by birth? If so, why had she seen no other family member? Very likely there was no town or shire for them to call home, no place to return to. Actually, she was in the same dilemma herself.

And the servants . . . what about them?

Suppose Mr. Docking should take it into his head to sell the house!

"Cory," she said to the tweeny when she met her at the dustbin at the back of the hall, "where is your home?"

" 'Ome, miss? Why 'ere. Oi was a foundlin', and verra glad Oi am to be 'ere. Miz Dockin' treats me good."

If Miss Docking did that, Dia could be glad for the girl.

What would be Dia's situation when her mama was gone? It did not bear thinking of! Perhaps the rector of All Souls would help her find a position as a companion or governess, although she had no talents for painting or drawing or teaching music. She would do best as a companion to an elderly lady, which was not a prospect to be anticipated with joy. After all, caring for her mama was a pleasure, while caring for a stranger might be burdensome.

"Mama," she said one day, "have we no family at all?"

Mrs. Carlisle, who was occupied in sewing yellow ribbons on her bonnet in preparation for Sunday at All Souls, murmured, "Um?"

"Family, Mama. Haven't we any?"

"Well, there were Marlows on my side, but not very healthy, I fear," replied her mother, ruminating vaguely. "I can remember only one ancient, cranky cousin. Oh, she must be long gone. Why, she thought your papa was a wastrel because he took more interest in philosophy than in improving his income. Imagine! Dear Papa being a wastrel!"

"Outrageous!" declared Dia. "I hope he ignored her."

"Rather, I fear she ignored us. Yes, she must be in her grave now, for she was at least twice your papa's age. I daresay she took her money with her, for I never knew her to give a farthing away—certainly not to Papa and me."

Dia said, "Shocking."

"Well, dear, whatever she had was her own. We expected nothing."

"And got nothing. What a nip cheese!"

Mrs. Carlisle shrugged philosophically. "She disapproved of me, too, you see, for she thought I should have made a better match, though I had so little to offer."

"A sweet disposition," reminded Dia, "which was something she could not appreciate, I suppose."

"Oh, well," said Mrs. Carlisle, "let us not speak ill of the dead. We have enough to live on I hope—haven't we?"

"Yes, if we are careful."

Mrs. Carlisle sighed. "It is so dispiriting to be careful! Besides, you need something new for Sunday. A shawl, I think."

"Why, Mama," Dia protested, "I have a shawl."

"Yes, an old one."

"Lord Knollton will not know that."

Her mother said, "I will."

"But you will not tell. Besides, Lord Knollton will be looking at these yellow ribbons on your bonnet."

"Ow!" protested Mrs. Carlisle, having stuck a needle into her finger.

"Here, Mama, let me finish that," her daughter said.

"After that, put the pink ribbons on yours," replied the elder lady, delighted to be idle.

Four

While Dia was being counseled by her defenders at Number 2, Lord Knollton was wondering how he could avoid escorting his stepmother to St. George's the following Sunday. Some idea of appearing to have a very late night of drinking and cards with certain cronies did occur to him, only to be rejected, for how would he be able to leave home at all if he were supposed to be nursing a "head" Sunday morning?

Then, on Thursday, Fortuna favored him by inflicting little Sara with a mysterious rash, and although the doctor, hastily summoned, declared it was nothing serious because Sara had no fever, and although the rash had begun to fade by Saturday, Lydia could not consider leaving home and child. His lordship was free to keep his appointment with the Carlisle ladies without making excuses at home.

On Sunday Lord Knollton had breakfast on a tray in his room. By doing this, he hoped to avoid his stepmother, who might ask questions, but would never invade his privacy. He came and went as he pleased, for she knew single gentlemen expected to do that, and after all, it was his house. But she might mention church in a way that would require some response from him, and he was not prepared to admit which (if any) he planned to attend.

Just why he had invited the Carlisle ladies to ride with him to All Souls Church he was not sure. It seemed the courteous thing to do, when they had been housebound for so long. It might be interesting to give enjoyment to that pretty girl, who obviously led a dull life. Besides, it would be amusing to raise a few brows amidst the congregation at All Souls. Yes, he enjoyed raising brows—though not in a way unbecoming to his position. He was not a hell-raiser. In fact, among his acquaintances, there were some who thought him abysmally tame; well, he thought *they* needed a lesson in decorum!

His valet, Shooker, brought a light breakfast on a tray and asked what clothes he would be needing.

"I will drive out soon," his lordship said vaguely, which was all the clue Shooker got, but he understood perfectly what was required. Francis seldom had to think about his garb, for Shooker was competent to judge what a gentleman should wear on any occasion.

"You left this in your pocket, my lord," Shooker said, lifting Dia's gold bracelet from the dresser.

So he had! After several days of being careful.

"Ah. Yes. A—uh—gift. Put it away for the time being," Francis said. He did not explain for whom it was intended or from whom the bracelet might have come, and Shooker, thinking ladybirds would expect more lavish presents, decided to drop the bracelet among his lordship's cuff buttons and forget it until his lordship asked for it.

The day promised to be fair; only a few puffs of snowy clouds were showing when his lordship set out earlier than he need have done. Undoubtedly he would reach Langham Court sooner than expected, which might make Adam think him eager—an idea that he would prefer the groom not to have.

"I want to make a swing through Regent's Park," he said. "They are saying Nash is doing wonders there. We have time to investigate and will not meet much traffic at this hour."

This sounded reasonable to Adam, who knew his master more frequently went to St. James Street, where his club was situated, or to Carleton House Terrace or Jackson's on Bond Street. His lordship, he was sure, would wish to keep abreast of London's development.

When, however, after the merest glance northward from the Outer Circle, Lord Knollton cut past Marylebone Road and turned south on Great Portland Street, Adam suspected Langham Court was to be their destination. His face remained impassive. Presently at Langham Street they were swinging left to reach the entrance of Langham Court, into which his lordship made a cautious turn.

"A bit tight, Adam," he said, manipulating the reins to swing his team about, so as to face the exit of the small court. "We will have two lady passengers."

Two ladies? This was titillating to Adam, who jumped down to steady the team. The well-bred pair being calm, he took the reins when his lordship passed them. Then Adam cooed to the team while watching over his shoulder to see his master mount the steps of Number 2. It was not a stylish neighborhood, nor even a prosperous one, but Lord Knollton had said, "ladies," and Adam did not think he would use the word loosely.

First from the building, on his lordship's arm, came a woman of middle years wearing a black bonnet enlivened with yellow ribbons. Though she was smiling and spilling pleasant chatter, Adam saw no distinction about her, yet his master was as attentive as to Lady Jersey or the Queen.

Then Adam's eyes fell upon a pretty and youthful creature who followed behind them, and all became clear. While he had never seen the young one's face, he did recognize the grey bonnet that he had pursued from Oxford Street, before its present embellishment with a pink bow.

This was all very interesting.

Lord Knollton handed the mother into his curricle, saw her comfortably settled, seated the radiant girl next, climbed aboard himself, and received the reins to thread through his fingers competently. "You are not crowded, are you?" he asked.

The ladies twittered, "No, indeed."

"Better lead us through the arch," he said to Adam.

This the groom did, the sleek pair lifting their hooves daintily. Then Adam sprang up behind, and they rolled smoothly and gently a scant two squares to draw up in the cluster of vehicles at All Souls Church. A ride had never been shorter or less necessary.

"Well, Knollton," said an aging *roué,* coming to assist Francis's ladies to the ground, "I never expected to meet you in church."

"Perhaps because you never attend," retorted his lordship. Obliged to present the man, he said, "Mrs. Carlisle, Miss Carlisle, this is Mr. Springborn."

Mrs. Carlisle simpered, and Dia, who realized that Lord Knollton had been forced into the introduction, nodded pleasantly. It was not clear to her which of the unacquainted persons Lord Knollton was reluctant to acknowledge as a friend, but since he had—of his own volition—escorted her mama and herself, she assumed Mr. Springborn was not someone he wished them to know.

Fortunately, the press of people separated them from Mr. Springborn as they moved toward the circular portico.

"Will seats here be satisfactory, madam?" Lord Knollton asked, indicating places halfway down the aisle. Any place would have suited Dia's mama, so pleased was she to be escorted by a titled gentleman.

She declared, "Yes, indeed!" and entered the stall. Dia followed, and Lord Knollton took a place (where he wished to be) beside the girl, at whom he stole glances when she was busy with her prayer book.

Delectable! he thought. If Dia was conscious of *his* presence beside her, she gave no indication. His ladies were probably recognized in the congregation, and any who were familiar with Lord Knollton were not surprised to see him, as he was to be seen most everywhere in London. The rector, who was facing a sea of faces, noticed no particular one, and he played his part serenely and—yes—tenderly.

Afterward, Mrs. Carlisle, exhilarated by her venture from home, thanked his lordship with smiles and hyperboles. "I declare," she said, "it is good to be out and about again. Why, I feel quite invigorated."

"Enough for a ride about Regent's Park?" Lord Knollton asked, handing her gallantly into his curricle.

"Yes, indeed, that would be delightful," she replied.

"Will it make you late for your dinner?" he enquired of Dia, holding her fingers a bit longer than necessary as he guided her to her seat.

"Things are less formal on Sundays," she replied, knowing perfectly well they were never *that*.

"Good. We must make the most of a sunny day."

Then he took his place, his broad shoulder touching Dia's, and soon they were bowling up Portland Place to reach the Outer Circle of the park. Mrs. Carlisle was astonished (so limited was her experience) by the fine terraces being built along the east side.

Dia said, "Why, the houses are quite beautiful—and how agreeable it must be to face into a park."

"Nash's idea, I understand, is to bring the countryside into town—into view," Lord Knollton explained.

Mrs. Carlisle, who had always lived in the city and had never experienced bucolic charms, murmured, "How odd."

So Dia was quick to add tactfully, "But a pleasant thought."

"I confess," said his lordship, "that I spend most of the year in Gloucestershire. The open countryside and clean air are refreshing. No soot or grime."

"But there cannot be much to *do*," objected Mrs. Carlisle, who was in the habit of doing nothing.

Embarrassed for her mama's attitude, Dia bit her lip, wondering how to ease the situation. But his lordship did not appear offended. He said quickly, "You cannot imagine how busy a manor is—or a village. If you admire the beauty of All Souls Church, Mrs. Carlisle, you would be sure to recognize another sort of beauty in our village church. Why, the ladies conspire to surround it with a lush and colorful garden."

"Yes," said Dia hastily, "you would like that, Mama. In the city we have man's creation, while in the country there is—"

"Woman's?" inserted her mother.

"I was going to say," admitted Dia, flushing, "God's."

Lord Knollton shot a side glance at her, never having heard a young lady talk this way. Seeing her blush, he thought her even prettier. "The peacefulness of the countryside," he said, "is very refreshing after the crush of a Season."

He meant, of course, the crush of a social Season, but the Carlisle ladies had no experience of that. A full circle of the park was made. Everywhere was evidence of work being carried on, and the roadway was not always smooth, though Lord Knollton's high-bred team did not falter as his lordship guided them in the safest track.

At the rear, Adam clung tightly to his perch, with his ears turned at right angles to his head, though they heard nothing to explain his master's attention to Unknowns. Would this be the last notice his master would pay these ladies or would he pursue the connection?

Dia Carlisle was wondering the same thing.

Lord Knollton was all graciousness. As he turned at last from the park to take them home, he did not seem hurried. When had the Carlisle ladies experienced such consideration of their enjoyment? Indeed, when had anything been a matter of pure pleasure? They passed the days in routine affairs, glad whenever Mr. Pond was in residence to enliven things.

Today, however, Mr. Pond and Mr. Whipple seemed bent on putting a damper on their spirits, for no sooner had Lord Knollton escorted the Carlisle ladies into the house—somewhat wind-blown but radiant—than the self-appointed guards of Number 2 had appeared upon the stairs and followed them into the parlor of suite A.

"Oh, it has been delightful!" exclaimed Mrs. Carlisle, not even seeking a chair. "I had forgotten that trees would be leafing out and looking so fresh and green."

"Yes," said Dia, glowing. "And the new houses are splendid."

"Houses?" pursued Mr. Pond. "I thought it was All Souls that you attended."

"All Souls was our target, of course," Knollton explained easily. "Then we drove up to Regent's Park for Mrs. Carlisle and Miss Carlisle—and myself also—to see the progress on new homes there."

Both men of Number 2 moved about London more often and more extensively than the Carlisle ladies, but new-cut stone and artistic shrubbery were not of great concern to them. In fact, it was not newness that exhilarated the Carlisle ladies, but the expansion of their horizons. Mr. Pond had the freedom of travels about England, and Mr. Whipple at least was able to browse bookstores of the city and sit over a hot cup in most any coffeehouse. How many hundreds of days had the ladies looked upon the sameness of Langham Court?

The ladies repeated their thanks to his lordship, to which he replied graciously that they must ride out again sometime. The Carlisle ladies, never expecting anything, were not dismayed when no plan was made to meet again.

His lordship bowed civilly and departed.

Mr. Pond and Mr. Whipple, reassured that Dia had not been compromised or deluded, retired to their own rooms after a light lunch, leaving the ladies to sleepless naps.

As Dia thought over the day, she could not settle upon what had been the special pleasure of it. Following weeks of gloomy skies and nasty dampness, sunshine was so welcome! Worship at All Souls refreshed her as it always did. And driving out in a smashing rig to see new and beautiful vistas was as delicious as whipped cream heaped upon raspberry trifle! Oh, she was elated! Even her mama seemed singularly invigorated.

Obviously, they could not expect every day to be like this. Dia would not be so foolish. Perhaps it was Spring, finally coming, that made everything fresh and new and interesting.

She was not a rebellious girl. The warnings from two concerned men and, yes, from Miss Docking, would not be soon forgotten, although Lord Knollton was everything courteous and sincere. She had not previously met a gentleman so fine, one so willing to be helpful and so unwilling to be thanked.

Naturally, she did not sleep, yet at teatime she arose refreshed and in such good spirits as to invite the two Froam girls down for late tea in Room A. Actually the Froams were older than she, but so giggly and frivolous as to seem much younger. Very little did Dia learn about their circumstances, except that Mary Ann's aspiration was to boat across the Thames to visit Vauxhall, while Jane would like to be presented at Court.

During this visit, Mrs. Carlisle occupied her particular chair to watch twilight overtake Langham Court. Mr. Whipple soon came in to accept tea, but they saw neither Mr. Pond nor Miss Docking, who generally saved Sundays to rest from her labors.

Lord Knollton kept invading Dia's thoughts while she made polite conversation with the visitors. It was just as well, she concluded, that old friends were on hand to keep unprofitable speculations subdued. She knew, without Mr. Whipple's reminding her, that a wealthy and noble gentleman, such as Knollton, was not for her. But of course her dreams were not subdued after all, for they bounced around her mind as she discussed gloves with Jane Froam and lace collars with Mary Ann.

The one male present, Mr. Whipple, did not contribute much except, "Yus, yus," and the rattle of his spoon against his cup.

Someone more frivolous than Dia might have thought the whole afternoon was a comic play with clowns soon to come on stage. This simple tea party was like many she had experienced in her life at Number 2, and ordinarily she could laugh a bit about it, but today was different: Today she had glimpsed other lives more rich. Oh, not rich in pounds, but in meaning—and interest—and aspirations. Mama did not seem to care, yet Papa had. At least, Papa had kept his simple life and undemanding spirit filled with scholarly study and the hammering of knowledge into young folks' heads.

"Knowledge, itself, is a form of wealth," he had often said, and in a way that was true, but surely life was meant to be lived with enthusiasm!

How filled was Knollton's life with things that mattered? Very likely he had Cambridge or Oxford behind him. Maybe even a tour abroad. He looked physically fit. Did that come from sports such as gentlemen pursued? Did he ride as well as he drove prime cattle? How incredibly different his life had to be from hers! On what level could they possibly communicate in a meaningful way?

Or did gentlemen expect to communicate to any depth with mere females?

She could recognize that Mr. Pond was wise in warning her against such a misfit as herself with Knollton. For heaven's sake! She did not even know his first name or what rank of nobility he enjoyed. And one thing was sure: She must stop thinking of him!

They heard the latch of the front door. Then Mr. Pond appeared at the open door of the Carlisles' flat.

"Do not come near me," he warned. "I have a vile something of the chest."

Mrs. Carlisle and her daughter exclaimed in unison, "Oh, do have hot tea!"

But he was backing away, saying all he needed was his bed. They heard him coughing as he plodded up the stairs.

The tea party ended abruptly, Mr. Whipple saying "Dear, dear—" and Mrs. Carlisle reminding them gloomily that her husband's death had begun just that way.

"For mercy's sake," exclaimed Dia. "A cough is not the end of the world. Mr. Pond should know if he needs a physician. Haven't we all had coughs?" Nevertheless, she did not object when Jane and Mary Ann began gathering cups, and Mr. Whipple surrendered his, which wasn't quite empty.

Twilight was creeping over Langham Court. One by one, the visitors took leave of Mrs. Carlisle and climbed the stairway on tiptoe, so as not to disturb Mr. Pond, who could be heard hacking now and then.

Dia's day, which had begun on such joyful note, subsided less happily, though she was able to hug to herself the precious parts of it.

Five

It was unsettling for the household to have Mr. Pond take to his bed. He had never ailed. In fact he scoffed at infirmities, very likely because of never having had firsthand acquaintance with any. Between coughing and growling powerfully, he made quite an uproar, especially when he refused to let Dia come near him with potions she had learned to make for her papa. The servants—Miss Docking and the others—tended him, on the doubtful theory that servants were hardier, more resistant to infection.

Dia could hear his coughing and begged to be allowed to bring him various of the concoctions that had eased her papa in coughing fits, but such a suggestion made him roar hoarsely, loud enough to be heard up and down the staircase. This, of course, was followed by greater coughing.

"I'm doing my best, dearie," Miss Docking told Dia. "You are only making him worse when you plead to wait on him— which would not be proper, anyway."

"Well, at least," Dia countered, "let me brew some of the things that soothed Papa."

Miss Docking did not think it was suitable for a young lady to come into her kitchen, although Dia had done so when her father was ill. Dia pled earnestly, and at last Mrs. Docking agreed, with the proviso that someone else deliver the concoction to the patient. When Cook had gone to her bed for the night, banked coals were stirred up by Dia to boil a kettle of peppermint with honey, as well as well as one of onions with garlic, which was simmered until the ingredients could be mashed to pulp. Spoonfuls of these things were fed to Mr. Pond by Miss Docking when coughing woke him from restless sleep. Mrs. Carlisle, peacefully dreaming on the floor below, remained unaware of Dia's tending pots in the kitchen at strange hours.

There was not much sleeping for Miss Docking or Dia. Next morning Miss Docking's boy was sent off by Dia to fetch a plucked chicken and also oranges, if he could find them.

"Mr. P. is resting better," reported the landlady, looking somewhat wilted. "His room reeks of garlic, and I suppose I do, too. At least he is not wheezing as much."

Dia, perhaps because she was younger, looked less frazzled, though her hair was noticeably untidy. "We want him to cough, but not so exhaustingly. Is he still fighting the broths? Something is needed to clear his lungs."

"There are strong enough garlic and onion fumes to clear the whole house!" the older woman declared. She went to wash her face and hands, while Dia prepared another kettle of water to receive the chicken when it came.

"Too late for cranberries," Dia mumbled to herself. "I wonder if Miss Docking has parsnips. . . ." Then she began to laugh a little to herself as she thought of the strange selection that was being forced on poor Mr. Pond. Would it not be a splendid bonus if he should lose a little weight?

Cook, coming on the scene to fix breakfast for the regular household, muttered about the use of her saucepans, but she was partial to Dia, as was the whole house, so she began to drag out kettle and skillet and adjust her plan for breakfast. "It'll 'ave to be fried eggs and oatmeal this mornin'," she muttered, banging what she could bang.

"Oh, Cook, I'm sorry you are overburdened," cried Dia. "Mr. Pond has been so sick, you see. Let me help you!"

But Cook retorted gruffly that she guessed Mr. Pond was the one as mattered. "Wot's this I smell? Are you trying to kill 'im with garlic—*ugh!*"

"But he is breathing *better* already!" Dia insisted.

"Well, don't let 'im see you with your 'air flying all this way 'n' that, missy, or 'e'll be fainting."

Clearly Cook was in a good mood. Dia laughed and said she would run up to freshen herself before the boy came back with the chicken, which had to be converted to a powerful broth.

Whether Dia's soups or Mr. Pond's constitution did the trick, in a few hours he was breathing more freely—coughing loosely but not wheezing—and even mending enough to complain of "high-handed" females.

Though the boy was not able to find oranges, from which Dia had hoped to extract juice for Mr. Pond to sip and clear away any troublesome mucus, he did bring back a nice young chicken, which went into the waiting pot.

Mrs. Carlisle came all the way to the basement for her breakfast, much surprised at what had been going on during the night, and she offered cologne for rubbing on Mr. Pond's chest.

"Thank you, Mama," Dia said. "I daresay he would think cologne just one more indignity to suffer. Besides, the aroma might not blend well with garlic and peppermint."

"Gor," said Cook, poking her head from the kitchen. "Let the poor chappie sleep if 'e can."

It was unusual for Mrs. Carlisle to eat anywhere but in her own parlor. Today, the general buzz of chatter about Mr. Pond was too interesting to miss—until someone asked if the infection might be "catching," at which point she retreated to the ground floor, calling Dia to accompany her.

Dia was too exhausted to carry more than a cup of tea for herself. However, Cook sent the tweeny up with a bowl of oatmeal when it was ready.

"Cook says you needs this, miss," the girl explained. "To give you strinth, seeing as 'ow you must be feeling wore down."

"Oh, how hot and fresh it is!" interrupted Dia. "Would you like some, Mama?"

But her mama said no and, going off into condemnation of the Scots' food, forgot to ask why her daughter needed strength.

Mr. Whipple, on his way to breakfast in the cellar, stopped off to say he had looked in on Pond and the fellow was dozing without a care for having upset them all last night.

"Of course he needs sleep," defended Dia. "He is not well yet, though I think he will come along nicely."

Evidently Mrs. Carlisle was oblivious to the commotion of the previous night. "I heard him cough as he went upstairs yesterday," she said. "You must not go near him, Dia. If you caught his ailment we might miss walking out in the fine weather."

Was it fine? Yes, just as Sunday and Monday had been, though Dia was almost too sleepy to notice.

Mr. Whipple shook a finger playfully at her. "Remember? The three of us are to walk to All Souls next Sunday. I shall feel very smart with a beautiful lady on each arm!" Then, overcome by his own gallantry, he cleared his throat and colored alarmingly.

Fortunately, both ladies were well acquainted with his timid social graces and thought nothing of them. It was impossible to dislike a creature so eager to please them. Mrs. Carlisle, in fact, found him more comfortable a gentleman than the elegant Lord Knollton, if less dashing.

Meanwhile, Lord Knollton went twice to his club in an effort to remind himself of his position in Society, but he found no one interesting there, and he had no inclination to doze over morning papers in a window on St. James Street like the old gentlemen habitués. At Jackson's he discovered he was winded more easily than he wished, so he went several times for sparring, though with the weather good, it seemed ridiculous to stay indoors. He might have driven along Langham Street for a glance into Langham Court—except for the presence of Adam beside him—and what would he have seen, anyway?

He wondered what Lydia would think of Dia, not realizing that in warmth of nature the two ladies were somewhat alike.

He felt sure Miss Dia Carlisle was respectable, yet was she someone he could present to his stepmother?

When Lydia dragged him—well, he went willingly—to Almack's on Wednesday, he surveyed the young creatures on display and thought none compared with the sweet freshness of Dia. But it was foolish of him to think constantly of an Unknown, with the pick of Society (as approved by the patronesses) eyeing him eagerly. So he fluttered several hearts and swelled the bosoms of several mamas by dancing every dance.

When he saw Lady Knollton dance twice with the Earl of Endfield, he was jolted enough to pursue her across the room and demand to know if she was determined to become a scandal.

"Mercy, Francis!" she hissed behind her fan. "Do you presume to teach me manners? I hope I am respectable enough to dance with whomever I please."

"Of course you are," he said, "but the Old Cats will have you halfway to the altar when you dance twice with the same one."

"Well, if you would settle down with some nice girl, as you ought, and raise an heir, the Old Cats would never give me a thought," she retorted.

This was all very true, he knew, though he need not worry about an heir for some years yet. What about his own pleasure? Should he tie himself to some "proper" female to please the patronesses of Almack's? Though he knew, as well as Lydia, that they would not suit each other, he wanted—yes, deep down he wanted someone similar to her.

When, after a dance with Francis, Lady Knollton accepted a second dance with Lord Marchmont, giving her stepson an arch look, he felt better, seeing that she had not blatantly favored Endfield. Lydia was really an enchanting creature, and he could not suppose she would stay a widow forever; moreover, he knew she would never desecrate his father's memory by wedding someone unsuitable.

Then there was the matter of little Sara. He would not want her to leave Knollton House, for he was quite enslaved by the precious bantling. If Lydia wed, both she and Sara would go. He could not like that.

By Friday he had had enough to bore him for eternity, so he summoned Adam and his curricle for a polite "call" at Number 2, Langham Court.

His welcome there was not all that he might have hoped.

Mrs. Carlisle and her daughter were at home to receive him in a building that reeked strangely of what he thought must have been garlic! The ladies' door stood open, and the odd aroma had penetrated their rooms also.

"Why, good day, my lord," Mrs. Carlisle said happily when he hesitated in their doorway. "Mr. Pond is much better. I do not think you will catch his throat. Come in!"

"You seem well, madam," he replied, advancing into the parlor.

"Oh, my daughter coddles me so I am never ill," she said blithely as Dia came from another room.

Dia, he noticed, was somewhat wan.

"Good day, my lord," she said. "We have had a time with dear Mr. Pond—that is, *he* has had a horrid time with his chest, but he is on the way to health now. I daresay," she added with a smile, "you can smell the treatment we inflicted on him."

"Surely not garlic?"

"Yes. Powerful for easing one's breathing. Also peppermint and chicken broth. I did want oranges for juice, but we were unable to find them."

His lordship asked, "Is Mr. Pond well now?"

"Almost," she said. "You need not be afraid of infection. We air the house every day."

His lordship then asked, "What about a physician? Does the remarkable treatment go on?"

Dia shook her head. "Mr. Pond would not hear of calling one. Miss Docking and the servants have been wonderful in caring for him."

Feeling sure he should not mention Miss Carlisle's peaked condition, and convinced she needed fresh air, his lordship began to address the "amazing days of good weather." Would the ladies like to drive out a bit?

They would indeed, though Mrs. Carlisle demurred that she was not dressed for such an occasion.

"What about you, Miss Carlisle?" he asked in a wonderfully offhand way. "Would fresh air be pleasant after days indoors?"

Dia was not fashionably garbed, but her cloak and best bonnet would cover much. The invitation was irresistible.

"Yes, thank you," she breathed, then sped from the room to make ready. She did not think Mr. Pond or Miss Docking would criticize her for deserting a post: One was napping, and the other was busy with a list for reviving her pantry.

When they went into the courtyard, Adam, who was waiting with his lordship's team, beamed to hear himself greeted by name. A real lady, this one was, sure enough!

Lord Knollton, who seldom bothered himself about what his servants might have thought, took over the reins and set his team down Great Portland Street to Oxford, and from there to Hyde Park, of which Dia had seen little, though she did not intend to admit this. From her father she had learned the wisdom of guarding one's tongue in unknown territory. Therefore, when his lordship called her attention to a horse or a building or a pedestrian, she responded with bland things like "Oh, yes" or "I see" and, when he maneuvered through an occasional tight spot, "Well done, sir."

For a time his lordship was busy with traffic, good weather having brought out many vehicles, and Dia, a bit nervous of their speed, held to her cloak to keep her plain gown covered, not sure if conversation from herself would distract him from control of his team. Adam she could not see, as he was balanced behind her, but she felt his presence, which both reassured her and tied her tongue. That Lord Knollton had heard enough frivolous female chatter to last a lifetime she did not guess.

His lordship liked having a pretty passenger beside him, though he did not think Oxford Street was a place for dalliance.

When they reached an entrance to the park, he slowed carefully and turned in, nodding casually to a few acquaintances, though managing to ignore Mr. Springborn, who tried to signal them from the walkway.

"That was the gentleman you introduced to Mama and me at All Souls," she reminded him.

"Yes," said Lord Francis, "but not the most gentlemanly of my acquaintance. Something of a gossip, I fear."

A gossip, she quite understood, was not to be relied upon, but she did not have time to deal with this thought, for they were receiving attention from a number of carriages drawn up on the edge of the roadway. To most, Lord Knollton responded by nods and greetings, though he did not stop. She was beginning to wonder if he was ashamed to introduce her.

Then they approached a barouche from which a beautiful lady was waving. She had a precious little girl beside her, and several gentlemen, on foot, were obviously vying for her attention.

Knollton halted alongside the barouche.

"Mama," he said roguishly to the ravishing creature, "may I present Miss Carlisle?"

"Of course you may. How do you do, Miss Carlisle? This is my daughter, Sara."

So exquisitely dressed was the youthful dowager that poor Dia—though admiring the other woman immensely—could really think only of her own passé cloak and resurrected bonnet. No one would have guessed her shame, since she responded, "How do you do, my lady?" in her pleasant voice, which had no uncouth timbre to shame Knollton.

"Fwancie, may I ride with you and the pretty lady?" asked little Sara, making them all laugh.

Two of the gentleman mimicked, "May I?"

Lady Knollton then presented the various beaux, who bowed and said exaggerated and agreeable things. Their names ran together in a blur. Nothing indicated if they were married or single; their manners were easy and friendly.

"We have no room for Court cards," Francis said, grinning at Lydia's admirers. "Adam, fetch Lady Sara, please."

Sara was already scrambling to her feet and holding out her arms to Adam. "To the big water, Fwancie, ple-ease!"

"Certainly, my lady," he replied grandly. "Miss Carlisle is sure to want to visit the Serpentine."

"Yes, indeed," said Dia, tucking the child between Knollton and herself. "But no wading!" she added, as a cool breath of wind blew a curl against her cheek. The sun went under a cloud, but came out almost immediately.

Dia thought Lady Knollton and her daughter were utterly delightful and wondered if one of these nobles who were hanging at her ladyship's sleeve hoped to carry them off to belong to *him*, leaving Knollton in an empty house. It was easy to see his lordship's affection for the two.

"Gallop!" commanded Sara.

"No such thing," retorted her half brother sternly. "Ladies do not gallop." He flicked his reins and the sleek pair set off at a smart trot.

When Dia glanced back, she could see that Lady Knollton's admirers were drawing closer, perhaps vying to see whom she would take up for a circle of the park. Lady Knollton's groom, Dia noticed, was large and intimidating. No daring beau would take advantage of her ladyship under his eye!

Dia looked over her shoulder to smile at Adam, who gave the merest of nods. Knollton, she thought, had not chosen his servant for brawn, yet she suspected Adam was clever and could give good account of himself if necessary.

How different were the servants at Number 2, Langham Court! Just as faithful as his lordship's, just as industrious, but somehow simpler—less status conscious, more resigned.

Was she equally different from Knollton's friends?

Papa had always said, "Be yourself."

She thought that was a good rule, for fakers were apt to be unmasked sooner or later.

The curving waters of the Serpentine reflected the blue sky

above. Little Sara wanted to get down from the curricle and dabble in it, but his lordship said absolutely not. It was interesting to note that nothing more had to be said. There was no whining or pouting. Instead, Sara was allowed to help hold the reins as they rolled back to rejoin her ladyship.

"Come to the house and visit with me," Lady Lydia invited Dia kindly.

Knowing this would mean removing her cloak and exposing her plain frock, Dia quite firmly declined, looking to his lordship for understanding.

"Some other time," he said.

They returned little Lady Sara to her mama. Francis saluted Lydia's enlarged circle of admirers, and they wheeled away.

"Did you like my stepmother?" he asked.

"Indeed I did," Dia answered warmly. "I expect everyone does so."

"Oh, yes," he agreed. "It was a shock when Father married her—so young, you see. I was stunned. They were obviously devoted. My nose was out of joint, though not for long. She twisted me around her finger as she did Father. She's a witch! An adorable witch. And Sara is going to be exactly the same."

Six

Both Miss Docking and Mr. Whipple came into the parlor when Dia returned. They fixed anxious eyes on her, not knowing whether to be glad or troubled that *her* eyes were sparkling and her cheeks touched with pink.

"It was so refreshing, Mama," she said, not at first aware of their anxiety. "The sun was shining the whole time, and the park—we went to Hyde Park, if you please!—was greening wonderfully. Oh, isn't Spring welcome!"

"Yes," replied Mr. Whipple heavily, "but we did not expect you to be gone so long."

"Was it long?" said Dia, untying the ribbons of her bonnet. "The minutes went so fast. Lord Knollton presented me to his stepmother, who is a most enchanting creature, and to several cordial gentlemen—but do not ask their names, for they are all quite scrambled in my head."

"There!" said Mrs. Carlisle. "I knew his lordship would behave properly to you. Made you known to Lady Knollton, you say?"

Dia laid aside her bonnet. "Yes. She is charming. No older than Knollton, I suspect, and she has an adorable child—little Lady Sara, who rode down with us to see the Serpentine."

"Was everyone gracious to you?" asked her mama, quite amazed.

"Yes. Lady Knollton invited me to return to her house for a *tête-à-tête*, but I could not go like *this*." Dia had cast off her cloak by this time, and they could see she was still wearing an everyday frock.

Miss Docking made clucking sounds. "Your frock—it's not one for visiting."

"No," said Dia. "I would have been mortified to remove my cloak and let her ladyship see me in this."

"Dear, dear," murmured her mother. "It is my fault that you had to miss such an opportunity. I should have insisted you change before leaving home."

"Well, Mama," returned Dia practically, "nothing could have come of such a visit, for I am sure Lady Knollton, though kind, has much grander persons to occupy her time."

Her three hearers could not dispute this.

"Papa would have said," she added irrefutably, "that nothing is more foolish than to get above oneself."

"At least," said Mr. Whipple with a sigh, "you had some fresh air and a bit of change from Langham Court. Pond will be glad."

Recalled to the kind friend in his bed above, Dia made a little distressed sound and asked, "How could I forget? Oh, do tell me I wasn't needed here!"

"No. Mr. Pond is well enough to be cross," Miss Docking said tartly. "It is a good sign. But you must stay away from him, miss, for we don't want another patient. Could you smell your soups when you came in?"

Laughing, Dia said, "No. That is, I did not think about them."

"The girls in Room C claim they have had to wash their hair to remove the smell before going out."

"Well, no one should reek more than I, who made the concoctions! Riding in fresh air must have blown me clean. At least, I hope so!"

Now Mrs. Carlisle had an opportunity to fret about the possibility of Dia's making a malodorous impression. It was much more engrossing than the possibility of puddles in the court, and she was heard to lament this several times.

"I will throw some cloves on Mr. Pond's fire," Miss Docking promised.

By this time, though keeping to his room, Mr. Pond was no longer wretched. He tolerated the cloves, and fumigation was the last of indignities he was forced to bear. No one else succumbed to infection; by Sunday Mr. Pond was allowed to come among the others, several pounds lighter, though not enough to necessitate alteration of his clothes.

Attention was transferred to Mr. Whipple, who brushed his best coat and polished his shoes for a visit to All Souls Church with a lady on each arm.

"I declare," said Mrs. Carlisle as they turned down Great Portland Street on Sunday, "our walk to church has never seemed so short or so pleasant!" She selected a pew as near as possible to where Lord Knollton had seated them, one that was not occupied by *habitués* of Mr. Lloyd's congregation.

Before the service had concluded they were troubled by rays of sunlight coming through a blue section of the nearest window, but it was not strong enough to be blinding, and the ladies' bonnet brims shielded them somewhat. It was Mr. Whipple who was obliged to squint one eye.

Lord Knollton did not attend.

Nor did Mr. Springborn, for which Dia was glad. Lord Knollton had intimated that he was not one with whom he wished her to be on terms. Lord Knollton was right in this case, although Dia did not know it, for Springborn already, with leers and winkings, was spreading the word about "Knollton's new interest—an Unknown, of course, but a tasty bit."

In such a way were reputations made or slaughtered.

"Did you know," said Lady Knollton to her stepson as they rode to St. George's that same Sunday, "that Springborn is insinuating things about Miss Carlisle!"

"Good God, is he?" growled his lordship. "I shall put a stop to that!"

"It might be wiser to ignore Springborn," she suggested. "Most people know what he is."

"A scoundrel," his lordship pronounced firmly. "Can't allow him to smear an innocent lady."

"But to make an issue of anything he says," Lady Knollton reminded him mildly, "is to fix it in people's minds."

Knollton knew this perfectly well. "Perhaps you are right," he said. "I would like to plant him a facer, though."

"That would only titillate the *ton* and lend credence to his horrid gossip." She hesitated, then added casually, "If you are not seen with Miss Carlisle again, her name will be forgotten."

Lord Knollton cast his stepmother a sharp glance. "I thought you liked Miss Carlisle."

"Well, I did. Too well to fan fires of a scandal."

"Scandal? There is no scandal!"

"No. Do you want to cause one?"

His lordship shrugged irritably. "No, of course not." Lydia was right, though. If he pursued acquaintance with little Miss Carlisle, he might harm her. But he did not stop thinking of her sweetness, her pretty face, and her complete lack of guile. Perhaps, if he let several days pass—until gossip focused on someone else—then he could renew the acquaintance cautiously. It was not just a matter of his defying criticism, he told himself. He genuinely liked the girl.

"Why did you invite her to our house?" Lord Knollton asked.

"Because I liked her," Lydia admitted, "and I had not heard Springborn's insinuations then."

Her stepson said, "Did a foul rumor change your opinion?"

Her ladyship shook her head. "No. But I cannot think it would be a kindness to ignite more gossip by giving Miss Carlisle too much attention."

Their carriage was nearing St. George's Church. Lord Knollton said no more. As they turned south from Hanover Square, the church bells sounded.

"Just in time," Lydia said.

Francis absently said, "Yes." He was not reconciled to Springborn's rearranging his social schedule and he would have liked to punish the other man—which was not the best thought with which to enter a Sunday service.

Afterward, busy with his thoughts, Lord Knollton had little to say, and Lydia, who knew him well, did not suppose him to be sulking. He was mulling matters over in his thoughts, she decided, and would come to a reasonable conclusion, because he was a reasonable man.

Lydia had seen Miss Carlisle for only a few moments, which meant she had little upon which to base her own judgment of the girl. What sort of home did the girl have? What sort of parents? Were they well mannered—or abrasive? Her own impressions of Dia were good. After seven years in the center of exclusive social circles she had seen all degrees of matchmaking mamas and calculating damsels. So far, Francis had not succumbed to any of that sort!

But would he be impervious to one without guile?

Miss Carlisle was refreshingly unaggressive which might be the very thing to win him. There was no doubt that Francis was interested. Did Lydia owe it to her beloved and now deceased husband to protect his son from an unequal match? For unequal it obviously would have been. She saw nothing objectionable in the girl, though her family might be less acceptable.

One thing was sure. Lydia had spent nearly an hour on these thoughts and the church service was ending, without her having heard a word.

"Would you like to drive about a bit?" Knollton asked as he handed his stepmother into their carriage.

"Oh, I think not," she replied, giving him an affectionate smile. "Sara is still fretful. I think I must go home and spoil her a bit today."

"Everyone in the household does that," he pointed out, "including me."

"You are the worst," she declared.

"Yes," said his lordship, "but it gives me so much pleasure." He was wondering if Miss Carlisle had been able to drag her mama to All Souls.

When they reached Knollton House, Lydia went upstairs at once to see if Sara was happy with her nurse, which of course she always was, for Nursie tended her worshipfully. His lordship, conversely, stunned the servants by going down to kitchen regions to ask if there were any oranges left of the ones brought from his orangery in Gloucestershire.

Cook said, "I 'spect so, m'lord."

"Good. Where is Harry? Ah, there you are, lad. I want you to take half-a-dozen oranges, or however many we have, to Number 2."

The boot boy knew what was meant. With an engaging grin he said, "Aye, m'lord," gave Cook a saucy look, and took the basement steps two at a time to the fruit cellar. He knew what Number 2 meant.

"Say they are for Mr. Pond," Knollton called after him.

Mr. Pond? Who was he? If Harry knew, his lordship's butler, Cook, two footmen, and three maids did not. Some freak start of the nobility, they concluded.

Lord Knollton returned to proper areas of his mansion, thinking how surprised Miss Carlisle would be. Pleased, too, he hoped.

When cocky Harry reached Langham Court, word of Mr. Pond's gift percolated through the house, and Dia, without any embarrassment, clapped her hands and exclaimed, "Lord Knollton remembered! How exceedingly kind! I will squeeze juice for you, dear Mr. Pond. It will be the very thing to complete your cure."

Orange juice sounded to Pond like ambrosia compared with what they had been forcing on him. He begged to be allowed to eat the pulp of one.

"His lordship has sent eight," Miss Docking reported.

"Then pray save four for me to eat," Mr. Pond said. "I am feeling better just thinking about it."

"You are not cross with me for forcing broths upon you?" Dia asked.

"No, no," he chuckled, "although you must not mention

broth to me again for a hundred years. How can anything as tasty as garlic become so oppressive?"

Mr. Pond did look better. Only a few random coughs rumbled from him. If he could laugh about Dia's soups, he was clearly on the mend.

Number 2 and its inhabitants fell back into the old routine, particularly as Lord Knollton did not appear.

Though Dia did not mention his lordship, she thought about him, marveling at the difference between his life and hers. London had never seemed so huge. What myriad life patterns the inhabitants of the city weaved! People in this house seemed unconcerned about what might be happening in Hyde Park or in Houndsditch or Cheapside . . . or Upper Brook Street.

Each time Dia squeezed an orange for Mr. Pond, or handed him half an orange with a spoon, Lord Francis crept into her thoughts—to be ruthlessly thrust out . . . until the next time. She was careful that no one should guess this.

His lordship did not return to All Souls Church, and Mr. Springborn did so only once, though fortunately Dia was able to evade him.

As Miss Carlisle did not ride again in Hyde Park beside the town's most popular bachelor, Mr. Springborn made no more gossip with which to discomfort Lord Knollton. Lady Knollton's prediction proved correct: Speculation turned to someone else.

Perhaps, thought Francis, Lydia was right again, as she always seemed to be about social matters. There was a boating party on the Thames to distract him, and several balls, and Lydia's musical evening, at which a soulful tenor performed.

Francis found himself wondering if Miss Carlisle would have enjoyed such a thing. He had no idea whether she were musically inclined. In fact, he knew very little about her—except that she was good-humored, softhearted, and very easy to look upon.

As if other damsels were not sometimes these things . . .

Meanwhile, Dia remembered him only two or three times a day.

After taking two weeks to recover his health, Mr. Pond prepared to set off for the Cotswolds with his samples, having admonished Mr. Whipple to keep a close eye upon their girl. Mrs. Carlisle, the two men felt, was next to useless. Oh, ladylike in her ways and a good example to Dia, but *not* awake on the subject of beaux. Actually, Pond and Whipple knew very little themselves about noble gentlemen; they were suspicious, however, and thought that the two of themselves were as effective as the one of Mr. Carlisle would have been if he had not unfortunately expired too soon to be useful.

The Froam girls came and went, blooming like flowers as the Spring weather progressed. They had very few expectations and consequently were not disappointed with their lot in life. They giggled, experimented daringly with the merest, tiniest bit of rouge, and walked briskly to and from the shop where they worked so as to trim themselves—though with what end in view was not known.

Dia had a little talk with Miss Docking about Mary Ann and Jane. Their mother, it seemed, was a widow at Stoke Poges, supporting herself and three younger children as a seamstress. She was thankful for her older daughters to be earning a living respectably as clerks of a draper to whom Mr. Pond had recommended them. Of course! Mr. Pond was eager to assist everyone.

Dia wondered why Mr. Pond had not placed Mr. Whipple in some comfortable situation. Perhaps he would find something gainful for herself, if the time came when she needed it.

She did not think about Lord Knollton. At least, not very much. Mr. Pond, after discreet enquiries, had mentioned casually that Knollton was a viscount. His father's widow, being so young and abhorring the label *dowager,* chose to call herself simply Lady Knollton. It was perfectly proper; she was regularly addressed that way, as Dia had noted.

Knollton was not an *honorable* or a *sir* but a real lord. Viscount!

No wonder that Mr. Pond and Mr. Whipple did not encourage the acquaintance. Dia quite understood. Lady Knollton, being such a gracious person, had acknowledged Dia kindly, but she and her stepson circulated in Society far above Number 2, Langham Court.

Fortunately, there was a great deal to do, no idle hands to cause mischief. Mr. Pond had given Mrs. Carlisle a length of blue muslin, which Dia undertook to stitch neatly into a frock for the elder lady. Planning a style and cutting pieces would keep them engrossed for several days.

"I expect to have something for you when I return, dear little physician," Mr. Pond had said on leaving for the Cotswolds by stagecoach.

"Oh, you are so good!" she declared. "We do miss you when you are gone."

Mr. Pond was under no illusion that this was an amorous sentiment.

"Well, I am leaving General Whipple in command," he replied, "though I daresay you are wiser than he! But a lady—especially a very young lady—needs a man to watch over her."

Knowing this was a veiled warning about dashing viscounts, Dia blushed, yet managed to reply firmly, "I have a hundred dictums from my papa to guide me."

"And wise he was," agreed Mr. Pond. He could not truthfully say Dia's mama was equally wise. At least she was fond, amiable, pretty, and other pleasant things, though utterly lethargic.

To Miss Docking he separately voiced additional warnings, and she promised no one would mislead "little missie" while she had an eye on her.

"Dear, dear," muttered Mr. Pond to himself as he set out for the coaching house. "What do I know about being a father? But I do know young men. . . ."

Seven

At Lord Knollton's mansion on Upper Brook Street the servants' table was presided over by his lordship's butler at one end and his housekeeper at the other, with Shooker occupying a place at the housekeeper's right hand and Lady Knollton's dresser at the butler's right. Others of the household filled in to make a long table.

Adam, known to be a favorite of his lordship, was honored with a seat at the housekeeper's left, which placed him opposite Mr. Shooker. During the course of the meal these two exchanged significant looks, which confirmed each in the necessity of private conversation. Consequently, as plates were cleared and others left the room, they remained seated.

"His lordship sent oranges to someone called Mr. Pond," Adam said.

"Oh?" returned Shooker inquisitively.

"Yes. A gentleman as resides in the same house with a very pretty young lady."

"Ladybird?" asked Shooker softly.

A maid came into the room to crumb the table, and Adam did not reply until she had gone.

"I think not," he said carefully. "Very pretty of course." The men nodded at each other, being in agreement that his lordship would not be interested in any female who was not that.

"Pretty manners, too," added Adam.

Shooker was remembering an unexplained bracelet—a modest bracelet—waiting in his lordship's dresser drawer, but he was reluctant to mention this. He said, "Ah?" and waited for more from the groom.

They understood each other very well, those two, being united in holding the highest hopes for Lord Knollton, though his lordship did not suspect this.

"It appears to be a genteel house. Number 2, Langham Court. The young lady has a mother whom I have seen. His lordship was—er—respectful to both of them."

"Interesting," commented Shooker. "Does Lady Knollton know?"

"Yes. We took Miss Carlisle driving in the park, and his lordship pulled right up to where her ladyship was stopped and presented Miss Carlisle to her."

Shooker said, "That bears watching."

"Just my thought. We are agreed in hoping his lordship will settle down soon, are we not? The wrong female would be a disaster. Generally, none seem to have raised a serious interest on his part, which is just as well, if you ask me. Not a one of Lady Knollton's quality."

"But this is odd enough to make us . . . wonder," said his lordship's valet.

"Aye," returned Adam. "If I had free time I would see if I could drop around to meet some of the staff at Number 2. Get on friendly terms, so to speak, but his lordship has uses for me most days."

Shooker nodded. "If he goes out of town—"

"He'll take me along," Adam finished.

"Unless some other gent invites him to go in his carriage," reminded Shooker.

"There's that," Adam said, pushing back his chair as two maids with brooms came into the room.

Mr. Shooker also stood, and the men went out, separating in the hall, each with the serious matter of his lordship's future upon his mind.

Young Harry, with an *entrée* to Number 2, could have told

the two men number of things, but they did not think to ask him. Only the two of them could decide what was best for his lordship, they thought, having had the care of him for nigh on a dozen years.

In delivering oranges for Mr. Pond, Harry had easily made the acquaintance of the tweeny, who was awed by ladies and gentlemen, but, having lived a number of years in an orphanage, was wholly at ease with cheeky boys younger than herself. They were on good terms immediately, which permitted Cory to learn that Lord Francis was "a foin gent," and Harry that Miss Dia was "an angel right out of 'eaven."

Shooker and Adam would have had mixed feelings about this description of Miss Carlisle, for the future Viscountess Knollton needed to be something more than a mere angel—a lady of dignity, poise, and culture. Someone who could entertain dukes and princes at soirees and talk easily with lords of the admiralty and foreign ambassadors.

Harry, however, went away from his meeting with Cory, the tweeny, thoroughly convinced by her that Miss Dia Carlisle was a perfect princess—if of no social standing. Had his lordship asked, Harry planned to report what he had learned, but Knollton did not ask, nor did his lordship's valet or groom.

The viscount threw himself into the typical activities of a young noble, losing a hundred pounds at White's one night and winning back a hundred and ten at Brook's faro table the next night. There were balls at which he danced dutifully with *débutantes,* amused to find that the partners he chose were immediately solicited for subsequent dances. Always he led out his stepmother, securing her for the supper dance if he was able. No viewer, intensely interested though he or she might have been could tie Francis to the future of a particular *débutante.* Mamas groaned over his elusiveness and wondered if anyone would succeed in attaching him.

Did this feed his lordship's vanity? Not at all, as he supposed ambitious mamas treated all single nobles with the same fawning courtesy. Actually, if he saw a young lady languishing on the side lines, he was likely in a good-hearted way to invite her to dance, thus setting an example for other bucks. He was not the only catch of the Season, there being on the scene two young barons and an earl who had lost his wife sometime during the previous year.

Lady Knollton watched her stepson covertly. His behavior was everything she could wish, yet she had the uncomfortable feeling that he was bored, and this alarmed her a bit, for she could not help wondering if he would kick over the traces in some outlandish fashion.

That was not his nature, but he seemed edgy to her.

She could not think of another suitable young lady to bring to his attention. How flat the Season would be if he should decide to escape early to his manor in Gloucestershire!

Little did her ladyship realize that fleeing London was the last thing on the mind of Francis. He had seen someone to catch his fancy, and he was wondering how it would feel to dance with her. Good Lord! Did she even know *how* to dance? If not, there were other things they could do. . . . He could escort Miss Carlisle and her mother to Westminster Abbey, or to Madame Tusseaud's wax collection, if it was not touring the provinces. He could propose a carriage ride as far as Merton or St. Albans for a change of scene. These activities would not pitch them into Society or make Mrs. Carlisle ill at ease. They were very tame activities, which ordinarily he would have spurned. He was not thinking of his own amusement now, being eager to bring some pleasure into Miss Carlisle's life, which he supposed to be monotonous.

Monotonous? Dia Carlisle had no such view of her circumstances. Did not Mr. Pond's coming and going spice things up, as he brought news and anecdotes? And did not the Froam girls add girlish giggles and the slamming of doors? Could Cook not be heard banging kettles sometimes and singing, "Glory hallelujah"? And did not the ash boy whistle at his work? Lord Knollton's home was considerably more regulated and serene than Dia's.

More than two weeks had passed without his lordship's having seen the tutor's daughter. Despite Lydia's hints, which she had been wise enough not to repeat, Francis decided to call at Langham Court with a bottle of excellent sherry purloined from the tray in his own study. Though the day was mild, Lord Knollton felt the need of a surtout to conceal what he must carry. Adam was allowed to steer the curricle, and this he did very creditably, even if "blind" to what his master was holding under his coat.

The Carlisle ladies were happy to receive his lordship, Mrs. Carlisle obviously expecting him to draw a chair beside hers. This gave him a poor view of the more interesting female, for he could see her only by twisting his neck, and that was too obvious a movement to do very often.

"We have been very dull," Mrs. Carlisle told him promptly, "as Mr. Pond has deserted us."

Fearing his lordship would misunderstand, Dia quickly explained, "Mr. Pond has gone on a business trip."

"He is well, then?" asked the viscount.

"Oh, yes, thank heaven," Dia replied. "Your oranges were just what he needed!"

"Such a cough," interceded Mrs. Carlisle. "For a time I thought he might be consumptive, so I could not allow Dia to go near him."

Lord Knollton cast Dia a horrified look.

"Well, it was only a nasty chest thing," she explained. "He never ails. That is what alarmed everyone. But you may be sure he is well now and gone about his business."

"What is his business?" asked Knollton.

"Cloth—fabrics."

"Ah," said his lordship, knowing nothing about such matters.

Dia explained that Mr. Pond had a kinsman with a loom business in the Midlands. Mr. Pond was able to offer shops good buys on the newest fabrics. "He is very generous to the ladies of this house in giving samples when he has finished with them."

"Yes," said Mrs. Carlisle. "Dia is making a lovely new blue gown for me now."

"Ah," said the viscount again, "talented as well as beautiful!" His compliment made Dia blush furiously.

She would have preferred that his lordship had not known they were unable to afford a dressmaker, but he was too bemused to be thinking any such thing, for he saw her as a young lady of talents.

Fortunately, Miss Docking, wanting to have a good look at his lordship, came in to ask if they wanted to have tea. Knollton stood and bowed, just as if she were a great lady, which quite won Miss Docking's heart for all eternity.

"Miss Docking's brother is the owner of our house," Dia explained.

"And a fine house it is," declared his lordship promptly. "So well maintained."

"My brother insists upon that," Miss Docking told him. "Shall I have Cory bring tea, Mrs. Carlisle?"

Ordinarily the Carlisle ladies made tea for themselves with a kettle kept on the grate; they were astounded at this offer.

"Thank you," Dia said with great presence of mind. "I had neglected to fill our pot."

"Why not have some of the sherry that I brought?" said Lord Knollton, indicating the bottle, which he had set aside with his greatcoat. He could see that the decanter from which he had been previously served was as low as when he had left, so at once he began to ease the cork from his bottle, walking toward the tray, where the Carlisles' glasses waited upside down.

Hastily, Dia moved to turn over the glasses.

His lordship seemed to think there was nothing unreasonable in her doing this. He gave her a small smile and began to pour.

"Do not go away, Miss Docking," he said over his shoulder. "You must share this." There were persons of his acquaintance that would have been shocked by his condescension to the keeper of a lodging house, but so secure was he in his station that he did not worry about lowering himself. His father, he knew, had been gentlemanly to everyone.

So easy were his lordship's manners that the three ladies ac-

cepted glasses quite naturally and prepared to sip when Mr.
Whipple came in from outside.

"Ah, Whipple," Knollton said, "you are just in time."

Mr. Whipple wondered if he were in time to protect Dia as
he had promised Pond to do, but seeing all persons relaxed and
holding glasses, he took the one urged upon him and smothered
a sigh of pleasure. He and Miss Docking understood that his
lordship was, for reasons of his own, endeavoring to set them
at ease, but it was well done. They did relax, sip, and murmur
polite comments as to the sherry's bouquet. Miss Docking, for
one, had never tasted any wine so smooth, and her estimation
of Lord Knollton soared with each swallow.

Mrs. Carlisle, whose palate was less discriminating, said,
"Nice." She was too busy holding her glass so as not to spill
any to watch her daughter closely.

With cheeks faintly pink, Dia avoided the warm glances of
his lordship as she drank daintily. She really did not care much
for spirits, but she had been instructed by her papa in the proper
drinking of them: *one* glass only for a young lady. When Knollton offered more, she declined and set aside her glass to prevent
further urging.

He, to do him justice, had no ulterior motive in inviting them
to drink. He wished to make them all feel comfortable, and he
did succeed in this, as was demonstrated by Miss Docking's
quite forgetting that she wore her housekeeper's apron.

"Would you like to take a drive, Miss Carlisle?" he asked.

But Dia, caught in an everyday dress, and not wanting to
make the mistake again of driving in public thus clad, declined
as gracefully as she could.

"Perhaps another day. What would you say to Richmond
Park, Mrs. Carlisle? Would you like to drive there? We would
take four horses, of course, to make a swift journey, with time
for tea at an inn that I know to be excellent." He did not include
Miss Docking, but he gave her a look that implied he expected
her approval of a treat for the Carlisle ladies.

"Mr. Whipple, if I bring a barouche, we will have room for you. Would you join us?" he added.

Who could say no to his lordship?

Certainly not Dia, who had never been to Richmond Park.

Mrs. Carlisle was doubly persuaded by the idea of tea at an inn, anticipating fresh-baked buns and homemade preserves; and Mr. Whipple was hemming and hawing, but mumbling, "Thank you, my lord," while feeling sure Pond would expect him to go along to watch over Dia's safety. A long carriage ride might unsettle his stomach, but it was clearly his duty to go.

"If the skies are clear," Mr. Whipple temporized.

"Only if clear," the viscount assured him.

Seeing that Dia would be doubly chaperoned, Miss Docking was eager to withdraw to the cellar to tell Cook what treat was in store for their girl. She knew Mr. Pond had been doubtful of his lordship's intentions. Knollton, who was a master at conning chaperons, though never taking improper advantage, had only to be his easy, charming self in order to win agreement from Miss Docking.

She bobbed a little curtsy and left the room.

Mr. Whipple took a seat near Mrs. Carlisle, then immediately was obliged to stumble to his feet in order to return Lord Knollton's bow.

"I am overstaying," Knollton said. "Good afternoon, ladies. Whipple"—he took up his surtout, retreating to the door—"I will send word when the weather seems propitious."

He bowed and was gone before the three inhabitants of Number 2 could move or speak.

Mrs. Carlisle was charmed; Dia was torn between apprehension and delight. Mr. Whipple found himself wholly unable to control matters as Mr. Pond had commanded him to do. But surely a carriage ride in an open barouche with two chaperons, not to mention a coachman and very likely a groom, could not give rise to scandal. He hoped he was not failing Mr. Pond.

As for Mrs. Carlisle, she had transferred from a mild father to an amiable husband, and she had had no experience with rakeshames. His lordship seemed a gentleman and so she judged him to be. Just like the grandes dames of elite Society, she was wheedled by him.

Dia was dazzled by his lordship's pleasing form and face, unable to be critical of one who was consistently considerate of her mother and herself. She could not believe ill of him, but enough of her father's wise dicta remained within her head to make her cautious.

Had not his lordship's stepmother invited her to visit in their home? Dia could see nothing diabolical in a carriage ride. The real danger, she thought, was in letting her emotions overrun her expectations. She must not, in fact, be swayed by timid hopes.

What would dear Mr. Pond have said? Surely her mama was protection against improper advances! What Dia must do was guard her emotions, for Lord Knollton was very beguiling, especially as he seemed interested in her.

Mr. Whipple was equally confused. He thought Lord Knollton was a splendidly dressed young fellow with pleasing manners, but was he genuine? Pond would have known. As for himself, Mr. Whipple could not imagine putting his foot down and forbidding the acquaintance when it seemed to please dear Dia. Her mother was not hesitant to accept Knollton's friendship, though Whipple had an uneasy feeling that Pond would not approve. So what was Mr. Whipple to do? Go along to Richmond Park, keeping an eagle eye on Dia. If a broken axle or some such thing stranded them somewhere and Mrs. Carlisle gave way to a spasm, Whipple told himself, surely *he* could keep his wits and watch Dia closely.

It was Mr. Whipple's nature to worry. On the other hand, Dia was inclined to view the proposed jaunt as something to anticipate with pleasure. If her mama were likely to suffer a spasm over their speed or a sneezing spell from dust, Dia thought she could cope with things like that. The prospect of being tumbled into a ditch did not occur to her. Since Lord Knollton's coachman was accustomed to driving Lady Knollton to and from their manor in Gloucestershire and other places, she thought she could trust herself and her mama to the excursion.

Eight

His lordship's groom and valet had no chance for consultation that evening.

Adam was late into the servants' dining room, having returned his lordship's team to their stalls and lingered to discuss with the coachman the steadier pair that were to be hitched to the closed carriage for transporting Lady Lydia and her stepson to an evening party.

Meanwhile, Shooker was early for his meal, so as to be prompt in attendance at a bath and careful dressing of his master in the restrained elegance that he preferred. Some valets might hope for snugger coats and intricate cravats, but Lord Knollton's inclination was more moderate, which—Shooker assured the household—was a sign of breeding and good taste.

"We don't need heavy padding on our shoulders," he had been heard to say time and again.

While Lord Knollton was being bathed, barbered, and eased into creaseless garments, his coachman was fortifying himself in the kitchen, much admired by Cook and her helpers for his digestive capabilities. He packed away a hearty meal, washing it down with strong tea (to keep him warm and awake while his lordship and her ladyship enjoyed a tedious dinner and concert, or whatever was supposed to entertain them).

As might be expected, Cook admired anyone who ate largely. She was a broad woman who enjoyed her own creations.

"Ye'll want a jug of tea, Wally. To keep ye warm while ye wait," she said.

It was a foregone conclusion. Except for midsummer, Wally always had his jug of hot tea stowed beneath his seat, and a woolly scarf for his neck. Damp rose from the river, along with poisonous vapors. Waiting could be chilly, though when Lady Knollton accompanied his lordship they did not linger excessively late.

Generally understood in service quarters was the fact that Lady Lydia could not stay away from her wee daughter long hours, and his lordship was almost as moderate. Rarely did he carouse with peep-o'-day boys.

The servants often forgot that Francis had reached maturity. Most of them had been employed at Knollton House since his childhood. But there was no doubt that they were proud to say "my lord" to him. Shooker, who was on intimate terms with him, was regarded by the other servants with awe. When Shooker said, "His lordship wants—" they rallied to their duties.

Most of the servants were older than his lordship, but his word was solid law, although he did not have the least idea of this.

Was Francis, Lord Knollton, free to do as he pleased? Certainly not. He was bound by the conventions of Society and by fondness for his youthful stepmother. But it all came so naturally to him that he had no inclination to kick up his heels or cause a scandal.

The Upper Ten Thousand expected him to choose a suitable bride and settle down to a life of ease and conventional pursuits. His papa had been a bit stuffy, though sufficiently gracious to be liked by most who knew him. Society supposed Francis would become the same, especially as he had no bad habits to embroil him in folly. They did not know, however, that Francis had discovered a little lady who looked for the best in everyone. Her papa had enough times told her that one must always do one's best, which was not necessarily what, in each case, came easiest. One should not coast through life, enjoying ease and dissipation, but must make the most of one's aptitudes and forgive the other fellow for his flaws.

"Give a man the chance to do good," Mr. Carlisle had said, "and generally he will do just that."

Perhaps this was a bit unrealistic in Regency England, but Dia's life had been so sheltered by her papa (and by Mr. Pond and Mr. Whipple) that she had no doubts. Even though warned by Miss Docking and by poor Cory, who had seen the seamy side of life before coming to the haven of Langham Court, Dia continued to look for the best in everyone. Her mama had cautioned that young men—especially handsome ones—were not to be taken seriously, and she understood this, but so few had come her way that she had none to compare with Lord Francis Dubois Milne, Viscount Knollton. And he, after all, had caused her no alarm.

But dreams and reality seldom meet.

Very likely she would someday be tending a counter in a draper's shop, like Jane and Mary Ann!

"They," she told herself, "are not at all unhappy. Mary Ann seems to speak often of someone she calls 'young Mr. Folkes.'" The son of the draper was described as being divinely handsome.

When the draper's son was displayed at last in Langham Court, Dia did not think him remarkable in any way, but a nice enough slim person with a sure future because his father owned the shop where he and Mary Ann worked. He could not be expected to wed both Froam girls, but apparently they thought one of them might nab him, and Mary Ann had the edge. Jane dropped hints about this from time to time, though no one at Number 2 saw him for some months. Perhaps it was wishful thinking. Was it possible that he would introduce a friend for Jane?

No suggestion was made of asking Mr. Folkes to produce a friend for Dia's benefit. Both Froam girls recognized that Dia was mysteriously several cuts above themselves. No hard feelings here. Place was something most people understood.

As for that, Dia felt no consciousness of Place.

The secret fifty pounds were comforting, bolstering what Mr.

Carlisle had left them. They were fixed nicely for a time, and if Dia could sew some simple dresses to sell or set up as a teacher of composition and arithmetic or something, the future would not be alarming at all.

Mrs. Carlisle was not troubled with qualms. Had not her husband always taken care of her? And was not Dia doing the same?

But Mr. Pond and Mr. Whipple were not satisfied with the modest future that Dia envisioned. She deserved better, they thought. And because Lord Knollton had not vanished from the scene, they began to have second thoughts about him. Privately, Mr. Pond feared Dia's sweet nature and the exquisite arrangement of her features would attract gentlemen who were more acquisitive than beneficent. Dia Carlisle must be protected at all costs! But Whipple had less discernment. *He* was beginning to imagine that Lord Knollton was just the one to elevate their darling to a position of respectable ease.

Though nothing further was said, all inhabitants of Number 2, plus Adam and Shooker at Upper Brook Street, maintained a quiet watch. Lady Lydia—seeing that her stepson stayed his usual attentive self to her and fond to little Sara—was lulled somewhat, though not perfectly easy; she would have liked to know more about Miss Dia Carlisle.

When, on a beautiful day, Lord Knollton discovered that his stepmama was expecting three ladies for luncheon and would be too occupied to think about his activities, he sent a note to Number 2 and ordered the barouche made ready. But her ladyship did hear this, too late to intervene, or even to discover the exact use intended for a four-person carriage. She did not know that Harry had sped off with a note for certain persons in Langham Court.

It was not that Lord Knollton wished to be secretive; he simply thought that the less said, the better. He had no ulterior motives, but he did not wish a simple drive in the country to be magnified to an assignation.

At Langham Court his note was received with pleasure. Mr. Whipple polished his shoes and brushed his best coat twice.

Mrs. Carlisle docilely put on what her daughter held before her, only asking if she should carry a parasol.

"I do not think so," Dia said. "The day is sunny, but mild. If there is any wind, you might find it a nuisance to hold on to a parasol. Let us rely upon the brims of our bonnets to shield our faces, Mama."

They were ready when his lordship came to escort them to the barouche, which was waiting in Langham Street because it was too large to turn in the court. This was a severe disappointment to Miss Docking, Cory, Cook, and the ash boy, who would have liked to see their three residents set out in such splendid style.

"I hope you will not mind," said his lordship, taking a seat beside Mr. Whipple, "that I decided to change our destination. Sometimes traffic is slow in crossing the Thames, so I thought St. Albans would make a more pleasant ride, and there are a number of antiquities to be seen."

Mrs. Carlisle cared little for antiquities. What meant most to her was the ride across London and being seen in his lordship's carriage, even if no one knew who she was. Mr. Whipple, in his self-appointed task of guarding Dia, sat very erect and watchful, though there was nothing to be criticized in the behavior of Lord Knollton or the young lady. Traveling mostly northwestward, as they were, the ladies had the sun to their right shoulders, with no need for the parasols that they had not brought.

Once out of the city, there was fresh spring-green countryside to be admired and enjoyed.

At the reins of his lordship's four horses was Wally. An immense figure almost overflowing his handsome livery, he was very pleased to be driving his master beyond the urban area. Seated beside him on the box was the favored Adam, who was wise enough to treat Wally with great deference, and who therefore was welcomed graciously.

"Ever drive a team of four, lad?" Wally asked genially in a low voice, being sure Adam had not.

Adam, who was no "lad," but a sharp fellow, replied softly, "Only with a lighter vehicle. Be glad to learn from you."

"Much the same," said the coachman. "Heavier vehicle, stronger horses, but his lordship cares naught for racing with ladies along." He chuckled. " 'Spect you see some swift runs."

"Aye," returned Adam, offering no details. Only to Shooker would he spill information about his master.

Behind and lower, Lord Knollton was enjoying a perfect view of a very pretty face. Dia's eyes sparkled with pleasure, and now and then a curl blew delightfully across her cheek. He could watch her without a thought to their progress, for Wally had his orders. As for the road itself, Lord Knollton knew the details of every road out of London and need not look about, except to note when they had cleared the city.

"I hope you are comfortable, Mrs. Carlisle," he said.

"Oh, yes, indeed," she replied. "It has been so long since I drove this way." So long, that it was doubtful if she had ever done so. And, of course, Dia had not, for how were they to have driven without horses or carriage? Of those residing at Number 2, Langham Court, only Mr. Pond ranged about the English countryside.

"If you do not mind our speed, Mrs. Carlisle," Knollton said, "we will head for St. Albans for a luncheon, and then have time to stroll about the town, before driving home."

"Oh—delightful," said the lady, assuming Wally had orders to be careful, for she was able to feel quite safe.

They spun smoothly along, seeing, now and then, a quaint hamlet, or the gates of a manor. Sometimes other vehicles wheeled by, heading for the city. Mr. Whipple, whose stomach was behaving well, had begun to relax. He now asked, "Do you ever drive a carriage and team such as this, my lord? I have seen you handle your curricle. But such a large equipage as this—?"

Knollton chuckled easily. "You are right. A curricle is more to my taste. Our driver today is very experienced. Mrs. Carlisle, you may be sure he is thoroughly competent."

As he spoke, a swift vehicle was approaching, heading in the opposite direction.

"Oh, yes," trilled Mrs. Carlisle. "I feel quite easy."

Even so, the other vehicle, not moderating its furious speed, surged by. Behind his lordship's back, Wally yelped and clapped a hand to the right side of his face, dropping the reins.

In a flash Adam had seized the lines to bring their horses under control.

"Good God!" exclaimed Knollton, twisting around. "What's the trouble?"

"Sorry, m'lord," groaned Wally. "Took a stone by me eye."

Almost immediately Adam had halted the team, who stamped their feet nervously. The viscount sprang down and went forward to see how badly his man was hurt, passing up to him a clean handkerchief. So concerned was he with his coachman that he did not realize Dia had scrambled down and reached his side.

"How bad is it?" she asked anxiously. "Let me see."

"Oh, miss," Wally mumbled. "It's nothing for you to be seeing. Just the hit, miss——took me sudden."

"Yes, yes," agreed Knollton hurriedly, "unfortunate mishap. You are in no shape to drive. We will go on to the next inn and get some cold water for you. Adam will drive. Miss Carlisle, let me set you back in the carriage."

Dia, having a view of Wally's swelling face, said, "This man must not stay upon the box. Suppose he becomes faint? Why, he could tumble down into the road! He must come in back. Can you not exchange places with him, my lord?"

Thunderstruck, Francis understood she expected him to yield his own comfortable seat to his servant. "Y-yes. Very well," he said. "Can you step down, Wally?"

As Adam watched and held the team securely in check, Wally lurched down to the road and was established next to Mr. Whipple. Mrs. Carlisle looked on, wide-eyed, as his lordship handed Dia back to her seat.

"But who will drive?" Mrs. Carlisle asked, confused.

"I am waiting for Miss Carlisle to tell me," the viscount replied. "Well, Miss Carlisle, what is your plan? Shall it be Adam or me?"

"You must decide, my lord," she said demurely. "Pray, let us find an inn quickly."

"It will be Adam," he said, turning away to climb to the perch. "Carry on, Adam."

The groom, pleased to be trusted with a carriage and four prime horses, not to mention five passengers, set about the business in a competent manner.

Within a mile or two, they had reached a small hostelry that was snug under a mantle of vines. Four mongrel puppies tumbled about the doorstep, and a mother dog ambled forward to greet them benignly. There was a reassuring calmness about the place.

Lord Knollton stepped from the barouche and went indoors to inspect the accommodations. He soon returned, followed by a rolling, pleasant innkeeper.

"Only one parlor," Knollton said, "but it's suitable for our ladies. This is Mr. Mix. Mrs. Mix will treat Wally in the taproom. There are no customers at present."

Wally was turned over to the innkeeper, Adam and the carriage to a gawking stableboy, and the viscount escorted his guests indoors, halting briefly while Dia stroked the mother dog.

"Such a sweet animal," she said of the canine matriarch. "I think this amiable creature would let me handle her babes."

"Oh, Dia, fleas!" protested her mother.

"But see how clean they are," Dia insisted, though she obediently followed Lord Knollton and her mother under a covered doorway and into the building.

They entered a room at left, finding a small, neat parlor, where a freshly kindled fire crackled in a friendly fashion. Mr. Whipple, feeling that somehow he should be arranging matters for the comfort of the two ladies, was relieved to find that no decisions or effort were required from him. The four travelers were ushered to seats about a table, and almost at once cups of tea were brought by a bonny, young servant girl.

Next, the innkeeper came to tell them that Wally's eye was not injured, the pebble having hit just beyond the corner of it.

"Very little bleeding, m'lord," he said. "The stone must have struck just next to the eye. We have a well with very cold water, and m'wife is applying wet packs to the bruise." Putting responsibility (or blame) upon his wife, he added, "Mrs. Mix feels your man should stay quiet for quite some time. Can we serve a nuncheon for you?"

"Perhaps we can leave Wally here to recuperate while we continue on our visit to St. Albans," Knollton said, not wishing to disappoint the Carlisle ladies. "I'll have a look at him."

Accordingly, his lordship accompanied Mr. Mix to the taproom, where he found Wally moderately comfortable with cold compresses on his cheek and temple.

"Oh, m'lord," said the injured man, "it's sorry I am to cause a fuss and spoil your day."

"But you have spoiled nothing," his lordship said kindly. "Fault lies with that speeding buck who passed us recklessly. Are you in much pain?"

"Not while the cold is against me head."

"Then we must keep the water packs on longer. Would you feel deserted if we continue our trip and pick you up on the return?"

"Oh, no, m'lord, but will you feel safe with Adam driving those horses?"

Knollton smiled. "Didn't he snatch the reins in the nick of time? I think he'll manage. We won't race, of course, and I will sit on the box with him. Will that do?"

Wally was not about to say his master could not take charge of his own carriage and team. "Aye, m'lord," he answered.

"Good man," said Knollton. "Stay quiet. Ask for anything you need. How about a mug of cold brew? We will not make a long stay at St. Albans, and we will fetch you as we return."

Nine

Knollton's decision to continue the little trip was not an easy one to make, for he did not like to leave Wally in the care of strangers. On the other hand, he did not wish to disappoint the Carlisle ladies. Dia, he felt sure, would understand the need to take his valuable coachman home, but Mrs. Carlisle might not be so easy to persuade to venture out another time.

The horses had had a good rest.

So they set out, his lordship climbing to the box beside Adam, and Mr. Whipple riding backward alone to face the ladies, though he had little to say to them.

All proceeded well. Adam demonstrated his skill. Another hour saw them rolling into St. Albans and stopping at a new hostelry, where the ladies went upstairs with the owner's wife to refresh themselves, while Knollton ordered a luncheon meal that he thought they would enjoy.

The day continued bright, with moderate warmth—perfect for exploring the town.

It was an ancient place, once called by the Romans *Verulamium,* but now taking its name from the first Christian martyr, Alban, who was executed in the early third century by the Romans for sheltering a Christian priest. The shrine, erected where he had died, became an abbey, and later St. Albans Cathedral, Knollton told his guests.

Knowing Mrs. Carlisle led a sedentary life, Francis took them on a gentle stroll to see an open-air market established by the Saxons, and a fifteenth-century clock tower.

"How do you know all these details?" Mrs. Carlisle asked wonderingly.

His lordship admitted he had been able to read a few facts before bringing visitors to this place.

Far from thinking this tour was only designed to impress them, Dia admired his taking the trouble to find out what they were sure to ask. She liked the easy pace, the casual air of the town, though her mother, accustomed to London, thought it was somewhat "slow."

"You are not seeing it on a market day," Knollton said with a smile. Bit by bit, so that the Carlisle ladies hardly noticed it, he led them up the slope to the cathedral. Once there, he commanded, "Look down the hill. Had you realized you'd walked so high? The River Ver looks no more than a small stream, doesn't it?"

"The Thames is the only river I know," admitted Mrs. Carlisle. "Why, that does not look like a *river* down there!"

"That is the Ver. Miss Carlisle, can you see it?"

"Yes. Is it as small as it seems from here?"

"Almost," his lordship admitted. "Isn't this a splendid site for a cathedral? But do not ask me to explain the building, for there have been centuries of tearing up and rebuilding. Off to the southwest was the ancient Roman town. I am afraid blocks of stone were stolen from it to erect the abbey and other churches."

Dia exclaimed, "Roman! Is this so ancient?"

"An ancient settlement," he admitted, "but there was much rebuilding over the years. My history is a bit shaky."

So easily had he brought them to the height, that neither lady could complain of shortened breath. They had walked enough, however, and were ready to descend to the carriage when he suggested it.

By now the sun was shifting to the west. Adam drove them to the inn, where Wally waited. All was serene at this place, the bitch and her pups rising from the doorstep to greet them. While the horses were being watered, Wally appeared, his temple beginning to turn shades of gray and green.

"I'm feeling fit to drive, m'lord," he insisted.

But Lord Knollton said, "Certainly not. Adam did well with your team. I will allow you to sit beside him again and see how properly he handles them."

Wally, mollified to hear the horses described as *his,* saw the passengers settled in their places, then heaved himself to the perch and gave Adam a nod to start. Adam, by this time feeling more secure as coachman, turned the horses onto the highway and set them at a moderate pace toward London. Both men knew ladies did not like breakneck speed.

"Your men understand how to give a comfortable ride," Mrs. Carlisle observed, as they slowed at the outskirts of London.

"Yes," agreed his lordship. "They have learned from my stepmother, who prefers comfort to speed."

As neither lady had traveled anywhere, they had no experience with which to compare this trip to St. Albans.

"Mr. Pond says," offered Dia, "that stagecoaches sometimes set a frightening pace."

"Yes," agreed his lordship with a grin, "and young bucks race one another, like the one who shot a stone at Wally. But you must not ask me if I have done that, for I would not want Adam to hear me tell a fib."

From this, she was not sure whether he had or had not raced. Ladies, she was sure, did not do so; of the notorious Lady Lade she had never heard. "Perhaps there are times when speed matters."

"Oh, yes, but not today," his lordship replied. "The sun is not so low, you will notice. We will have you ladies safe at Langham Court before dusk. Are you warm enough?"

Mrs. Carlisle answered for both of them. "Yes, indeed. The sun is still warm."

"Like a gentle shawl," Dia added whimsically.

Mr. Whipple, with a pleasant expression attached to his face, said nothing, for he was thinking that his stomach had behaved very well and that it might hold out until they reached Number 2. By keeping his eyes on the ladies opposite him and not watching the slipping away of the road behind them, he was warding off the queasiness that often assailed him in rapid vehicles. In company, he seldom had much to say, and did not feel equal to anything now. As they entered the city, a slower pace made him much more comfortable, and at the entrance to Langham Court he breathed a small sigh because the trip was finished.

With twitterings of thanks, Mrs. Carlisle and her daughter crossed the court, each one with an arm of his lordship's to steady her, and Mr. Whipple followed thankfully until—at the very door of Number 2—a frowning Mr. Pond confronted them, saying, "Where have you been?" in militant accents that startled all but Mrs. Carlisle, who immediately exclaimed:

"Mr. Pond! You have made a short trip this time!"

"Yes," he replied. "But I relied upon you, Whipple, to—"

Here his lordship, only half understanding, but realizing the need to smooth matters, said firmly, "We have taken Mrs. Carlisle on a little drive to St. Albans to give her the benefit of fresh country air."

Even an irate, suspicious Pond could see the need of that. Though he shot a disapproving look at Mr. Whipple, he stood aside so that they could enter the house.

Pink with embarrassment, and understanding Mr. Pond's attitude (if her mama did not), Dia said, "Let us see if Miss Docking can give us tea. It was a revitalizing day in the country, Mr. Pond. You are not the only one who can enjoy good weather and fresh scenes. Have you seen the cathedral at St. Albans? Do come in and let Mama tell you how impressive it is."

Knollton, assessing the situation, said with appropriate solemnity, "You will understand my need to take my injured coachman home. Good day, ladies, Whipple, Mr. Pond." He bowed and left them at the doorsteps of Number 2.

Mr. Pond, having second thoughts about his own hasty jumping to conclusions, led the ladies inside.

"You did not expect to see me back in London so soon. Oh,

I am feeling fit enough, but it seemed wise not to overdo it on a first business trip after such a bout of chest problems." Miss Docking met them in the hallway. "Ah, Miss Docking, would you be so kind as to make tea for the ladies, Whipple, and me?"

"Aye, sir," she replied, heading for the cellar stair. Well did she know that Mr. Pond was her brother's most prosperous tenant. Besides, he was a man whose principles she could respect.

The four boarders went into the Carlisles' sitting room, all removing their hats. Mr. Pond added two coals to the grate and gave it a good shaking up, while Dia drew closed the curtains at the courtyard windows. She saw no reason to apologize for accepting the attentions of Lord Knollton. Had he not proved himself a friend in more ways than all the residents of Number 2 suspected?

Mrs. Carlisle had subsided into her customary chair, and Mr. Whipple chose a stiff, straight one; surely, Pond could not be cross with him. Had he not been watching over Dia closely for hours, despite the effect of travel on his digestion?

Miss Docking brought the tea tray herself, then went back down to the nether regions again to tell Cook and little Cory that fresh air had raised a bloom in the ladies' cheeks.

"Well, missy," said Pond, stirring his tea briskly, "did you enjoy St. Albans?"

Miss Carlisle's conscience was clear. "I certainly did. The antiquity is astonishing. The whole day was perfect, except for Wally's accident."

"Who is Wally?" demanded Mr. Pond, neglecting his tea for a moment.

"Poor man," said Mrs. Carlisle, entering the conversation. "Some madcap fellow passed us on the road at a horrid pace and threw up a stone, which hit Wally in the head—Knollton's coachman, you know. We did not see it happen. Everything went so fast, but Wally was hurt so unexpectedly that he lost control of the team—that is, would have lost control, if Adam—the groom—had not grabbed the reins. Dia and I could not see from where we sat, but that is what Knollton explained to us later—and certainly we were thankful for Adam!"

Mr. Pond was accustomed to Mrs. Carlisle's way of talking.

"You could have been wrecked!" he objected, shooting a look of disapproval at poor Whipple, though what he might have done to rescue Dia and her mama was not clear.

"But we *were not!*" replied Mrs. Carlisle triumphantly. "Did I not just say that Adam seized the reins and stopped his lordship's four horses as quick as anything? Oh, it was neatly done, and I daresay Knollton will reward him suitably."

Mr. Pond scarcely looked convinced, but Dia added calmly, "We were not traveling fast."

"No, we were not, but even so, Wally might have fallen from his perch, which was quite high above the road. Why, he might have broken something!"

Whipple, who was withdrawing into his cravat, was relieved to hear Dia say pacifically, "A horrid bruise was all Wally received. It spoiled his day, but ours was in every way delightful. You, Mr. Pond, who travel so much, cannot know what pleasure Mama and I had from a day out of town."

Mr. Pond was then obliged to say he was glad to learn of their enjoyment. "Well, Whipple, they will be calling us to dinner soon. Shall we go up to our rooms now?"

It was the same as a command, though Mr. Whipple did not relish the prospect of a private chat with Mr. Pond, of whom he stood somewhat in awe. He feared he could expect chastisement for having allowed their ladies to go off anywhere with Knollton, though he did not know how he could have prevented their going.

But upstairs, being invited sternly into Pond's room, he found Pond only wished to hear details of the day's outing.

"It could not have been more—innocent," Mr. Whipple said. "You know my uneasy stomach, but the drive was not reckless, and I got along fairly well."

Pond said it was Dia he wished to hear about. "Was his lordship proper in his behavior?"

Glad to affirm this, Mr. Whipple declared, "Perfectly. Except for the accident to Knollton's coachman, all went well. I had been to St. Albans once, though not up the slope to the cathedral. Quite a view from there, quite a view. As for Knollton, if you think such a gentleman should overstep himself, you are wrong." Rather proud of himself to suggest Pond could have been wrong about anything, he added, "Perfect gentleman. Paid more attention to his injured servant than to either lady!"

Mr. Pond did not sigh, but his manner eased. "I am glad," he admitted, "for the Carlisle ladies to have pleasure, however small. The weather was fine. They got fresh air. But we cannot relax our vigilance, Whipple. You and I do not know Knollton well enough to judge his character. Heaven knows I would like some respectable fellow to rescue Dia from this place, but a nobleman is not likely to do so. You and I must put our heads together and think of someone suitable to introduce to her."

Whipple was willing enough, but he knew no one superior in sense and pence to Pond, and Pond would be first to admit himself no "catch" for a beautiful girl of eighteen. Perhaps if Pond married *Mrs. Carlisle,* it would stabilize those ladies . . . but even Whipple could see that would not lead to happiness or advancement for anyone.

While Mr. Whipple was drifting off into these unprofitable thoughts, Mr. Pond was thinking more sensibly. "A hint to Knollton may not be enough," he said. "I will have to think further about this. Meanwhile, keep an eye on our pretty girl and let me know if the viscount comes again."

"I cannot jump in his curricle with them," Whipple protested.

"No, of course not." Mr. Pond sighed. "I suppose I shall have to warn Mrs. Carlisle, but it will be like talking to a mist on the downs."

"She is a sweet lady," Whipple defended.

"Yes, but a vague one. Ah, well, let us stay alert." Mr. Pond would do so himself, but he was uncertain of Mr. Whipple's capabilities. Nice enough fellow, but soft as a custard pudding. Perhaps he would have to have a strict word with Knollton, who would undoubtedly take offense. How had he, a middle-aged bachelor, fallen into this difficulty? Mr. Carlisle had not empowered him to act as Dia's father . . . but *somebody* had to protect the girl.

Ten

"I think I will go down to dinner tonight," said Mrs. Carlisle after the men had gone.

This surprised Dia, though she thought it best to give no sign of its being a departure from daily practice.

Both went to wash road dust from their faces and hands, by unspoken agreement not changing their dresses. If a drive in the countryside had such a convivial effect upon Mrs. Carlisle that she did not wish to dine alone in her parlor, Dia could only be glad. Besides, she was not anxious for a private *tête-à-tête* on the subject of Knollton's attention.

"I will go down now and tell Miss Docking, so that she can set a place for you. Come along when the bell rings, Mama."

Mrs. Carlisle said, "Well, of course."

Was this going to be the beginning of a new lifestyle?

Dia went quietly away to find Miss Docking setting out utensils.

"A bit of excitement you had, Miss Dia—the coachman's being hurt, I mean."

"Yes. We are so thankful it was not worse," Dia replied. "Let me lay out forks for you. Will we need knives?"

Miss Docking said, "No. Yes. I mean, you must not help me, but we are having fish tonight and I daresay Mr. Pond will want a knife to deal with skin and bones."

With a smile Dia asked if Mr. Pond made decisions for the whole house.

"He knows what's what," Miss Docking replied, giving Dia a sharp look. "Better listen to him, miss."

"Are you hinting something about Lord Knollton?" said Dia. "Oh, dear. Cannot Mama and Mr. Whipple and I go for a simple drive without the whole house raising alarums?"

"But it wasn't a simple drive," countered Miss Docking. "It was a barouche and four horses, and a genuine coachman, and a footman. I hope you have at least suspected that his lordship might have ideas!"

Dia bit her lip. "I cannot read minds," she admitted, "but you must believe his lordship has never said the least improper thing to me. Ever. Were not my mama and Mr. Whipple with me the whole time?"

"Well, yes, Miss Dia, but those two need someone to watch over them, as you and I both know. And the carriage wasn't a pumpkin, either. But I ask you this: How many lords find the way to Langham Court for any reason? But I beg your pardon for speaking when maybe I shouldn't."

Dia could not be angry, nor could she face the supposition that his lordship had improper designs upon herself. In a way it was amusing—probably the result of nobles never having been seen in Langham Court before now. But she was not inclined to dream castles. If the whole house manufactured impossible romances (or foul deceits), she would keep the good sense that Papa had instilled in her. Somebody must maintain a sense of proportion.

Mr. Pond was the one she would have selected for that, and look how he was acting now—toplofty—almost throwing a scene. Mr. *Pond?*

Fortunately, it was Mr. Whipple who was first down to the cellar when Miss Docking sounded the gong. He said, "All those wheels—round and round! I would not have thought I could face a meal, but here I am—actually hungry."

"You did not eat much at St. Albans," Dia reminded him with a smile. "Mama and I appreciate the sacrifice you made in accompanying us."

"Ah! No sacrifice when it is for you, my dear," he said.

She knew he, at least, had no designs on her. When he spoke flowery things, he was only falling back on the custom of a courtlier era.

"I do not want you to suffer on my account. Mama and I are always glad of your company, and look what travel has done for you—created an appetite!" Sometimes she wondered if Mr. Whipple went without meals when he was gone all day; she very much feared his spare coins were spent for wine. At least Lord Knollton had provided a luncheon today.

The Froam girls came next, followed by Mr. Pond, who escorted Dia's mama. If everyone was surprised to see Mrs. Carlisle, they said nothing. Jane Froam did once mention young Mr. Folkes, and her sister muffled a giggle with her napkin. Mrs. Carlisle actually ate four bites that Dia saw, and perhaps others. The meal passed peacefully.

At Upper Brook Street, warning bells for dinner were not even sounded until long after Number 2 had finished.

Knollton's stepmother was looking particularly beautiful when she ventured into uncertain territory by saying, "You drove out of town today. Which way did you go?"

"Northwest," he replied briefly.

"What on earth is that way?" she exclaimed ingenuously.

"St. Albans, Mama dear. And if you want to know why, do not hesitate to ask."

She promptly said, "Why?"

He had known that sooner or later she would discover he had driven out of the city. "To give Mrs. Carlisle and her daughter something to see besides London streets. Mr. Whipple, whom you do not know, accompanied us. A very pleasant fellow, if sometimes a bit fuzzy."

Lady Knollton laid down her fork. "Fuzzy? I know you have friends who are eccentric, but why a fuzzy one?" It was Miss Carlisle she was most interested in hearing about, yet she endeavored to approach the subject indirectly.

"Because he is their friend and he was available to lend Mrs.

Carlisle an arm when we walked—although I seemed to get that duty."

"And you intended to escort the young one."

"Naturally. I see you know me well, Lydia. Did you learn also that Wally was hit by a flying stone?"

"Yes. That rumor reached me. Well, was the day worth the effort and Wally's discomfort?"

He replied that he was thankful Wally was not seriously hurt, and sorry for the accident, but he had not considered these things a purchase price for pleasing the Carlisle ladies.

"Now you are sounding like your father!" Lydia exclaimed. "Being lordly!"

"Thank you, Mama," he said, leaning back in his chair with a teasing grin.

She was not diverted. "You know I thought highly of your father. Even when lordly, he did not tease me. Or try to dodge issues. What is there about Miss Carlisle to make you evasive? Take her driving anytime! No need to pass it off as a kindness to her mother." Two could play at the game of keeping secrets, she thought, forming an idea of investigating Miss Carlisle privately herself. The little she had seen of the girl was satisfactory—neat, well behaved, modest. Also the girl had won little Sara's approval. Others might have laughed at Sara's having any discernment in the matter, but Lady Knollton did not underestimate one who seemed to appeal to her small daughter. There was a way to make sure.

When her stepson had left home the next morning, after warning her not to expect him for dinner, Lydia went from the breakfast room to her chamber, where she changed to a simple blue frock and a straw bonnet with sky-blue ribbons that complemented the limpid blue of her eyes.

Then, having sent her maid out of the way on a nebulous errand, she went swiftly down the stairs and out the street door, to a jarvey at the corner. "Langham Court, please," she said, entering a hackney. A casual word from Adam to her maid had produced that much of an address. "Court" did not sound large; she could knock at every door, if necessary.

The jarvey knew a lady when he saw one. He touched his cap, and headed for Langham Court as instructed to do. Lady Lydia found that they had not far to go beyond All Souls Church. Most houses there appeared well kept. If the neighborhood was not elegant, certainly it was respectable.

"Please wait for me," she instructed, when they had halted in Langham Court. Like the boot boy on his first visit to Langham Court, she was confronted with three houses. Which was she to enter?

Luckily, at that moment, two young women came from the central house and stared with interest at her. Lady Lydia had thought her outfit modest, but they recognized someone of superior class.

"Were you wanting someone, my lady?" Mary Ann asked.

"Mrs. Carlisle," she replied. So struck by her beauty was the girl that she gawked. The other one said, "Oh, yes. Room A—on the left, my lady."

"Thank you," said Lady Knollton. She nodded in a pleasant manner, passed them, and entered the door from which the two had come. After that, it was easy; the inner door at the left bore a card bearing the Carlisles' name. Lydia knocked.

In the few seconds before the door opened, Lady Knollton was able to notice the good quality of the building (Mr. Docking's investment) and the well-kept interior (Miss Docking's responsibility).

Then there was a small, neatly dressed woman confronting the poised and beautiful Lady Knollton, eye to eye, since they were of even height.

"Mrs. Carlisle?" said her ladyship in a pleasant voice. "I am Lady Knollton. I believe you know my stepson."

The elder lady stepped back, drawing wide the door. "Well, I do and I don't, my lady," she said her usual unclear fashion. "He was kind enough to give me a ride in balmy air—Mr. Whipple, and my daughter, and me—and we saw St. Albans, though

Wally was hurt. So I cannot say I know Lord Knollton well, but Mr. Pond says that he is a very fine gentleman."

Being willing to accept that estimation, Lydia said, "Of course, I agree with that opinion. Your daughter is quite enchanting; she has bewitched my small child."

"Oh," said Mrs. Carlisle immediately, "there is nothing of a 'witch' about Dia, although her papa thought her quite something out of a myth—or some such thing. I know nothing about myths. He insisted on the name, and I thought 'Why not?' "

Fey, decided Lady Knollton.

Then Mrs. Carlisle belatedly said, "Do sit down. I will call Dia, who is in another room sewing something." A dress for her mama, though fortunately Mrs. Carlisle did not reveal that.

Her ladyship chose the chair that her stepson had several times occupied. She looked about the salon while Mrs. Carlisle went to summon Dia. There were some good pieces of furniture, a bit shabby, and a handsome decanter on a tray at one side, all of which indicated respectable origins. There was not time for a closer scrutiny, for Mrs. Carlisle returned with her astonished and gratified daughter, who curtsied prettily, saying, "My lady! Good day! How did you find us?"

"It was simple. I had heard a mention of 'Langham Court,' so that is the direction I gave the jarvey, who brought me straight here, where I encountered two young women just coming from what turned out to be your door. Men think they are the only ones who know their way about the city. Pooh! I managed very well without them." She turned her head to Mrs. Carlisle. "You and I are both widows, I understand, so we must shift for ourselves, must we not?"

"Well," replied Mrs. Carlisle, "Dia has a better head than I."

Dia said with a smile, "Mama does not like decisions. I make most of ours—relying on Mr. Pond and Mr. Whipple for advice, of course."

"Who are they?" asked Lady Knollton.

"Two older men who live here—they have the kindest hearts, and Mr. Pond is wise. He does not think I should . . ." Her voice trailed away, as she was unable to complete the sentence. "They think of me as their child," she added hurriedly.

"Dia," declared her mama firmly, "is wonderfully sensible. Takes after her father. Knows all about Latin, and astronomy, and things like that."

Lady Knollton listened with interest. What her stepson cared about Latin and astronomy she could not imagine, but there was no doubt that Dia had a piquant face and gentle poise that made one feel comfortable with her. *Not* the sort of empty-headed damsel one met at Almack's. Perhaps it would be more accurate to say, not a meek soul cast upon society by an ambitious mother. Lydia could sense a poise that came with serenity. Was Francis becoming enthralled?

Because Lady Knollton loved her stepson, she did not wish him to be entangled with a girl (however beguiling) who did not have dignity.

"May I give you a glass of wine, my lady?" Dia asked. "I can promise that you will find it very good, because Lord Knollton brought it."

"Very smooth on one's tongue," inserted the mother, though Lady Lydia could not imagine her to be a judge of such things. Perhaps it would be wise to see if Francis had brought their best stock. "Why, how kind of you. I am a little dry. Just half a glass—"

Dia at once stood up and went across to their decanter, in which the balance of Knollton's gift was waiting. Because he had supplied it, she knew Lady Knollton could find no fault.

And she did not; one sip told her that Francis had brought a bottle of their choice sherry. "Very nice," she said with aplomb.

"I have told Mama what a precious child you have, my lady," Dia said, choosing a topic that was sure to please her guest.

Lady Knollton replied briefly, "I am blessed."

"Yes, I think his lordship must feel the same. She was adorable on the drive that we had down to the Serpentine. He seems to deal with her beautifully."

Lady Lydia laughed lightly. "Spoils her, you mean."

"No," contradicted little Miss Carlisle calmly. "It was wonderful to see how smoothly and firmly he turned her thoughts from wading in the water."

"Did he do that? Thank heavens. He hates to deny her anything, and I would not have been surprised if he let her pull off her shoes and stockings at once—in front of all the *ton.*"

"He allowed her to steer the horses, instead."

"Mercy! Were you alarmed?"

Dia laughed. "Oh, no. He was holding the reins, too."

Shaking her head, Lady Knollton said she did hope he would not give Sara a curricle of her own any time soon.

"Do you drive, my lady?" Dia asked.

"Yes, but I am more than five."

The two of them smiled at each other.

"Five what?" asked Mrs. Carlisle.

"Years," replied her ladyship. Then she handed Dia her empty glass, saying, "The hackney is waiting for me. I must go. Such a pleasure to see you, Mrs. Carlisle, Miss Carlisle. Perhaps we can meet another time."

Mrs. Carlisle murmured "Er—yes," and Dia accompanied their visitor to the exterior door of the house, which, upon being opened, revealed Mary Ann and Jane still lingering in the court, waiting for a conflagration or something cataclysmic to occur.

The Froam girls' curiosity would make them late to work.

When Dia returned to her mother, that lady, who spoke what was on her mind, even if not clear to others, said, "There now. Have I not always said a lady is a lady anyplace?"

"You mean even in Langham Court?" asked Dia.

"I mean, in a rented parlor."

"Why should she not be? Is ours not clean and neat and paid for?"

"It is those things," agreed her mother, "but I should be very much surprised if Lady Knollton has ever been in such a place before."

Dia was silent for a moment. Then she said, "Lady Knollton does not despise us."

"No," returned her mama, "we are not important enough to despise."

This made Dia shiver. When had her mama ever spoken so much like a hammer striking a nail? But she rather thought her papa would have said much the same, though in gentler terms.

Was her mama unhappy with their circumstances? She had never indicated so before. She was never caustic. Perhaps her mother was regretting the situation that her daughter amiably accepted. Did she want something better for her daughter?

Always her papa had said, "One makes one's own happiness."

Eleven

Deep in thought, Lady Knollton rode home in the hackney. Once she had reached the modish house on Upper Brook Street, she went up to her boudoir and summoned her maid.

"I want to change, Becky," she said, turning her back so that the maid could unbutton her frock. "These shoes and stockings will suffice but I need something handsomer."

"The deeper blue silk, my lady?"

"Yes. That will do nicely."

The servant lifted away the pretty dress, which had struck Jane and Mary Ann Froam as very fine, and went to a wardrobe to take out the desired silk one. It had tiny vertical tucks that emphasized Lady Lydia's slim midriff, and it spilled out to send ripples down the skirt. Not knowing where her ladyship intended to go, the servant hesitated to suggest a particular bonnet.

When Lady Lydia asked for her blond straw with bluebells, the woman knew her mistress was to make an appearance somewhere important, for this bonnet was new and especially exquisite.

"Shall you be wanting the carriage, my lady?"

"Yes. Please send for it." Lady Lydia surveyed the servant. "You will do nicely to accompany me, Becky. Pray fetch a bonnet and shawl."

As Lady Lydia was never disagreeable, the servant thought she must have serious business on her mind to be so solemn;

and this was indeed the case. Lady Lydia intended to call upon the toplofty Mrs. Drummond Burrell, with whom she was so fortunate as to be on excellent terms. Actually, Lady Knollton was on good terms with everyone who mattered, for she was warm and charming, liking everyone and being admired by them in return—even by such arrogant persons as Mrs. Drummond Burrell. This patroness of Almack's had looked with favor on the late Viscount Knollton, perhaps because he was as perfectly mannered as she thought desirable, and when he had married the youthful Miss Lydia Heywood, Mrs. Burrell had chosen to recognize the new bride as a personal friend. For this she was rewarded well by Lydia's actually liking her. Of course, Lydia's disposition was a friendly one, and as Mrs. Burrell was respected and feared more than she was loved, the charm of Lydia's liking someone so prickly won Mrs. Burrell as no other person had done. Mrs. Burrell terrified *débutantes,* but she approved of Lydia.

To speak to Mrs. Burrell of an unknown girl from Langham Court would require immense courage, and Lydia was not hopeful of any attention to Dia, but she was not unhopeful that her crusty friend could give her some clues for dealing with Francis's growing infatuation.

Lydia loved her stepson dearly. If he was becoming serious about this Unknown, then for the sake of her late husband she could accept her without harsh words. After all, the girl was pretty, amiable, soft-spoken, and well behaved—so far at least. But would the girl be a handicap to Francis? Even more to the point, would her mother be a handicap? Lydia hoped Mrs. Drummond Burrell would tell her what action to take.

In her carriage, riding to Mrs. Burrell's home, Lady Knollton felt some qualms about baring her thoughts to that severe lady. She must tread cautiously and not cause horrid gossip. Perhaps if she merely hinted at her concern . . .

They had reached Mrs. Burrell's residence. Already, as Lydia and her maidservant mounted the outer steps, a door was being opened to her.

Lydia left Becky in the lower hall, and went up a flight to Mrs. Burrell's drawing room under escort of an admiring butler.

"Well, Lydia," said the dragon," you are just the medicine to cure me!"

"Are you feeling ill?" asked Lydia sympathetically.

"Dying, my dear, of boredom," replied her hostess. "I hope you have good news, or a juicy bit of scandal to cheer me . . . but *not* that you have accepted some unworthy gentleman."

Lydia said she would never do that. "It is Francis. I am worried about him."

"You do not mean it! That perfect gentleman? Not making a fool of himself with light skirts"

"No, not that," Lydia answered. "But I very much fear he is playing with the affections of a young and inexperienced girl named Carlisle."

Mrs. Burrell said, "Pshaw! He is too kind to do that. Besides, what inexperienced girl would catch—or hold—his attention?"

Lydia hesitated. "She is young and quite green. I have the feeling that she thinks my stepson is a—a prince of some sort."

"Very nearly is," asserted her hostess. "Have you met this girl?"

"Twice. Sara likes her."

"Sara does! What does a child have to say to anything?"

Lady Knollton smiled at that. "Sara," she said, "adores her brother. She receives a great deal of attention from him and in general would, I am afraid, not wish for anyone—who was not delightful—to take his attention away from herself."

"Spoiled? I thought you were on your guard against that."

"Yes, I am. Francis and Nanny and I are agreed upon certain standards of behavior. Sara is imperative, but really very good and loving."

Mrs. Burrell said "Yes, yes. But this girl—?"

Lydia bit her lip. "Sara did seem to approve of this girl. I like her myself. She has a warm manner, no pretensions at all, and—"

"No pretensions?"

"None. And I was going to add a beautiful face with serene hazel eyes. Her mother—"

"So," interrupted Mrs. Burrell, "you have seen the parents."

Lydia shook her head. "Only one, a widow, and rather—er—vague. I believe the daughter looks after her."

Mrs. Drummond Burrell made a humphing sort of noise. "Then who is to protect the girl from profligate males? I do not mean Francis. If she is modest and chaste, what has saved such a beauty from lascivious attentions?"

"A miracle," replied Lady Knollton. "Though perhaps there are other persons in the house to keep watch over her."

"Kin?" asked her hostess.

"No, no. Older men, one hopes, who live in the same rooming house."

"Rooming house!" cried Mrs. Burrell, horrified.

Lydia hastily assured her it was a genteel house.

"Where?"

"Langham Court."

"Never heard of it," sniffed her hostess. "But how did you meet this girl, and why?"

"Well, as to how," said Lydia, "Francis took her driving in Hyde Park one day, and introduced her to me there."

Mrs. Burrell looked scandalized. "With your permission?"

It was true that Lady Knollton had been a bit surprised for Francis to bring an unknown female to her attention—within the presence of several high-placed gentlemen. She answered, "Yes. I could not insult the girl by refusing to acknowledge her existence, could I? She was very young, quite modest of manner, and so kind to my Sara, who rode down to the Serpentine with them." Lydia hoped she need not mention visiting the Carlisles' home in Langham Court, a location Mrs. Drummond Burrell appeared to disdain.

"Well, you want my advice?" said the elder lady. "I would not encourage Knollton's pursuit of this female. If he is sowing wild oats, better that you appear not to know."

"That is what bothers me," Lydia explained. "I do not think it is wild oats."

"Better hope it is," advised the most stiffly starched of Almack's patronesses. "Now, tell me if you intend to stay a widow indefinitely."

Lydia had no desire to tell anything about that subject. She laughed lightly and replied that she had made no plans.

"My dear girl! You must arrange something for yourself. Francis will not stay single forever. You do not want to spend the rest of your days as a useful relative, do you? What a waste that would be!" The dragon rapped Lydia with her fan. "I hear rumors that Lord Marchmont and the Earl of Endfield are vying for your favor. Endfield has the higher rank, but Marchmont is richer, they say. Are you about to choose one of them?"

"No," said Lydia sharply. "That is, no, Mrs. Burrell. It is Francis that I have on my mind."

Her hostess took no offense. "Well, dear girl, you are wasting your time. Francis will do what he pleases. This is something that annoys us ladies. But I have a high opinion of Francis—very like his father, you know. I do not think he will do anything outrageous, and if this girl—this Miss Carlisle—is as admirable as you seem to think, she will not be party to scandal. I *cannot* abide upstarts, but neither can I abide mewling, sanctimonious, bootlicking snobs."

"Oh, yes," returned Lady Knollton with a sigh. "Neither can I. You think, then, I must trust Francis's judgment?"

"Indeed, I do. You will not be able to turn him from his purposes—or even find out what they may be."

"He is very l-lovable," Lydia managed.

Her hostess nodded. "Young men are sometimes as nonsensical as children. However, family pride should keep Francis from making a scandal. His father startled everyone by marrying a very young second wife, but it worked out well, did it not? It was not a mistake, was it?"

"No. Oh, no. No mistake," returned Lydia happily. She smiled mistily and stood up. "Thank you, dear Mrs. Burrell."

"I like giving advice," the lady admitted.

"And I will follow it," said Lydia. "Perhaps I am only imagining difficulties. Francis *is* somewhat like his father. You may not have realized it"—she blushed rosily—"but my husband was something of a romantic—"

"Oh, yes," agreed Mrs. Burrell, with a fond smile. "That was obvious. With all his proper ways and formal manners, he had a soft side. Not everyone may have noticed it, but obviously you did."

"Yes," said Lydia. She stood up, collecting her reticule and shawl. "Thank you, dear Mrs. Burrell. You have been wonderfully helpful."

"Push-tush," returned that lady. "I am glad you thought well enough of me to come with your problem. Oh, yes, I do exert some influence in the *ton,* though I am not popular. Power can make one lonely. Do not try to strip Francis's self-determination from him."

Lydia was lost in thought as she rode home with Becky. They did not exchange two words. When little Sara greeted her with hugs and pleas for a walk around Grosvenor Square, Lydia agreed at once. Langham Court was not so many streets away, yet it seemed very distant from Lydia's walk with her child.

At Number 2, Dia Carlisle was creating a blue frock for her mama. She sewed, as she did everything, unhurriedly, wanting the garment to be free of puckers and crooked stitches. Her handiwork was as meticulous as her mind, though the latter was showing a new tendency to wander. Perhaps it was just as well that her mama talked in a ramble of the lunch at St. Albans, the direction of a breeze, Mr. Docking's long absence from Number 2, the first wearing of the dress that Dia had under construction, and the sunken paving stone in the court—just waiting for the next rain.

"Do you not think Mr. Docking should fix that stone?" Mrs. Carlisle demanded.

Dia murmured "Um-hmm."

Her mama continued the one-sided conversation: "At any rate, I shall remember not to walk there. Even if there is not water, one could twist an ankle. Perhaps I should speak to Mr. Docking myself . . ."

But Dia knew her mother would never challenge their landlord about anything. She held up the frock. "Do you think you will like this?" she asked.

"To be sure, I will," replied the elder lady. "Thank you for sewing so nicely, dear."

"Better thank Mr. Pond, who provided the fabric," Dia said.

There was a brief silence, while Dia wondered what her mother would say next.

"Lady Knollton was gracious to call upon us, was she not?" Mrs. Carlisle asked.

Dia murmured, "Um-hmm."

"I wish you would not talk with pins in your mouth," objected her mama.

Dia removed a single pin and held it up to prove that it was not plural. Usually her mama did not expect answers.

"Where will I have occasion to wear that lovely dress you are making?" Mrs. Carlisle asked.

"At the next Drawing Room of the Queen," her daughter replied naughtily.

"Now you are funning!" objected Mrs. Carlisle. "Though perhaps if Lady Knollton invites us for tea one day, I can wear it then."

Did her mother really think that might happen? Dia had no such expectation, though she was glad of her ladyship's brief visit, for it gave her a chance to verify that Lydia Knollton was as beautiful and unaffected as she had seemed at their meeting in Hyde Park. Perhaps all great ladies were cordial, though common sense suggested that some might be haughty. Princess Esterhazy, whom Dia had once seen riding by, was said to be disdainful of lesser persons, and sometimes cartoons appeared of other great ladies. But, really, Lady Knollton seemed very kind. Though not as exalted as the patronesses of Almack's, Lady Knollton certainly associated with them, which put her far, far above Carlisles—and Whipples—and fubsy Ponds—and good-hearted shop girls like the Froams.

That evening at the supper table, Dia looked around her and thought how fortunate she was to share a house with such truly pleasant persons. She supposed her papa had chosen their home carefully. Even though the tenants of Number 2 had changed somewhat over the years, decent persons seemed to find a haven there. She could not believe good people were limited to the Upper Ten Thousand.

"The lady—your visitor—was very beautiful," Jane Froam said between courses.

"I think," Dia replied, "that she is as kind as she is lovely. Kindness must run in her family, for it was her stepson who took Mama and Mr. Whipple and me for a pleasant drive to St. Albans."

"How fortunate that you had a drawing room in which to entertain her," said Jane. "Mary Ann and I think Mr. Folkes would come to call if we had a place to receive him, but there is no parlor here, and the hallway would scarcely do."

"That does seem a shame," Dia agreed. "Would you like to use our sitting room? Mama and I could play least in sight, for we have two more rooms. Why, we could even take a walk!"

"Oh," breathed Jane, wide-eyed. "That would be *wonderful*. Do you mean it?"

Dia said warmly, "Of course I mean it. Any afternoon or evening—though it would have to be early if an evening is planned, for Mama soon settles for the night and voices might—"

Jane protested that they did not wish to disturb Mrs. Carlisle. "Perhaps teatime—after the shop has closed. I think Miss Docking would let us fix tea!"

"I am sure she would," said Dia, "though you are welcome to use our cups and the kettle on the grate."

"Perfect!" declared Jane happily. "We will furnish the tea and sugar, of course."

Dia did not argue. It seemed a good plan, though she wondered if Mr. Folkes was being entrapped. Well, the Froam girls were merry, good-hearted persons, and he would be fortunate to attach either one, even if it meant attaching both.

In less than twenty-four hours the invitation was extended and accepted, and Dia had only to explain to her mama that it would be necessary to remove themselves for an hour or so. She must think of something to keep her mama occupied in the little pantry/bedchamber at the back of the house.

Twelve

Dia and her mother had not vacated their parlor when Mr. Folkes arrived two days later. They were both curious to see him, having heard only hyperboles from the Froam girls, which necessitated the exercise of imagination to identify the "splendid chappie" that had been described to them. He was tall and neatly dressed, rather colorless until a warm smile had brightened an undistinguished face. Quite clearly he was glad to have come, and since the girls were happy to receive him, Dia could only suppose that the tea party would be a success. Indeed, her mother must have found him agreeable, for Dia was twice obliged to remind her that they had "things" to do.

Leaving Jane and Mary Ann to chatter eagerly, fill cups, and pass around a tray of biscuits Miss Docking had contributed, the Carlisles made their way to Dia's cubbyhole at the back of the house.

"A nice young chappie," said Mrs. Carlisle. "Too bad there is only one of him, or they cannot cut him in two."

"I think the girls hope he will have an unattached friend," Dia replied. "Even if he does not, those are fond sisters, and I do not think they will battle for possession of him."

"You should be having callers, too," said her mother regretfully. "You are prettier than either girl . . . though I could not like to see you tied to a shopkeeper's son. Oh, dear, I fear we are neither fish nor fowl."

"Who," said Dia, laughing, "would want to be a fish?"

"Or a fowl?" added Mrs. Carlisle somberly.

Dia gave her mother a hug. "Let us put your new dress on you to see that it fits properly. If the Queen should invite you to a garden party, you must look perfect."

"I fear, if I went," said Mrs. Carlisle, "I would be directed around to the buttery or the still room, and your handiwork would be wasted."

"Ah," said Dia bracingly, "you will too grand for that. We must send regrets to Her Majesty. Perhaps Mr. Whipple will take us to the theater."

It was an idle suggestion, for Mrs. Carlisle would never consent to face the crush of a theater, even if Mr. Whipple could be brought to such an idea.

So Mrs. Carlisle was coaxed into the blue dress and her daughter marked the proper place for the hem with pins.

"It is a pretty dress, Dia. If Mr. Pond had not given me the material, I would say the dress should be for you. May not Lord Knollton invite you to go somewhere important? And do not say Mr. Pond gave *me* this material. He would be just as glad for you to have it."

"But he did not give it to me, Mama. Besides, your eyes are blue and mine are not. He meant this for you."

"Perhaps you are right," sighed Mrs. Carlisle. "Well"—resignedly—"neither one of us is going anywhere, and Mr. Pond may bring home something to suit you better."

"He said he would bring something," Dia said, stepping back to have a full-length view of her mother. "I do not think the Queen will invite me to anything."

"Yes, but Lady Knollton might," her mother reminded happily.

Dia shook her head. "You must not depend upon that, Mama."

The noncombative discussion continued as Dia helped Mrs. Carlisle to remove the dress. Then the faint sound of laughter from their parlor turned their thoughts.

"Those are cheerful girls," Mrs. Carlisle said.

"Yes," agreed Dia. "I hope Mr. Folkes will offer for one of them, but what will become of the other I do not know. They are both too young to live alone in London." It was true, yet Dia was thinking of her own situation. Suppose she had not had Mama!

Mr. Folkes must have had similar thoughts. In almost too few days to count, he offered for Mary Ann, saying that Jane must make her home with them, and he set off for Stoke Poges very properly to seek the agreement of Mary Ann's mother. Folkes Senior knew a good thing when he saw it; his son would be decently settled, and two excellent clerks were thus bonded to his shop.

No one could suppose that Mrs. Froam might object. She did not. Young Mr. Folkes was obviously respectable. Having learned courtesy from dealing with his father's customers and being a genuinely kind young man, he spoke of Mary Ann just as was necessary to please a mother.

Mrs. Froam agreed, and offered her own wedding ring for her daughter, but Mr. Folkes (while not overwhelmingly handsome) spoke graciously, saying that she must not part with something so precious to her, especially as she had other daughters. His own deceased mother's ring should go to Mary Ann, which would please his father.

As Mary Ann was without dowry, Mrs. Froam was glad to be able to please Folkes Senior. She gave Robert Folkes her blessing and promised to come to London for the simple ceremony before Mr. Lloyd at All Souls.

At Langham Court there was a great deal of excitement with a bride-to-be in their midst. Cory was thrilled, saying, "Coo! Isn't it romanik?" She was invited to the ceremony, along with everyone in the house; only the ash boy took no interest.

Mr. Lloyd was asked to conduct a small ceremony before the altar of All Souls Church on a day when nothing else was planned. Few would attend, but it must be a proper marriage service.

Only one impediment confronted the eager couple.

No home had been found for the soon-to-be-wed pair.

Mr. Folkes offered them a room of his flat, but Robert felt (just as he should) that it was up to him to provide a place for his bride. As for the upper story of the draper's shop, it had two vacant rooms, long neglected, and needing myriad things done to make them habitable.

Robert said, "I must keep looking. We want to be convenient to the shop, but the neighborhood must be clean and safe, I hope, with sunshine to make it agreeable." Whatever he decided was all right with Mary Ann, as long as it had a parlor with space for Robert's desk, two bedchambers, and a kitchen all their own. To share a kitchen with another tenant might mean crumbs and mice.

Dia wondered if the girls had any idea of planning meals, for they never cooked at Number 2, but Jane reassured her by saying that they had often helped their mother to prepare meals and knew a thing or two.

"But how to feed a man?" questioned Dia, doubtfully.

Not to worry, Jane had said. Two of their siblings were brothers, so they knew what men liked to eat: potatoes often and meat twice a week, if possible.

Both girls had already learned about tasty economies from what Miss Docking put before the boarders of Number 2. Robert was a thin young man and obviously did not expect to be fed bountifully, they declared. Dia thought they might learn something different in a very short time . . . but it was not her problem.

One by one, the inhabitants of Number 2 began to look forward to the next return of Mr. Pond, who had gone off on another selling trip after seeing that Dia was safely watched and still uncompromised. Because he was one who Got Things Done, they hoped he would return in time to discover rooms for the bridal couple and Jane.

Meanwhile, what the Froam girls had hoped came to pass. Robert, overflowing with connubial plans and joy, soon realized that Jane was missing something vital, and he wished her (and everyone) to be as happy as himself. The answer was James Middledore, whom he presented to Jane, asserting he was a fine fellow. Jane was perfectly willing to be pleased. Although James was shorter than Robert and somewhat rounded, he was accepted as a good chap to make a foursome. There was a deal of tromping from male feet upon the steps of Number 2—a welcome sound to all but Miss Docking, who thought her brother might suppose the tone of his house was growing giddy. But no one complained, so she had Cook make sweet muffins for the young people, to dull their appetites after business hours.

"Just as well," Mrs. Carlisle said privately to her daughter, "that Robert Folkes has not found a set of rooms for his bride. Your papa and I were betrothed several months before we married, which allows time to be sure. Oh, I was sure enough, for he was a lovely gentleman, as you know. But it is best to be certain of making the right match." She sighed and added, "Where am I to find a husband for you?"

Dia understood that this was no slur upon herself. Marriage was the only suitable situation for a lone female. At least her mama was a buffer of sorts between her and the world, though wholly without practical discrimination. Yet when Mama was gone, Dia would be utterly unprotected. Here, at Number 2, there were Pond and Whipple to advise her, but both were nearly thrice her age, and where could she look for help when she dwindled into her forties and fifties?

Resolutely, she put such morbid thoughts aside and volunteered to sew a wedding dress for Mary Ann. Fabric was no problem, for Mr. Folkes Senior offered anything in the shop.

Robert came every weekday to escort Mary Ann and Jane to work. At teatime he brought them home, going on himself to look for possible rooms to rent. He seemed to feel, very properly, that he must not impose on the Carlisles for the use of their parlor. If he were not such an amiable young man, Mary Ann was quick to explain, he would have lingered in the hall or on the stoop, boring everyone in the house—except herself, of course.

Mrs. Carlisle would have let him in the parlor anytime, but she had no idea of making herself invisible, and Robert had no desire to share his courtship with a middle-aged lady, which everyone understood except Mrs. Carlisle.

"Your papa visited me almost every day before we were married," she said to her daughter.

"But, Mama, was it in a parlor belonging to someone else?" Dia asked, laughing.

"No, it was my home, but surely Robert Folkes understands he would be welcome in our parlor."

"Mama, Mama, it is Mary Ann he wishes to see, not you and me."

"Doesn't he see her every day at the shop? If he wishes to see more of her, why does he drop her at the door and go off to where she is not?"

This circular argument made Dia shake her head.

"They cannot be married until he has found rooms. Rooms, Mama. He cannot move in with Mary Ann and Jane."

Mrs. Carlisle declared, "I should think not!"

Despite the frustration of finding no flat to rent, the Froam girls were in top spirits. With London so big and full of buildings, they knew Robert would discover the perfect place.

"I feel a bit guilty," Dia admitted to her mama. "Here there are two of us with three rooms, and the girls have only one."

"That is true," her mama admitted, "but they are here less than half the day. Think how uncomfortable we would be in one room. Besides, your papa chose this for us; he would want us to be nicely situated."

"I am not suggesting we relinquish Room A," Dia explained. "I am only wishing Robert Folkes could find something. He is bound to do so, but the three of them will be in a twitter until he does. In a way, perhaps they enjoy agonizing about it."

"Yes," agreed her mother, "that must be more interesting than the weather or the state of the King's health."

"Yet we should care about His Majesty's health," Dia reminded.

Mrs. Carlisle said, "Yes, as good citizens, but look at poor Prince George—neither fish nor fowl, just like you and I."

"I cannot see the similarity," Dia declared, trying not to burst with laughter. "He is *royal,* after all."

Her mama frowned. "What do you find so amusing? His Royal Highness must feel very unsettled. I think that explains why he eats so much and has become so fat."

"Perhaps so," replied Dia, choking with mirth. "We should not be laughing."

"He won't know," her mama said.

Prince George had many friends, of which Lord Francis was one, though not an intimate. His manner toward the Prince was everything proper, but Francis could not be really sympathetic to a man who had to be raised to his saddle with a hoist. The chaps whom Francis considered his friends were bruising riders, excellent shots, and competent dancers. Lady Knollton, for all her affection, did hope he would be more serious in his thoughts.

And he was.

Francis was thinking a great deal more than Lady Lydia realized about a certain little blonde creature whose serene hazel eyes seemed to see into his head. Why was her manner pleasant, yet distant—as if she were not sure she approved of what was glimpsed there?

Because of this, with another Sunday being overcast though not stormy, and Lady Lydia sleeping late, his lordship slipped off to Langham Court to ask if the Carlisle ladies would enjoy a stroll to All Souls Church with him. He gambled that grey clouds would deter Mrs. Carlisle this day, and—sure enough— she declined. The most appealing facial expression that Francis could assume was successful in persuading Dia to walk with him, which would be his first chance for a private talk with her—no groom, no mama, no Mr. Whipple.

In addition, Miss Carlisle suggested Adam fasten the horses to the rail of the step and call the ash boy to watch them, so that he could go down to Miss Docking's kitchen, where he would be welcome to drink a cup of coffee or tea.

When had his lordship's other acquaintances ever offered this? Adam would have something to report to Shooker this day.

Then the couple walked out of the courtyard and strolled toward All Souls Church.

"My friend, Miss Mary Ann Froam, who presently lives with her sister, is to be married at All Souls," Dia told his lordship.

"Indeed? Will this be soon?" The wedding of an unknown female meant little to him, yet his manners were perfect.

"No one knows for sure," she replied. "She is to wed the son of a draper by whom she and her sister are employed. Robert—Mr. Folkes—is trying to find a flat for them first. Her sister, Jane, is to live with them, you see. Such dear girls. We will miss them at Number 2."

By this, Francis understood that Miss Carlisle was speaking of two who lived presently in the house with her. He could not quite believe that shopgirls were suitable friends for Miss Carlisle.

Yet she continued, saying, "No father, you see, and they have been very anxious to be no burden to their widowed mother, who has three younger children to care for."

It was with a twinge of shame that he realized self-reliant daughters like the Froam girls would have been a blessing to their mother. How difficult some lives were! And how wonderfully some persons adapted to them!

Pondering what trials this small, sweet girl might, herself, have been enduring, he escorted her into the church and found her a seat, where she took out a prayer book and appeared to forget him.

"Will the wedding be here?" he whispered.

She nodded with a little smile.

There was something special about this church, he thought. Something different from the fashionable St. George's, and far different from magnificent St. Paul's, where his father and Lydia had been wed with due pomp and tolling of bells.

If, perhaps, the difference was his own attitude, he did not suspect that.

"What do you think of St. Paul's Cathedral?" Francis asked.

Dia touched a finger to her lips; the service was beginning. She seemed quietly attentive to what Mr. Lloyd had to say; Knollton began to listen, too, halfway thinking how fine it was that a shopgirl could be married here, just as piously as any peer of England.

The only impediment was the need for a flat.

On Monday Francis summoned Hull, his man of business, and required him to find a modest suite of rooms for three persons, something in the neighborhood of Oxford and Great Titchfield.

"It is needed by Mr. Robert Folkes, who does business as a draper in that area. Think you can locate him, eh? I cannot give an exact address. His shop is within walking distance of Langham Street, at any rate."

"It should not be difficult to locate the shop, if it has the name Folkes on its sign," Mr. Hull said calmly, though wondering why his lordship took an interest in a draper.

"And, Hull," Lord Knollton warned, *"keep me out of it."*

"Certainly, my lord. Will you wish me to report to you what I have found?"

"Oh, yes, yes. But tell Folkes simply that you heard he was in need of rooms and can suggest something. Did I say that a parlor, two bedrooms, and a kitchen are required? Folkes will be paying, not I. I do not know Folkes and have nothing to do with the whole thing."

Except, thought Mr. Hull, *arranging Folkes's life.* Odd. Still, no stranger than other of his duties, for which he was well paid. If he had been asked to find accommodations for a ladybird, he would have understood more readily—though Lord Knollton had never requested that.

Thirteen

Mr. Hull returned to his office and, as a first step, summoned his runner, who came at once with a nod of his head.

"Boy," said Hull, "have you heard of a draper in Bloomsbury named Folkes?"

The youth looked surprised. What contact had he with drapers? "No, sir," he said. "Do you want me to find 'im?"

"That is the first part," Hull replied. "I suggest you work along the north side of Oxford, from Portland Street to—say—Tottenham. That is an expensive stretch for a draper, but we must not overlook him. Then work northward on intersecting streets. Folkes has a prosperous business, I think. It should not be a small shop. Ought to have a noticeable sign." He did not explain what need he had of a cloth merchant, and the boy did not ask, because he did not care. Errands like this were ways to earn his bread and keep him out of a gutter.

"Hop to it," Mr. Hull ordered. He then replaced the boy by calling one of his clerks.

"What's the situation on flats in Bloomsbury?"

The young man wiped his inky fingers upon a grimy cloth. "Folk seem to come and go, sir. My mother has a nice bright attic going to waste. Would you be wantin' it?"

"No, I wouldn't," snapped Mr. Hull, stung by the suggestion. "But I might know someone who does. Jot the location, and I will have a look."

"Yes, sir." The man made a note for him and then returned to his desk work.

When Mr. Hull had dealt with matters waiting on his own desk, he put on his hat and set out to find the building at the address his clerk had written down.

This turned out to be a respectable street, but a slightly shabby one, which he did not think would appeal to Lord Knollton's friend (whom his lordship denied knowing). He'd better have a look at it; his clerk had called it "nice" and "bright."

The clerk's mother was a well-cushioned female with a keen look in her eye. Mr. Hull had an idea that she would be smart enough to make her attic appealing, which it turned out to be: sunny and clean, with the rooms he required, but with the drawback of one chamber's needing to be entered through the other. Since he did not know who would occupy the flat, he was dubious that Lord Knollton would approve of it.

Nevertheless, he reported to his lordship, who lost no time in saying such an arrangement would never do.

"Might help, your lordship," Hull volunteered, "if I knew what persons have to be accommodated."

"Mr. Folkes, his wife, and his wife's sister. Keep looking, please," the viscount replied.

"Very well, m'lord. If you are wondering about the shop, it is just off Oxford, on Wells Street."

Knollton thanked and dismissed Mr. Hull. For a while he sat nibbling on the end of a pen, as he thought about the situation. Dia Carlisle had not asked for help. Neither had the two shop-girls—whom he had not even seen, though he expected to see them sooner or later. Nevertheless, to be of help to someone in whom Dia was interested seemed a good way to win her approval of himself. Young women of his class, Francis thought, needed no help from him, and Miss Carlisle, he felt sure, would ask nothing for herself. Yes. Meeting this need would make him feel better about himself, even if the persons concerned did not know he had a part in the matter.

Francis sent for Adam to bring his curricle to the door, then descended to meet it.

"You may drive, Adam," he said pleasantly. "I will be watching for a particular shop—a draper's place—on Wells Street."

They proceeded along Oxford at a slow trot until they reached Wells Street. Here Adam turned the team, and presently they had come upon a prosperous shop that occupied the lower story of a two-story building. A sign streamed across the wall above two mullioned display windows flanking a green door.

Folkes and Son
Fabrics
Since 1792

That was the place.

"Ah!" said Knollton.

"Would you wish me to stop, m'lord?" asked Adam, having almost done so.

"No, no. It is here. We have found it," Lord Knollton replied. "That was all I wanted. Drive on."

Adam did as bid, though puzzled by his master's interest in such a place. This was strange enough to report to Shooker, when they met, as usual, for their evening meal.

"What can it mean?" asked Adam.

Mr. Shooker had nothing to suggest. "Not where his lordship obtains his clothes. Meinrad tailors for him—has for years, same as for his father, with sometimes a coat from Weston."

Neither man connected a draper's shop with little Miss Dia Carlisle. Even his lordship did not, for he was thinking only of an engaged couple whom he did not know, hoping to be helpful to them in a way that might please Miss Carlisle.

"We haven't been nigh Langham Court for several days," Adam said. "Nor near any other young lady."

Shooker chewed thoughtfully. "At least his lordship has stopped talking about a bolt to his manor. Her ladyship likes his company when the Season is in full blow."

"Likes to oblige her, he does," Adam said, casting a sideways look at his cohort.

"Don't we all? She's a fine lady, though you needn't imagine romance there. They are just plain friends—fond, don't you know?"

Adam agreed with a sigh. "Will we ever get his lordship buckled?"

"What's wrong with things the way they are?" Shooker asked, before putting a slice of carrot in his mouth.

"His lordship is edgy," the groom replied, not knowing Lady Lydia had used the same word in her thoughts. "I don't know when I have seen him this way."

"What is the Unknown like?" Shooker asked. He meant unknown to Society. After all, Adam certainly knew her.

Adam said, "Mighty—sweet. You should have seen her concern for Wally. Stood right there in the dirt of the road and said his lordship must give up his seat to make Wally comfortable."

Shooker's knife and fork halted in midair. *"His lordship?"*

Adam said, "Yes, and he did it!"

There was silence between them for a few minutes. Then Shooker said, "Bears watching." Still, he did not mention a particular gold bracelet, hiding with Knollton's cuff buttons. Nor did he approve of his lordship's interest in anyone beneath him. He had the uneasy feeling that Adam was beginning to relax his guard of their young gentleman, who deserved, Shooker thought, the best.

As if Adam guessed Mr. Shooker's different opinion, he ventured to say, "If you was acquainted with Miss Carlisle, you might feel better about her. A prettier creature you never did see, and downright thoughtful as to the comfort of everyone."

Shooker said he could appreciate those things, but he held that a viscount should look higher.

"How high?" demanded the groom. "There's no princess we would welcome into the family. Lots of snobs and Devil's Daughters out there who wouldn't make his lordship happy."

The valet conceded that with a nod. "Have to remember, Adam, that gents of the peerage don't marry for happiness."

Fortunately, the other servants had left them alone at their supper table.

Adam burst out, "Well, don't tell me his lordship's pa didn't marry our Lady Lydia for love! So young, she was. It worked out very well, too."

"Yes," admitted Shooker, who, being older than Adam, thought he knew more. "But many of the kind don't. We want our lordship settled comfortably, don't we?"

Cooling a bit, Adam agreed, pointing out that they could not be sure what would make his lordship happy, though they could spot a troublemaker, which Adam was sure Miss Carlisle was absolutely not.

"Not many are like our Lady Lydia," Shooker reminded.

"Well, that's true enough, but I say it's for *him* to find the right one—wherever she may be," Adam declared.

They parted then, neither pleased with the other's point of view. It made a little rift between them, though both wanted Lord Knollton to be happy. He was the chief interest in their lives. Neither supposed he was languishing . . . but he was certainly not his customary self.

Even Lord Knollton knew that. Dia Carlisle would simply not stay out of his thoughts, and though he was familiar with a fellow called Cupid, it did not occur to him that a naughty Roman bloke could have been making trouble in London, England. At least, not for him!

Since Hull, upon whom Francis relied for almost everything in the way of business, had not been able to find a flat for the draper's son, his lordship began to ride most mornings on his hack, Intrepid, roaming Bloomsbury, and watching for signs in windows that declared rooms were to let. The few he saw did not seem comparable to Number 2, Langham Court. Once or twice he entrusted Intrepid to an urchin while he went indoors to inspect rooms, but none were satisfactory. His respect for the unknown Mr. Docking's standards began to grow. Also, he thought that Mr. Carlisle had been wise in establishing his wife and daughter in Docking's house.

Perhaps the depth he saw in Miss Carlisle's hazel eyes—which were sometimes green, and sometimes dark grey or amber—signified a thing he could not recognize. Plenty of young girls had cast out lures to him, and he remained impervious. How, then, did one young girl not flirt, nor give him sidelong glances, yet keep his attention? If Francis compared her to his stepmother, who was his ideal, he saw two ladies of the same size who otherwise did not appear to match. Lydia he adored wholesomely and admired her town bronze. For a long time she had been his ideal. Yet here was Dia Carlisle, who had no bronze, or any other metal facade, but who seemed to be able to look critically into his core. It was . . . unnerving.

Francis would have liked to see the Carlisles move to a smarter neighborhood, one of the smaller squares with a park in its center. If they did that, then perhaps their suite at Number 2 would accommodate the Folkes; about kitchens he was unsure. However, he was already aware of Miss Carlisle's pride—or call it "self-respect"—which would make it impossible for him to offer any help to her. If—if he found a better situation for Mrs. Carlisle and her daughter, would it be possible for him to make up privately the difference in rents? But no! Such things always leaked out, to the ruin of those concerned. How could Francis be thinking of such a thing? Well, then, could he have Hull buy a nice flat and rent it to them for what they had been paying? He need never come into the picture. *Hull* would act as their landlord.

Great heavens! What was he thinking of? Setting himself up for extortion, that was what. Although he trusted Hull, someone in his office might whisper information, and cause the Carlisles terrible embarrassment. Any number of men in his set kept *chères amies* living in ease, while their wives turned blind eyes, but that was not his style. He had his father and Lydia as an example of what married life should be.

Marriage? Was he ready for that? No, no, he must not get carried off in shackles.

What he did not realize was that all these thoughts meant matrimony was actually nudging his inclination.

Francis concluded, at last, that he needed a good gallop to clear his head. Any relationship, other than one like his father's with Lady Lydia, would have been impossible for him to tolerate.

If Lady Lydia had been able to read his mind, how reassured she would have been. Astute though she was, she could not read minds, and so she was pondering what steps she should take to protect her stepson. Mrs. Drummond Burrell had advised doing nothing; and Lydia, in truth, did not wish to interfere in his life. It was obvious to her that Dia Carlisle was no schemer, and the girl's mother did not have wits enough to plot anything. She also knew that Francis's closest and most influential friend, Lord Collingwood, was a sound gentleman who dealt ably with the estate that had come to him, and who was securely wed to a delightful lady. That marriage and her own with Francis's father, which were the only ones of a special sort that he could know, must surely have affected her stepson's attitude to matrimony in a positive way.

She began to wonder if she could introduce Dia to Lady Collingwood in some casual manner . . . perhaps a drive to Kensington Palace Gardens.

Totally unaware that Adam, Shooker, Lady Lydia, Mr. Pond, Mr. Whipple, and Miss Docking were fretting about her relationship to Lord Knollton, Dia completed her mother's blue frock and began another for Mary Ann Froam. There was no hurry. Part of the pleasure for her and Mary Ann was examining swatches of luscious fabric. Mr. Folkes told his future daughter she might have anything she liked, and as Mary Ann felt the wedding gown must be practical for later uses, they did not consider satins and laces. It must be muslin in pink, or peach, or lavender, Mary Ann decreed.

Mr. Folkes had a well-stocked shop with row upon row of choices; he smiled benignly while Jane attended customers and

Mary Ann conferred endlessly with Dia. Both girls enjoyed the search immensely, and at last they settled upon a deep pink muslin embroidered with scattered florets of a paler shade. They were able to find thread of the lighter pink with which Dia hoped to create an edging for the neck and sleeves. It might be weeks before a flat was found for Mr. Folkes and the Froam girls, but making the wedding gown could proceed.

Meanwhile, having secured Lady Collingwood for a drive with her, Lady Lydia sat down to write a note to Dia. Then it occurred to her that she might have been expected to invite Dia's mother to fill the fourth seat in the barouche. Instead, Lydia prettily (and daringly) solicited the company of Mrs. Drummond Burrell. That invitation accepted, she jotted a note to Dia Carlisle and required the Knollton butler to see that it was carried at once to Langham Court.

The footman who particularly served her ladyship being absent on another errand, the boot boy was sent loping to Number 2, where Dia Carlisle (surprised, delighted, and willing) hastily penned an acceptance.

Soon after luncheon, a footman Dia did not know escorted her to Langham Street, where Lady Lydia waited in a familiar barouche. Wally, fully recovered from his injury, was at the reins, and he beamed when Dia used his name in asking if he was quite well, before joining her ladyship.

"Good day, my dear," said her ladyship cordially. "We will be collecting two other ladies, and I hope you will not mind a backward seat when we take up the elder one, Mrs. Burrell, who is next."

"No, indeed," returned Dia. "I ride comfortably in any position. How delightful to be visiting the gardens on such a lovely day!" The name Burrell had no significance for her, and when they presently took on the third passenger, she smiled sweetly, though the lady gave her a piercing look and repeated her name doubtfully. Then they added Lady Collingwood, a young matron of sparkling blue eyes and amiable expression.

Dia had no suspicion that she was sitting opposite to a social dragon, especially as the dragon welcomed Lady Collingwood warmly, saying, "My dear Julia! It is good to see you. Have you come up to town for the Season?"

"Not the whole Season, ma'am," Lady Collingwood replied. "My husband has business that will take a week or so, and he brought me with him."

"Could not be separated from you that long, I will be bound," said Mrs. Burrell. Obviously, she approved of this young lady and had some fondness for her, for she added, "You are an example to the young buds having a first Season."

Dia knew no details about "Seasons," but certainly she was aware that this was the time of year for them. Did not news sheets report in flowery terms on various activities of the *ton?* It was obvious that Lady Collingwood, if an example now, must have been presented to the *ton* a year or two before this.

When the young matron, in an encouraging manner, asked Dia if she were having a Season this year, Lady Knollton quickly answered for her. "Miss Carlisle and her widowed mother live quietly just now."

The young matron said softly, "Oh, I see."

At the same time, Mrs. Drummond Burrell was alerted. Did she suspect that unknown young lady was the one to whom Lord Francis was attracted? She scrutinized Dia covertly as the girl turned her head to respond to something Lady Collingwood had said. Very pretty. Sat without fidgeting. Did not chatter, but answered Mrs. Collingwood easily at appropriate moments. Her garment was modest and becoming, not expensive, yet not crudely made (obviously from a skillful dressmaker). All in all, the toplofty Mrs. Burrell found nothing to criticize, though she was a stickler of the most intimidating sort.

Lady Knollton, having gone through all the same hesitancy and reached the same conclusions, smiled slightly. Her anxiety about her stepson had not evaporated solely because the girl was very appealing. Who *was* this girl?

Lydia heard Mrs. Burrell say, "Carlisle? Carlisle? There is a family by that name in York, I believe."

"My father never talked to me of York, Mrs. Burrell. I believe his people were from Scotland, though we never traveled there. My mother does not think there are any relatives living now," Dia said. It did not occur to her to fabricate lofty connections. She smiled and added, "Papa had no burr."

Dia, herself, had no uncouth accent in her voice.

Lady Knollton had been holding her breath lest Dia should say something to annoy the powerful patroness of Almack's; now she relaxed a trifle. It was not that she wished to *promote* the girl socially, but that the danger to Francis could somehow seem less.

They reached Kensington Palace, and drove slowly past it, commenting that it was more like a country estate than a palace.

"We have Queen Caroline, wife of George II, to thank for these beautiful gardens," Lady Knollton said. "This is a perfect time of year to view them. Would you like to step down and stroll a bit, girls?" She was still a girl herself, though she had been a widow for several years.

"Oh, yes!" exclaimed Julia, just as though she had not recently come from blooming gardens of her husband's estate. "Do come with me, Miss Carlisle."

Dia was not only willing, but eager, for she seldom had an opportunity to enjoy Spring air and walk among blossoms.

Accordingly, the two were set down, as Wally had found a tree under which to draw to a halt. The groom sprang down to assist the young ladies in descending; then he took charge of the team, and Wally heaved his bulk down to stretch his legs.

"You see my dilemma?" said Lady Knollton softly.

"Something of a mystery," Mrs. Burrell replied. "I cannot find fault, except—"

"Unknown?"

"Yes. Looks and talks prettily. But of what origin?"

"A genuine lady—or a consummate actress?"

Mrs. Burrell nodded agreement. "Neither seems likely. I ought to have heard of the family. Shall I write a few discreet enquiries?" Even if Lady Lydia did not encourage this, it was not Mrs. Burrell's nature to remain in doubt. "What was her father's first name?"

"Francis has not said."

Lydia wanted very much to know something about this girl with whom her stepson was near to being entangled, and yet she feared, perhaps, a disgraceful reason for Mr. Carlisle's having cut himself off from his roots. She wished to think well of him; indeed, she did think well of him, for there was the evidence of his daughter, who was delightful. And she did not think the girl's mother was the one who had shaped her graceful ways and intelligent mind. A few minutes with Mrs. Carlisle had revealed only vapid discourse. It was true that, in choosing wives, men often overlooked the matter of intelligence, and Mrs. Carlisle did have a pretty face. It could be possible Mr. Carlisle had been influenced by that. At any rate, Dia did not flutter and utter inanities. Also, she made no attempt to impress anyone. What attracted Francis, Lydia thought, was the girl's uncritical nature and a certain serenity.

If Mrs. Drummond Burrell did not set herself against the girl, and she had not yet done so, which was surprising in view of the fact that Miss Carlisle was a Nobody, perhaps Francis was not headed for social disaster.

The girls circled back to the carriage, and a return trip was made, as Lady Knollton had previously instructed Wally to deliver each guest to her abode in the reverse of the order in which they had been collected, thus concealing from Mrs. Burrell and Lady Collingwood the respectable but utterly unfashionable neighborhood in which Dia Carlisle made her home.

Fourteen

Lady Knollton was enough of a realist to know that Francis would hear about Dia's little drive with her, but the news reached him sooner than she expected, for Julia Collingwood mentioned to her husband that she had met a very pleasant young lady with Lady Knollton.

"Not a houseguest, I believe," Lady Collingwood said, "and not someone having a first Season. Who could she be? I liked her very much."

Lord Collingwood promptly forgot the matter, until he came upon Lord Knollton at their club a day or two later, and asked if there was a houseguest at Upper Brook street. "My wife spoke of meeting a friend of Lady Lydia and would like to see the young lady again."

"I don't keep up with all Lydia's social affairs," the viscount answered, not much interested, but wanting to oblige his friend. "Did you get a name?"

"Yes," said Collingwood, "Carlisle."

His lordship, holding a glass, splashed wine upon the ruffle of his sleeve. "The deuce you say! When was this?"

Collingwood was uncertain. "Within the week. Do you know the chit?"

"Yes, I do. Un-unexceptionable."

"Seems they shared a drive to Kensington Gardens. I recall m'wife said Mrs. Drummond Burrell was one of the party."

Francis exclaimed, "Good God!"

When his friend asked if something was wrong, Francis hastily said, "No, no. For a moment I was forgetting Lydia had met Miss Carlisle in the park. Drove to Kensington Palace recently, you say? Lydia did not mention it to me."

"Didn't think you would be interested, perhaps," Lord Collingwood replied. "Can you say where the girl lives?"

"Er—" replied Francis, "north of Oxford Street, I believe. Julia should ask Lydia. How long are you staying in town?"

"Only a day or two more," his friend answered, and the subject of Miss Carlisle was dropped. In fact, the Collingwoods left London without having made contact with Dia Carlisle.

Lord Knollton was able to breathe more freely. It was not that he was *hiding* Miss Carlisle, but he was uncertain what to do about her. He even wondered if he should do anything. There were monumental impediments between Dia and himself, at least, social impediments . . . though Lydia's seeking out Dia seemed to erase some of them. What was Lydia's motive? If she wished to separate him from the girl, taking her driving with Mrs. Burrell (of all people) was not the way to go about it. For any of the *ton,* seeing them together, would assume Mrs. Burrell had approved a new face upon the social scene. Oh, clever Lydia! Was this her way of stilling Springborn's tongue and establishing Dia? Why would she do so?

Francis did not know whether to be angry or pleased.

Mrs. Burrell's apparent condescension was astonishing, though he knew Dia was a perfect little lady—if without suitable connections.

When his stepmother did not mention Dia to him, he asked nothing, and let nine days pass before approaching Number 2 again. This time he met Miss Docking in the hall as he was about to knock upon the Carlisles' door.

"Beg pardon, my lord," she said. "Were you wishful to see Miss Carlisle? She has gone to purchase ribbons for the wedding gown."

Wedding gown!

"Whose gown is that?" he asked, taken aback.

"Miss Froam's, of course. Miss Carlisle sews very skillfully, you see."

Knollton said hastily, "Miss Froam's, to be sure. Did you say the Carlisle ladies are not at home?"

"Only Mrs. Carlisle is there just now."

At this point, Mrs. Carlisle, having heard her name mentioned, opened the door of Room A. "Lord Knollton!" she exclaimed. "Were you looking for me?"

"No," he babbled, feeling a fool. "That is, I am delighted to see you, ma'am. Is your daughter . . ."

"Come in. Come in. Dia went for buttons, I think. We can have a chat—and a cup of tea—while you wait. The kettle is hot."

Willy-nilly he found himself entering the Carlisle parlor and laying aside his hat. It was not Mrs. Carlisle he had come to visit, nor had she said how long her daughter might be gone, but his gentlemanly instincts required him to accept the situation gracefully.

"Sit here, my lord," she said, indicating the largest chair, before turning to fetch a cup and saucer from a side table, where the bottle of sherry that he had brought some days ago waited half empty.

"Or would you rather have sherry?"

"No, no. Tea will be perfect. Will Miss Carlisle be gone long?"

"Oh, no," she replied. "But long enough for us to have a nice chat." She poured tea and continued to chatter while he sipped it. "Your mama gave Dia such a pleasant ride to Kensington Gardens. She told me about the flowers she saw, though the names of them run in a mix. Nothing grows in our court, of course, it being all paved—nicely paved except for that stone that is sinking and makes a puddle when it rains."

Here she took a breath and Lord Knollton was able to ask again if she expected her daughter to return soon.

"Yes. Just went for pins—or did I say buttons? But not far. A little hole in the wall a block or so away. She has made a fine dress for me, and now is sewing a wedding dress for Mary Ann—Miss Froam, who is to be married when Mr. Folkes has found a place for them to live."

"Are you not having tea, too?" he asked, hoping to stem the flow of words.

"Not just now," she replied. "You have a charming mama, my lord. She called upon me, you know, which was most condescending of her."

This so surprised Lord Knollton that he dropped his spoon upon the carpet, and Mrs. Carlisle insisted upon giving him another. "Dia says you have a precious sister. I wish I could say the same. Dia and I are quite alone in the world, though very comfortably situated here where my husband settled us."

Feeling he must set facts straight, Francis hastily explained that Lady Knollton was his *stepmother* and Sara his half sister.

"Well, half is better than none at all. Dia has no one but me, which is to say I have no one but her, and we rub along very nicely. It is comforting to me that Mr. Pond and Mr. Whipple are here to watch out for her. Treat her like family, don't you know?"

Francis had the uncomfortable feeling that the two gentlemen just named were quite jealous of anyone who approached Miss Carlisle. Perhaps Pond more so than Whipple, who had seemed pleasant enough on the drive to St. Albans. Pond, he thought, must suspect him of having designs on Dia, which he didn't . . . at least, not improper ones. Actually, he did not know what to think about himself, and he wished Dia would come along and extricate him from this odd sort of interview.

Instead, it was Mr. Pond who knocked next and came in to look at him—Lord Francis Dubois Milne, Viscount Knollton— with disapproval unmistakable in his manner.

"Oh, Mr. Pond, do sit down and have a cup of tea," said Mrs. Carlisle happily. She did not notice that he was wearing a severe face.

He made a stiff little bow and took a chair. "Where did you say Miss Carlisle is?"

"Oh," she replied, "you must ask his lordship, for I have forgotten if she went for thread or pins. What did I say?"

"Buttons, I think," supplied Lord Knollton, "though Miss Docking said ribbon."

Mr. Pond did not care, one way or another, but he was determined to outwait his lordship.

"How pleasant to have visitors!" declared Dia's mama, quite unaware of Mr. Pond's chill manner. She herself could not imagine being uncivil to a viscount. Mr. Pond and Mr. Whipple, who came after Pond, were old friends; one didn't need to stand on ceremony with them. Lord Knollton, however, whom she supposed to be on terms with Mr. Lloyd of All Souls Church, was someone she could respect, whether he had a title or not.

Whipple was no help to the conversation. He had survived a backward trip to St. Albans and a luncheon there, for which he had dutifully thanked his host when they took place. There was nothing more to say. Let Pond do the talking!

"What *can* be keeping Dia?" wondered Mrs. Carlisle aloud as she handed out cups of tea.

Nothing was keeping Dia, for she was just coming in the doorway, wreathed in smiles because of having seen his lordship's curricle and Adam.

With some scraping of chairs, the oddly assorted gentlemen stood up to receive her.

"Why, Mama! Do you entertain while I am away?" Dia asked, laughing easily.

"Yes, indeed," agreed Mrs. Carlisle. "Isn't it delightful?"

Her daughter did think she seemed less lethargic than usual, though not one of the gentlemen looked as if he were enjoying an impromptu party.

There was a bit of color in Dia's checks, which made her even more lovely than usual, though it faded away as she endeavored to bring about communication between her guests.

"Who has seen a news sheet? Or heard some interesting rumor?" she asked brightly. "Is the Regent planning a dinner for nine hundred at Carlton House?"

"If so," volunteered Knollton wryly, "I have not been invited."

"Nor I," added Mr. Pond firmly, clearly unwilling to be seen at such a dissolute place.

"I do not know him," said Whipple. "That is, he does not know me."

Lord Knollton asked with a twinkle in his eye if Mrs. Carlisle expected to be one of the nine hundred.

"No, indeed," she asserted promptly. "What would I wear? The new blue that Dia has made? Doesn't one wear white when presented to royalty?"

"Oh, Mama," interrupted Dia, "presentations are made at the Queen's drawing room, not Carlton House."

"I believe you might say Carlton House is less—er—formal. There is no throne or anything like that," Knollton explained. "With five or ten hundred intimate friends invited, one might not even be noticed."

Mrs. Carlisle said, "Then why go?"

"Exactly!" approved Mr. Pond in a disapproving voice.

Dia thought, "Oh, dear," and quickly said, "Who, beside me, has seen the gardens at Kensington Palace this spring? They are utterly breathtaking, Lady Knollton and I thought."

"Yes, so Lady Knollton has told me," agreed his lordship. "She did not say you visited them together."

Dia thought that was quite odd, but did not like to say so.

"My friend, Collingwood, told me that his wife enjoyed meeting you," Francis continued carefully.

"Oh, yes. Such a dear girl."

"And," he added, somewhat pointedly it seemed, "I understand Mrs. Drummond Burrell was one of the party."

This made Mr. Pond prick up his ears like a wary fox; of everyone at Number 2, he was most alert to significant London names.

"Are you acquainted with Mrs. Burrell, my lord?" he asked.

"Forever," Knollton replied with an easy grin. "She had a particular fondness for my father. In fact, she encouraged him to wed Lady Lydia. I believe she is also fond of Lady Collingwood, whom you—Miss Carlisle—say you met on the drive to Kensington. So you admire the gardens?"

As Mr. Pond and Mr. Whipple had no opinion of gardens to insert, Dia was able to express her delight. "You can see, my lord, that we have no flowers or shrubbery around here. I did so like visiting Hyde Park with you and Kensington with your mama." She turned to her mother, adding, "The pretty little garden where we strolled on our way to St. Albans, while poor Wally was being treated for the blow to his head, is nothing to compare with Kensington."

"Perhaps we should visit Richmond park, as I believe I once mentioned. Have you seen that, Mr. Pond?" Knollton said civilly to his apparent adversary. "Or you, Mr. Whipple?"

"But that means crossing the river," objected Mrs. Carlisle, as if she thought she would be expected to swim. "So much wider than the Ver!"

Lord Knollton answered her gently, though there was a smile plucking at the corners of his mouth. "There are bridges, ma'am, and boats of all sizes."

"Oh, I should not trust a boat," Mrs. Carlisle declared. "They are very tipsy, I believe."

"Not all boats," he assured her. "Will you trust a bridge?"

"Well, a stone one, I think," she allowed. "None of metal, which might *bend*."

Here Mr. Whipple inserted a frivolous thought. "Our river has been known to freeze solid enough for one to walk upon it."

Dia's mama declared she would never allow her daughter to walk upon ice, for no one would be able to judge how thick or thin it might be. She was reinforced by Mr. Pond, who said firmly, "True enough."

There being no hope of speaking sense to one who had little, or to another who was determined to resist anything he might propose, Lord Knollton rose to his feet, bowed to each person in the room, took up his hat, bestowed a singularly sweet smile upon Miss Carlisle, and removed himself from where he was not wanted by two, though admired by two others.

"Such an elegant gentleman," sighed Dia's mama.

"Oh, yes, elegant," agreed Mr. Pond, "but we cannot know his real character."

Dia thought this was unfairly critical of one who had always behaved like a true gentleman in their presence. Who but a gentleman would condescend to deal courteously with nobodies such as the residents of Number 2? She started to say, "Oh, I think—" and hastily revised it to, "His lordship has been both kind and uncritical, hasn't he, Mama?"

"Yes, indeed," Mrs. Carlisle responded promptly. "Very solicitous of his coachman's welfare, too. I think that is a sure sign of his good character."

"His servant was the recipient of his lordship's attention. Of value to him, obviously," Mr. Pond pointed out sharply. "One wonders if he has equal concern for other people."

Dia was shocked to hear dear Mr. Pond, who was always so kind to others, speak thus critically.

As if he read her face, Mr. Pond modified his position by adding more peaceably, "Well, well, one is always most considerate of one's own. Whipple and I are partial to close neighbors named Carlisle."

"Yus, yus," Mr. Whipple intoned.

Thereupon, Pond and Whipple departed for upper regions of the house, and Dia began to gather empty cups. She did not at once speak.

"Well!" said Mrs. Carlisle, settling into her favorite chair before the window. "That was a nice little party, even though it was unplanned."

"Nice?" echoed Dia. "I thought it was most difficult—Lord Knollton being unexpected—and Mr. Pond being pointedly ungracious. So unlike him!"

Upstairs, Mr. Pond was saying to Mr. Whipple, "Well, we brushed through that. Knollton is gone—for the time being."

"I do not understand why you are so set against him," Mr. Whipple ventured to say.

Mr. Pond frowned. "Come now, Whipple. Do you really think there is any chance of a nobleman's offering marriage to our Dia?"

"It would be so fine," mumbled Whipple.

"Too fine. I cannot believe it would ever happen. Lords look for wives in their own circle. Would it make you happy for Dia to be offered a *carte blanche?*"

Mr. Whipple said, "She wouldn't know what was meant."

"Yes, she would," Pond contradicted, "and it would crush her. I must think of what to do."

"Pond! You would not speak to his lordship—warn him off!"

"I may have to. Unprotected females are fair game to bucks of the first head."

"Do you really think Knollton is one of those?" persisted Mr. Whipple. "I have never seen a sign of it. On our trip to St. Albans he was the perfect soul of good breeding."

"Oh," responded Mr. Pond, "his breeding is excellent, but what do we know of his character? You and I must watch closely. Besides, there is the danger that Dia might fall in love with him and believe he means well, when he only pursues his own pleasure."

Looking distressed and being aware of Pond's superior mind, Whipple said, "She had a wise father, don't you think? He surely planted standards by which she is to judge—"

His friend interrupted ominously. "When love comes along, judgment flies out the window." As Mr. Whipple was looking dashed, he added, "Well, well, if Knollton falls in love, he might lose his judgment and offer marriage."

"But Dia might feel unequal to his station—might decline—sacrifice her own happiness. She's a modest girl, for all her pretty face and sweet ways."

"Yes," assented Pond. "It would be like her to put his family's wishes ahead of hers, and turn him down." He sighed. "Well, well, we are not at that point. What you and I must do is see that he doesn't take advantage of her. Mrs. Carlisle, unfortunately, cannot see danger ahead any more than she could see an elephant."

By this time, Mr. Whipple was utterly confused, not understanding how elephants had come into the picture. At least he and Pond were agreed that no one must take advantage of the dear girl whom they loved like a daughter.

Although they understood Dia's nature very well, both overlooked one aspect, which was the keen mind bequeathed her by her father. Deep down Dia knew Lord Knollton was attracted to her person, with little concern for her thoughts or her principles. She also recognized temptation when she met it, having heard Mr. Lloyd speak repeatedly on the subject at All Souls Church, and she was determined to resist. A drive in the open air, with her mother and Mr. Whipple along, could not be dangerous; nor could serving tea in her own home to several callers be wicked. And there was Lady Lydia Knollton, so gracious, so kind. Dia did not believe she could be party to a shameful plot.

But Dia also overlooked one thing. The excitement and happiness of Mary Ann's betrothal to young Mr. Folkes, with plans for a wedding, had created such a cloud of romance over Number 2 as to make rational thought difficult.

Fifteen

When Mrs. Carlisle and her daughter were reunited with Mr. Pond and Mr. Whipple for the evening meal in the cellar of Number 2, there were no embarrassing mentions of a certain member of the peerage. Jane and Mary Ann were bubbling with talk of "Mr. Folkes" and "wedding clothes," and both Miss Docking and her little slavey, Cory, moved busily in and out with dishes and cups.

"I am keeping a list of good things that Miss Docking serves," said Mary Ann.

Miss Docking, overhearing, smiled in appreciation. "If you wish to be economical," she said, "you must visit meat shops and vegetable stalls to learn about prices and values."

"We shopped sometimes for our mama, before coming to London," defended Jane.

"That's true," agreed Mary Ann, "but there were fewer choices in Stoke Poges than here, I expect."

No one else had had the experience of both markets.

"Perhaps there are numerous more items to be found in London," Miss Docking suggested.

Because of his travels throughout England, Mr. Pond was considered to have had more worldly experience. He said, "More variety here, but fresher vegetables and fruits in rural markets."

There was no one to dispute his view.

"Miss Docking plans well," Dia said appreciatively, smiling up at the woman.

"In *everything,* planning ahead rewards one," Pond said firmly, but Dia wondered how one could plan matrimony or estimate the number of children that might arrive. She suspected that a flat for three might have to accommodate twice that number sooner or later, but of course it would be indelicate to suggest such a thing.

"We are most comfortable," Mrs. Carlisle announced.

There was a general murmur of agreement, which warmed Miss Docking's heart, causing her to ask, "Who will have something more?" Though watching pounds and pence carefully, she provided savory meals.

When they had finished eating, little Cory brought cups of coffee, and Mrs. Carlisle, in an excess of goodwill, invited all to bring their cups to Room A for a small visit. This was something of a surprise to Dia, although she was delighted for her mama to be in a convivial frame of mind. Except for Jane, who needed to write her parent, and Cory and the ash boy, who were expected to assist Cook in washing dishes, everyone else took cup in hand and climbed the stairs.

There was something of a scramble for seats. Miss Docking tilted herself into a windowsill, and when Dia had brought a stool from her mother's room for herself, all were settled after a fashion.

"I really cannot like for Miss Mary Ann to move away," said Mrs. Carlisle. "Such a pleasant group we have."

"Yes," said Mary Ann gloomily. "And sometimes I think Robert will never find an equally good arrangement for us."

"He is being careful to seek the best situation for you, my dear," said Mr. Pond to encourage her.

"Oh, yes," agreed Mary Ann, "but it seems hopeless."

"Hundreds—thousands have found homes in London. Sooner or later something will turn up," Pond said. "I'll keep an eye out for a place when I go about my business. Meanwhile, have you learned to cook? Cannot live on ambrosia and kisses, you know."

Mary Ann giggled. Embarrassed, but pleased, she replied daringly that she knew which would be nicest.

"I daresay Mr. Folkes would agree with your choice," Pond teased.

Watching Mary Ann's reaction, Dia thought it would be wonderful to have a beau camping on her own doorstep, though she could not find Mr. Folkes exactly exciting. Well mannered, neat, polite, probably reliable, yes, but not . . . dazzling. Mary Ann's flush seemed to show that she found Robert Folkes more than satisfactory, even if Dia did not view him in the same fashion.

"Why does sparkle ever have to go out of marriage?" asked Mary Ann, anxiously revealing a worry. "Being betrothed is, well, merry. I hope to keep Robert's and my relationship that way!"

Her hearers looked at each other doubtfully.

"You do right to think positively, my dear," said Mr. Pond kindly. "Make Robert truly welcome when he comes home every day."

"But we will be returning together from the shop," she protested. "Do you mean act glad to see him when I have seen him already the whole day?"

"Of course," said Pond forcefully. "Will you not be glad, he is there with you instead of applauding painted females at some tawdry theater?"

"Oh, that would not be like Robert at all!" she exclaimed. "He is a gentleman."

And all understood what she meant, though none of them had acquaintance with a real English gentleman, other than Lord Knollton, of course, and *him* they could not claim to know well.

"Certainly, Folkes is gentlemanly," Mr. Pond said tactfully so that Mary Ann was satisfied. Pond was well aware of Lord Knollton's social ease and impeccable dress; also the man was known to act with consideration and kindness . . . but what was his personal view of gentle creatures like Dia? Mr. Pond did not intend to relax one iota in his protection of Dia Carlisle.

He hoped this little conversation, without names called, would warn her to be on guard against possible abuse.

Dia was surely warned. She understood Mr. Pond's hints, but she could not condemn his lordship, when he was so perfectly considerate of her mama and herself—and of everyone at Number 2, Langham Court. Mr. Pond had not warned Mary Ann against Robert Folkes, and indeed everyone could see he was a person of merit; but why had Pond taken such a dislike to Lord Knollton, whose manners to her mama and herself were consistently perfect?

Was it possible that Mr. Pond had not entirely recovered his good nature after his spell of sickness? Was he still irritable enough to be suspicious of everything and everyone? Had not the viscount helpfully sent oranges to speed Mr. Pond's recovery?

It was all very puzzling. But Dia's nature, which made her see the best of Lord Knollton, made her accord Mr. Pond the same consideration. He had proved a good and true friend, upon whom two ladies alone in the world might rely for protection. As for Miss Docking, she was less experienced than Mr. Pond, yet upright, steady, and a comfortable sort of friend to have. Dia's feelings about Mr. Whipple were less clear; she could not call him "strong," yet she was fond of him and suspected he had a soft spot for her in his heart. Yes, it was very good to have these friends . . . but why could they not trust her to keep her head secure atop her shoulders?

Though no one noticed, Dia sighed slightly.

Miss Docking finished her cup and went below to be sure that Cook was putting away scraps carefully, and that Cory was not frittering time in vocal skirmish with the ash boy.

Soon Mrs. Carlisle was ready to be assisted to her bed. There was only one candle left burning in the Carlisles' parlor when Dia at last settled curled in her papa's armchair to do some serious thinking. Occasionally she could hear Mr. Pond's footsteps overhead, though not a set for Mr. Whipple, who must have gone to his own room above Pond's.

Dia's mood was a bit blue, despondent, which was not her

natural condition. Then she shook herself, mentally, remembering that she must not begrudge Mary Ann's happiness. She stood finally to extinguish the candle here and grope her way through her mother's room to reach her own. Her pantry chamber had a separate door to the hall, though she generally kept it locked.

Papa would have said she must think positively. "Change what must be changed," he had told her often enough, "and do not fret over what you cannot alter." There had never been a sign of his regretting more affluent days.

Her chamber being at the back of the house, she could not hear any sounds from Mr. Pond or Mr. Whipple.

Whipple, for one, was awake and straining his mind to think of protecting Dia from a handsome fellow of the nobility. He thought she deserved a splendid match, but he did not think she yearned for such, perhaps only for someone to love her, fill a gap in her life. And Knollton was interested; he could see that. Perhaps Knollton found her gentleness soothing. Even a smashing young buck on the town might deep down crave for peace and affection and appreciation. The peaceful atmosphere of Number 2 was what kept Mr. Whipple here. He had no family to care for him, and no prideful ambition. He was contented here. But Dia was a different matter—so beautiful she was, yet no marble statue. He could not bear to think of her withering away into old age.

What could he do? Well, one thing. He could find out more about Lord Francis Milne, Viscount Knollton.

Upon this thought, he went peacefully to sleep, having decided to locate his lordship's home on Upper Brook Street and see if he could scrape an acquaintance with someone of its staff. He had had some contact with his lordship's groom, Adam, and his coachman, Wally—enough for them to remember him. It was a starting point.

And he had an idea that Adam was approachable.

In the morning, Mr. Whipple was the first down to breakfast, and the first to leave the house. No one noted that he was meticulously dressed. Pond had not appeared when Mr. Whipple set out to walk to Grosvenor Square and beyond. Nine or ten squares was not far to walk for one who relied upon his feet for all his locomotion. It was a bright day with breezes to dispel the fetor of the river.

At Oxford he turned west until he had reached Duke Street, where he had a long wait to cross Oxford safely. Oxford was always busy. Then south on Duke he went, a long stretch, to come upon Grosvenor Square. Mr. Whipple was on familiar ground here, for he walked a great deal and explored London for lack of other things to do. Westward along the Square he went, and at last was looking down Upper Brook Street. Now he had only to determine which was Lord Knollton's house, and luck was with him, for approaching from the opposite direction was Adam tooling his lordship's curricle. When Adam had halted before a high, narrow, well-kept house of cut stone, Mr. Whipple went forward, saying, "Good day, Adam. This where you attend your master?"

"Mr. Whipple, sir!" returned the groom. "Yes, this is his lordship's town residence. You are far from home."

"I have an errand this way," Whipple responded vaguely. "This is a chance for me to tell you that you did a quick thing in controlling his lordship's horses on the St. Albans road."

"It's me job," the groom admitted.

"But you did it well," said Whipple, adding carefully, "I daresay his lordship rewarded you."

"Aye, he did. He is a good master." Adam rubbed the nose of the horse nearest him. "These are fine cattle. Wouldn't want them to break—and run—and mayhap hurt themselves and the passengers."

"Well, you did splendidly," Whipple insisted. "We could not see from the back what was happening, but I would not want anything to harm the ladies, especially our sweet little miss."

This was Adam's chance to get information. "Sweet as she is pretty, eh?" he asked.

"Yes," said Whipple. *"We* would not want anything to hurt her." He thought Adam got the plural of the message, for the groom grinned and replied earnestly, "No, sir. Not to be thought of!"

This was about as far as Mr. Whipple was able to go in subtlety. He presumed that Adam had caught his warning, and—for his own part—he felt reassured.

The door at the top of his lordship's steps opened. Mr. Whipple gave Adam a slight nod and proceeded down the street in a direction that would hide his face from Lord Knollton if he should turn his head that way.

Whipple knew he was not clever like Pond, yet he had established a connection with Lord Knollton's groom. He even thought he might have won another protector for Dia Carlisle without insulting Adam. Of course, the groom would never admit to a flaw of character in his employer, but Mr. Whipple believed Adam now understood that Dia had protectors. Pond might have made the matter clearer, being braver and more skilled with words. The most Whipple could do was sound a mild warning and hope for the best. He did not guess that Adam was quite ready to promote the welfare of little Miss Carlisle.

Secretly, Adam was pleased. He wondered if he should tell Mr. Shooker that Miss Carlisle had some who cared about her, but he feared Shooker would scoff at her needing them and make him feel a fool.

Lord Francis, sensing no undercurrents, entered his curricle and gathered the reins. "Want to have a look at Richmond Bridge," he said. "Take a seat."

Adam joined him.

"I thought I would examine the bridge to see if it would alarm Mrs. Carlisle to cross the Thames there," his lordship explained, though Adam could not imagine what spasms a bridge could cause.

"Same as new," Adam said reassuringly. "Built only forty years or so ago."

This amused his lordship, who knew Adam was younger than the bridge by at least ten years. "Westminster is sturdy masonry but a good deal longer and carries heavier traffic, which might make Mrs. Carlisle nervous," he replied. "She would like Richmond Park," his lordship continued to mumble half to himself. "I could cross one of the larger bridges like Westminster and approach the park from the south side of the river . . . or I could circle north and west of the river and cross eastward at Richmond Bridge. That is what we will do first, Adam. I will feed you at Richmond."

"Beg pardon, m'lord," said Adam carefully. "Why take the old lady on such a ramble?"

"Eh? It is not far as St. Albans, and she did all right then. Mrs. Carlisle is not really old, just—well, accustomed to looking through a window on a very limited world. So dull for the young lady! The whole point is, Adam, to take *Miss* Carlisle somewhere pleasant—somewhere she has not been—that has fresh air."

"How about the Tower, sir?" Adam ventured. "Daresay you would not have to have the Old One coming along for *that.*"

Knollton chuckled. "Very true. But would the young lady come?"

"Sartin sure, m'lord. Would like any place as has sunshine and people and breezes. Not a blade of grass can she see in that Court!"

Knollton shook his head, but he was smiling. "Now, why did I think I could plan a pleasant outing? Your ideas are better than mine. And I heard Miss Carlisle speak of enjoying the flowers at Kensington Gardens! Well, let us continue to Richmond and come back by Westminster Bridge to test the traffic. Kew Gardens is another possibility. Richmond has shops, too. Ladies always enjoy those."

"If they has coins in their reticules," Adam muttered, which his lordship thought it best not to hear.

"One thing I am sure of—we will not cross on London Bridge," said Knollton, "for the traffic there is sure to be so slow as to hardly move, even though all the old buildings have been cleared away."

At Richmond they agreed the bridge would not alarm nervous

ladies; it was securely built and the river was less wide here. When they topped Richmond Hill a splendid vista lay before them.

"The ladies must like this view!" the viscount exclaimed. "And there is the whole of Richmond Park to see." He did not mention shopping in the village of Richmond as—like his groom—he wondered if Mrs. Carlisle and her daughter would have money to fritter away. *Can't have idle money to spend,* he thought, *or they would not be living in a neighborhood such as Langham Court.* "Let us find an inn where we can rest the horses and have a bite to eat. Hungry, Adam?"

"Yes, m'lord. It's all this fresh air," the groom replied.

"Cleaner than in the city," Knollton agreed.

Accordingly, at the next wide place, where the road branched, his lordship turned the curricle and headed back into the town, stopping at the first respectable inn they reached. Adam, though an admitted favorite of Knollton, knew his place was in the taproom, so he went there after leading the team around to the stable and turning them over to a cheeky boy who grinned and said, "Prime uns! Oi'll pamper 'em like me childr'n."

Lord Knollton, meanwhile, had found a table at a window of the dining parlor. There were no other patrons at this early hour, which suited him just as well. Leaving the innkeeper to feed him the best he had, he fell to pondering about two ladies named Carlisle who lived reclusively in a lodging house in an unprepossessing neighborhood, yet displayed no ungenteel behavior or speech. He did wish he could have known Mr. Carlisle, who might have explained the ladies that bore his name. The whole of Number 2, in fact, was unexpected. Perhaps voices and inflections were a bit uncouth—no, not that, just less smooth, less refined. All inhabitants seemed free of coarseness in dress or grammar. But of course Francis had never had contact with a rooming house before now and did not know what to expect of one. How could he judge? His appearance there had been politely accepted; until this moment the absence of a butler or any other servant had not struck him. Even Miss Docking's appear-

ance in an apron had not seemed remarkable, as his own dear
nanny had regularly worn one.

What he could not visualize was Lady Lydia's visiting in
Langham Court. Perhaps that should have been a signal to
him—the inappropriateness of her ladyship's calling there! But
she had done so, as he knew now; her impression of Langham
Court had not prevented her from inviting Dia Carlisle to drive
in the exalted company of Mrs. Drummond Burrell! Perhaps it
was Mrs. Burrell's opinion of Miss Carlisle that he should discover . . . though he shuddered to think what it might be.

The idea of calling upon Mrs. Burrell to—to sound her out
did flit through his mind, yet he was not sure he was brave
enough to make the attempt. He would rather face a hostile gun
at thirty paces than Mrs. Burrell! Then he remembered that the
delightful wife of his friend, Collingwood, had been in the party
to drive to the gardens of Kensington, and this was one lady he
could question without his head being blown off. Collingwood
did say (didn't he?) that his wife would have liked to see Miss
Carlisle again.

By this time he was contemplating a gallop to Collingwood's
manor. Then Adam appeared at his elbow, saying the horses had
had a good rest, so although his meal was only half eaten, Knollton got to his feet, tossed down a generous amount of money,
and said he was ready to get along to Westminster Bridge.

This they did, slowing only through a few boroughs—Richmond, Putney, and Battersea—to reach the roads converging on
Westminster Bridge.

"Here, Adam, take the ribbons," he said, handing them to a
pleased groom. "Take whatever street you please, after we have
crossed the river. I need to think." There was no doubt in Adam's
mind about what his lordship was thinking.

The pair drawing the curricle took some exception to the
crowded bridge and at first tossed their heads disdainfully, but
they recognized the groom's hand upon their ribbons, it being
as familiar as Lord Knollton's, so they behaved politely as they
had been schooled. Very little of the river could they see; what

they noticed was the clatter of their hooves upon the solid sur-
face of the bridge—somewhat different from the crunch of road-
ways. Adam murmured soothingly, and they responded with
manners far superior to those of other animals among which
Adam maneuvered them.

As they came off onto the north bank, Knollton stirred himself from his thoughts to say, "You mentioned ladies liking to
shop—for amusement, if not to buy anything. Take us home by
way of Bond Street so that I may see if a visit there would
appeal to Miss Carlisle and her mother."

"Yes, m'lord. It is my understanding that females—of any
age, sir—like shopping," his groom replied. "There are some
interesting shops along Oxford, if you would be wanting to look
there, too, before going home."

Knollton said, "Yes, yes. Why not?" He was remembering a
small jeweler's place on Oxford, which the groom, who had also
remembered, was planning to pass casually.

Adam was not exactly sure of the significance of Mr. Hendrick's small place of business, but he knew it had some connection with pretty Miss Carlisle. He resolved to find some
necessity to go slowly by it, to nudge his lordship's memory . . .
if it needed nudging, but of course Adam would not say anything to him.

Adam had not forgotten his own surreptitious pursuit of a
particular grey bonnet that had led him (and his lordship) to
Langham Court. From Piccadilly Adam drove first up Bond and
New Bond, then turned right on Oxford and allowed traffic to
slow him until he had casually let the team plod past Mr. Hendrick's small shop.

After another square, Adam asked solemnly, "Any further,
m' lord?"

His lordship replied heavily, "No. Home."

At Wardour the groom turned the horses right, and right again
onto Noel Street, and continued in a westward direction until
he had reached Brook, which took him into Upper Brook.

"Be thinking where we had best drive the ladies," Knollton said as he stepped from the curricle.

Adam understood he meant Carlisle ladies.

Sixteen

Having spent most of the day in exploring access to Richmond, Lord Knollton went in a thoughtful mood to his room, prepared to strip and wash off the dust of travel before dressing for dinner. It was now his lordship's plan to invite Miss Carlisle and her mother for a drive to Richmond.

He opened a dresser drawer to return stock pin and ring to their niches and choose ornaments for the evening. Then what should he see, snuggled with cuff buttons, but a lady's bracelet of gold links, which had been casually laid there by his valet.

The bracelet that had started everything.

It looked innocent and insignificant amidst his jewelry, but not tawdry. A lady's simple keepsake.

The fifty pounds he had paid for it passed right out of his mind. "Damned if I feel right about keeping that!" he muttered.

Then Mr. Shooker entered to assist with his dressing, and Francis closed the drawer. "Have I an engagement this evening?" he asked.

"I believe so, my lord. There is a note of Lord Tilbert's name on your calendar," returned Shooker, whose intention it was to know everything, completely, that concerned his lordship. "I have had your evening clothes pressed. A dinner, my lord. Lady Knollton is expecting you to escort her, I believe."

"Oh, yes," said the viscount. "That's correct. I did promise to bear her company." Evidently, neither Endfield nor Marchmont was invited. He was rather glad that he did not, for once, have to watch either of them—or both—hanging over his stepmother.

They were decent chaps, of course, and he supposed he ought to be getting to know them better—if Lydia was likely to wed one of them.

But while Shooker continued to prepare Francis, via bath and clothes, his mind lingered on Dia Carlisle. For someone so young, she had a great deal of poise, a calm demeanor. Although her eyes were bright, aware, it was not the sort of contrived vivacity he saw in new young buds each social Season, but an intelligent alertness, a readiness to listen to him and respond without self-consciousness.

He was sure the bracelet was important to her, even if she avoided mention of it.

"Her ladyship likes to be seen with you, my lord," Shooker murmured, bringing him back to earth with a final brisk brush of his shoulders.

Lord Knollton thanked his valet, as he never failed to do, and went down to the parlor on the ground floor, to await his youthful stepmother, who was beautiful enough to set the beaux of London at each other's throats . . . if she chose. Francis could find no fault in her, yet he was beginning to think he preferred for himself an unsophisticated, gentle creature with hazel eyes and tranquil nature. The hundreds of young ladies, with whom he had become acquainted over a number of Seasons, he had dismissed as either gauche or predatory. It did not occur to him that the poor girls might be timid, their mamas being the marauding ones.

Lord Knollton enjoyed balls well enough, and he did his part at them good-humoredly. But he did not wish to be manipulated. Dia appealed because she was simply herself, serene, without simpers or coyness. Though he had not yet thought this through, he found her easy to be with. Who would want to be embroiled in emotional brangles?

As Lydia soon joined him, Francis gallantly offered his arm to lead her out to their carriage. Not until the evening at Lord

Tilbert's mansion had ended, and they were on their way home again, did he conceive the idea of inviting his stepmother to join his proposed excursion to Richmond.

"If you do not think only one gentleman for three ladies will be dull, it will give you a chance to form an opinion of the Carlisles," he said.

"Remember, I have met both," her ladyship answered mildly, giving no clue to her sentiments.

"But not in an open carriage," he reminded. "And have you shared a meal with them? I think you will be agreeably surprised."

His stepmother reminded him that she did not like surprises. However, she did not refuse the invitation. "I have not forgotten that Sara prattles of riding down to the Serpentine with you and the young lady. Surely you remember that I invited Miss Carlisle to tea. And certainly, I will go with you, if that is what you wish." She was rather curious to see how the girl and Francis would react to each other. "Am I included for the purpose of distracting Mrs. Carlisle's attention from your flirtation with her daughter? How jolly."

"Nonsense, Mama dear," he retorted. "I want you to watch so that you can give me your opinion. You have seen so little of Dia—"

"Have you reached first names already?" she interrupted.

"Of course not. Without you to chat with Mrs. Carlisle, I will have to include her in every sentence, and Dia will not say anything."

Lydia sighed noticeably. "Oh, very well. Shall I have Miss Carlisle sit beside me so that you can look at her without twisting your neck, or do you wish to have her beside you?" There was a twinkle in Lydia's eye, so he knew she was teasing him.

"Beside you, so I can admire both of you," he said grandly. Lydia shook her head. "Now you are trying your wiles on me. But you haven't considered this fully. That arrangement will force Mrs. Carlisle to ride backward."

"Good God! But someone must do that," Francis pointed out.

"Well, Francis, we are not at the altar yet, I hope. Only going for a ride in fresh air." She added soothingly, "The matter is simply arranged. Miss Carlisle has already told me that she is perfectly comfortable in a backward-facing seat. That is the way she rode with me the other day. You can have her next to you, and therefore also admire a full view of her mama!"

"I would be more apt to admire you than Mrs. Carlisle," he said.

"Cozening me!" she mocked. However, they were both satisfied with the plan, and she said the invitation would properly have to come from her.

"Fine," approved the viscount. "Wally tells me the weather will be good for several days."

As a rule, some malevolent spirit held sway over the rain clouds of England, but Wally was a Knowing One, and he approved the day Lady Knollton chose.

A note was dispatched to Mrs. Carlisle, who responded with polite acceptance. "Is it not delightful of Lady Knollton to invite me for a pleasant journey?" she said to her daughter. "You are to be included also."

No mention of Lord Knollton was made, but Dia suspected that he would be a fourth in the barouche, and a wee smile tugged at the corners of her lips. She could not—really she could not—honestly suppose his lordship took a serious interest in herself. She would have to guard her heart and simply enjoy something so new and interesting as Richmond Bridge and the pretty town and parklands.

Lady Knollton, though she did not mention it, at first had some idea of taking her daughter along. Then she decided that a wiggling child (however precious) would crowd the ladies and perhaps disturb them with childish prattle.

As Wally had predicted, the day dawned beautifully, almost cloudless, and not too hot. They set off northwest to follow the looping river, sometimes seeing it, but more often not. Wally, at the reins, and Adam, beside him, wore their smartest livery, of which Mrs. Carlisle saw only the backs; but she cared little for that, being more interested in her ladyship's lavender ensemble and dove-grey bonnet, which dripped violets so perfect that they looked almost real.

"I declare," said Mrs. Carlisle, "I have always lived in the city, and you would say I am a city person, but new scenes—this wonderful fresh air—we have left the chimney pots behind, haven't we?—is most refreshing."

"Yes, we could not have chosen a better day," Lady Lydia agreed. "Francis lives mostly at his manor, but I must admit to being addicted to the pleasures of the city—libraries, theaters, concerts, shops. They hold me to Upper Brook Street most of the year."

"You have a young daughter, haven't you?" queried Mrs. Carlisle. "We have always lived in London, and fortunately Dia has been healthy, but I have wondered if country air might not have been better for her."

Lady Lydia explained that she liked to keep Sara near her. "We spend summer months at Knoll Hall to make sure Sara has oceans of fresh air and can run about in sunshine."

"Ah, I might have liked that for Dia. Her papa preferred London, where there are shops full of books and where his students could reach him easily. He was a teacher of young men, you know," Mrs. Carlisle explained. "Dia, I think, learned more from him than any boy did."

Feeling it was time for her to interfere, Dia said gently, "Papa inspired me. He liked to talk about history—literature and things like that."

"This was interesting to you?" enquired his lordship. "Then you will like Richmond. It is a quaint town, charming buildings, a pretty green . . . and of course there is Richmond Park, which we will visit."

"Historic, too, is it not, my lord?" Dia asked.

The other ladies appeared to have found something else to discuss, but Lord Knollton realized that Dia was interested in what he could tell her, so he said, "I thought at first of planning a visit to Kew. We are near it now. However, I was not sure what features are open for viewing. The mad King lives there, you know."

"Yes. So sad. At least one can be glad that he befriended Mr. Harrison, who was so mistreated by the Board of Longitude. It was before His Majesty fell ill, as I expect you know."

"Er—yes. But how do you know?"

"Why," replied Dia, "Papa told me. Mr. Harrison made those wonderful clocks, so incredibly accurate, and solved a way to calculate longitude. Just think of the ships lost at sea over the centuries because of not knowing!"

"Very true," murmured Francis, hardly following this.

"It was here—at His Majesty's private observatory, that Mr. Harrison's newest clock was tested and proved wonderfully accurate. Have you ever visited the observatory?"

Francis said, "Well, no. But it is something to think about."

Dia nodded. "Papa always wanted to see Mr. Harrison's clocks."

Lady Knollton, watching them as she responded to Mrs. Carlisle when needed, was interested to see how much at ease Dia was. The girl spoke knowingly, and Francis seemed satisfied with what she had to say. After all, he had been well educated; his father had seen to that. And if several seasons in the *ton* had been frivolous, it was time—wasn't it—for him to begin serious thoughts. Oh, not just about settling with a wife, but maturing to carry on the Knollton line, duties, and gentlemanly standards. Lydia wondered what her husband would have thought of a Nobody who was beautiful, yet obviously serious minded.

At the same time, Mrs. Carlisle was paying no attention to her daughter, whom she had heard talk innumerable hours with Mr. Carlisle in an equally serious and noncombative manner. Even if father and daughter had separate points of view, they debated peaceably, as if aware of multiple points of agreement.

Fortunately, Francis had remembered (when his brain had

been nudged) that Harrison was the name of the man who had handcrafted clocks that kept time to a well-nigh-perfect degree. Captain Cook was said to have praised them, Francis recalled. He could answer Dia sensibly, while noticing the earnestness of her expression as she spoke.

Then the carriage was turning onto Richmond Bridge, and presently they had reached Richmond Green and were circling it slowly for a view of seventeenth- and eighteenth-century houses, which delighted the London ladies. Then Wally was reining in his team at a picturesque hostelry, and all stepped down to be received by a bowing host.

Although Mrs. Carlisle seldom went anywhere, seldom did anything ruffle her; her kind husband had always been ready to smooth her way, and now Dia was accustomed to doing the same. Mrs. Carlisle was never inclined to create scenes; they required too much effort. As eldest lady of the party, she followed the inn's host to a table and accepted the chair offered to her. Lord Knollton then indicated that his stepmother should sit at Mrs. Carlisle's right, and Miss Carlisle at *her* right, which placed him between the Carlisle ladies.

"Would you like to order for us, Mama dear?" he asked, almost as if challenging her.

Lady Knollton drew off her gloves gracefully, saying, "I will leave choices to you, my love."

He nodded and began to consult the host in a low voice. They were to be surprised, it seemed.

"Do you find the village charming?" he asked Mrs. Carlisle when he had finished his order.

"Indeed I do," she replied. "I hope nothing ever changes it."

He shook his head regretfully. "It will. It will. Miss Carlisle, I expect your father would say the same."

"You are right," she agreed, "but Papa also said change is not always bad. Poor art and distasteful architecture may be overruled in time."

"It may be overruled," said Lady Knollton, "without being wiped out. One sees horrid examples."

"Hopefully," suggested Dia, laughing, "overgrown with moss!"

"One does not see moss obscuring bad ideas," Lady Knollton objected. "The bad old ones keep popping up, I fear."

"My papa would say they are dug up."

Dia's mother was clearly puzzled by this conversation. "It seems to me that whatever will be will be. Why worry about it? Here today and gone tomorrow."

"But, Mama, that is so pessimistic, for good things would not last anymore than bad ones," Dia objected. "Surely, your outlook is more hopeful than that!"

"Oh," responded her mother, who never seemed to worry "I not only hope but am sure that the worst things cannot stay bad forever. Look at the weather today. One might have thought the rain would never end, but it has. And the sunlight will end, too, sometime. I cannot worry about it."

"Mrs. Carlisle," declared Lord Knollton, "you are an original thinker!"

"Oh, no, I never think," she replied, which may have been the simple truth.

Her hearers were struck dumb. Knollton, the one male present, wondered if the same theory could be applied to worry. At any rate, he introduced a change of subject by asking if everyone had finished eating and whether they could not move on to their carriage and a circle of Richmond Park.

They went out from the inn to find Wally and Adam waiting with his lordship's barouche, the team well rested for the drive home.

Now the road led up to rolling parkland with both wooded areas and wide vistas, even an occasional house.

"What a change from crowded city streets, and yet convenient to the city," Dia said.

"If you appreciate this, you can understand why I live most of the year at Knoll Hall," Lord Knollton said, "and, Mama, admit you always come to the Hall for a visit of some length!"

Dia's voice was wistful. "It must be wonderful to walk where there are trees and blooming things."

"Yes," admitted Lady Knollton. "Unspoiled nature is restorative, I think."

"Partly because the air is fresher in the countryside," the viscount explained. "Watch for the grey pall above the city as we approach it. At least it is not as bad as at mill towns. In winter, when more fires are spewing smoke here, it is time for good Englishmen to return to their lands."

Dia, who had no choice of homes, thought an estate, or a farm, or even a small villa in the countryside sounded very pleasant, but she did not say so for fear of making her mother feel at fault for clinging to London and Number 2.

Seventeen

Dia's return to Langham Court was both bitter and sweet. Home, however plain it might be, was always warmly familiar, and friendly faces were waiting to be seen by her, yet she had tasted the elegance of travel and obsequious service—not to be spoiled by them, but to be made overly conscious of the modest way in which she and her mother lived. How remarkable that Lady Lydia would condescend to befriend them!

She was thankful that Mr. Pond was not at home when she arrived, for while she knew he was wise and strong and concerned for her welfare, it did seem that he had a certain blind spot, due to deep conviction that the nobility was scornful of plain, honest men who earned an income. But was that scorn any more unreasonable than Mr. Pond's own resentment of the titled elite?

Number 2 was the same as always, the same as when she had left it earlier in the day, and maybe it would stay that way. At least she could be sure that her mama was unchanged by rubbing elbows with nobility. As for herself, she knew common sense was good sense, for her father had convinced her of that. Obviously, it was necessary for her to provide the common sense that her mother lacked.

Dia's mother had a regular message for everyone in Langham Court. Never borrow trouble. It is free. Available to everyone who wants to waste time worrying. It is much more agreeable to let someone else supply the worry—a husband—or a daughter.

When Lady Knollton and her stepson had reached their residence on Upper Brook Street, by unspoken consent they had handed an assortment of hats, shawls, and gloves to waiting servants, and drifted into the family sitting room behind their formal drawing room.

Small Sara was often to be found here, though today she was enjoying a bath, after digging happily with a wooden spoon in the soil of a small garden behind the house. She had not heard her mama arrive, and so allowed that lady a sort of reprieve.

Francis flung himself back in a deep chair and asked, "Well? What do you think of Miss Carlisle now?"

Lydia sank more gracefully into an open arm chair. She did not have to delay answering, for she had been forming her response for the last forty-five minutes. "I like her. For that matter, I like her mama also, though their minds operate on different levels."

"May we guess Dia is like her father?"

"Yes. One wonders who—or what—he may have been."

"Something rare, do you think?"

"Or odd," Lydia said with a smile. She sighed then, and leaned back, waiting for him to say more, which of course he did.

"Does that mean you are going to set yourself against her?"

"I am going to wait and see, which is what I advise you to do. Don't jump into her net too fast."

Francis frowned. "Do you think she has a net—set to catch me?"

"I do not know, which is a sure way to get one's self caught."

Francis retorted that he was willing to take the gamble.

"But are you willing," his stepmother said, looking him in the eye, "to remain entangled?"

He threw up his hands. "Yes—no. First I have to find out what she is." He went off to amuse himself by teasing his adoring wee sister.

Lady Lydia spent a restless night in wondering if there might be some way she could test Dia's conduct in a social setting; she told herself that it was best to be prepared, in case Francis should consider making the girl an offer. To accept the match might be preferable to risking the scandal of a breach of promise claim! By noon of Saturday, when he had left the house, she sent a note, written to invite Dia and her mother to come to tea on Sunday afternoon. Not a great deal happened on Sundays; she enlisted Mrs. Drummond Burrell and another lady with two daughters, and Miss Angela Wetherall, who was a cousin of her own. It would be interesting to see how the Carlisles fit into the group.

Surprised, yet pleased, Mrs. Carlisle returned an immediate acceptance from her daughter and herself.

"How glad I am to have my new blue dress!" Mrs. Carlisle declared. She was as delighted as a child by the idea of a party, and had no qualms at going. She did not think very far ahead about anything. Already she knew Lady Knollton, and Dia would be beside her to fill pauses and explain anything that might puzzle her. Sherry might be offered, but she thought she should accept only tea, which was sure to be of the finest, not the twice-used sort.

Dia was less easy. She thought it unlikely that the viscount would attend a ladies' party, but did not know how many strangers they would be required to face, nor who of them would willingly acknowledge her and Mama. But Lady Knollton she knew to be kind, and she had—well—a secret curiosity to see where Francis Knollton lived, though she feared she and her mama would look like fish that had somehow got past the weir and were in the wrong pool. At least she would not have to face his lordship on his own turf, and she both hoped and expected her ladyship's other guests would be civil to strangers.

Lady Knollton had not offered to send her carriage for them. Mr. Whipple (Pond being absent) insisted Upper Brook was too far for them to walk, although Dia assured him they could do so easily, if they did not go too fast. Her mother, having no clear idea of the location of Upper Brook Street, insisted she could do whatever her daughter could.

"But, Dia, you know your mother is not a great walker," Mr. Whipple said with unusual firmness, and he went out to hire a hackney for them. He suggested that when Lady Knollton considered the darkening sky of evening, she might send them home in a carriage belonging to her stepson.

"If it is to be a party, perhaps some other guest will offer us a ride," Dia countered. "I doubt gentlemen will be invited, but ladies are sure to consider the need for some sort of conveyance, and may offer to bring us to Langham Street." She did not say that, if worse came to worse, the two of them could hang on to each other for a few blocks. At any rate, she tucked coins into her reticule in case she should have to pay for a hackney to return home.

Before they could go anywhere, a bonnet must be provided to set off Mrs. Carlisle's dress. Miss Docking came to the rescue, by lending one of blond straw, around which Dia hastily twisted a scrap of the blue fabric from which she had cut her mother's newest dress.

"Do not worry, Miss Dia. No one will be looking at *your* bonnet, for they will be admiring your dear face," said Miss Docking.

Dia blushed, and thanked her, thinking how heartwarming it was to have kind friends. Even though she felt somewhat nervous about going among strangers, she remembered how pleasant the drive to Kensington Gardens had been with Lady Knollton. Mrs. Drummond Burrell and Lady Collingwood had been cordial then; would they be present today?

Julia Collingwood, unaware of what was in store for Dia Carlisle, was not there. Her ladyship's cousin, Miss Wetherall, was at Brook Street when they arrived; Mrs. Burrell came next after them. Dia greeted her happily and presented her mother, whom the exalted Mrs. Burrell eyed sharply but offered a civil "How-do-you-do."

They had gone up to the drawing room when another lady

came with her daughters. Seeing Mrs. Burrell apparently on good terms with the Unknowns, these three spoke cordially. Then Lady Knollton was settling them in a loose circle near a small fire in the handsome grate. As usual when visitors came, Lydia's elderly Cousin Emalie remained upstairs. A butler and footman came in with the trays of tea and coffee, followed by comely maids with platters of dainty sandwiches and cakes.

Much as Dia wished to stare about the chamber to admire the paneling, somber portraits, and gold draperies closed against fading daylight outside, her attention was divided between what Miss Wetherall was saying on her right and what her mama, two seats away, might be saying to Mrs. Burrell.

Actually it was harmless. "These are pretty sandwiches, are they not? I do think pretty things taste best, don't you?"

"Prettiness improves everything," returned Mrs. Drummond Burrell largely. "You have a beautiful daughter."

"Do you think so?" said Mrs. Carlisle, pleased. "I could not have a dearer one. Why she even makes—"

Then a servant came between Dia and the older ladies to offer sweets, so that Dia could not hear if her mama was guilelessly revealing who had sewn her blue dress. Miss Wetherall was asking which cake she should try, so Dia said hastily, "Oh, take the pink sort. Anything pink must taste good."

Mrs. Burrell was now addressing the lady on her other side, who was her hostess, and Mrs. Carlisle was safely sipping tea. Dia would have liked to talk with the two girls who looked to be about her age, but they were beyond both Miss Wetherall and their mother. They were very subdued in manner, though they looked alert; probably, Dia thought, this was their first visit to the residence of an eligible viscount. The pleasure of knowing other young people made her wonder how she might move nearer to them.

As she handed her cup to a servant, shaking her head to deny wanting more tea, she glanced past her mother and saw Mrs. Burrell start to set her own cup upon a nearby table. The cup skidded in its saucer, splashing tea upon Mrs. Burrell's wrist.

Dia sprang to her feet, clutching her lacy serviette, yet managing to rescue the cup and convey it to a table.

"Ma'am," she exclaimed, "was it still hot? Are you burned?"

Looking as upset as if she had been scalded, Mrs. Burrell protested faintly, "No, no, only a drop or two."

Immediately there was pandemonium, on a par with the Exeter stagecoach's being toppled into a gully. Most of the visitors stood up, clustering about the injured one. "Some butter," said one. "Or honey," said another, but Dia, not thinking at all where she was, said, "Nothing. Nothing, just a clean cloth, please."

"Better listen to Dia," advised her mother comfortably. "She is as good as a physician."

There was a babble of voices, so Lady Knollton signaled for her personal maid to be summoned. Meanwhile, Dia was dabbing gently near where the hot tea had splattered. "Is it painful?" she asked.

Mrs. Burrell refused to make a scene, at which she was generally very adept. "Hardly at all."

"There is a little pink area, ma'am," Dia said, indicating it. "With your permission, I will cover it to keep the air from it. We will need a clean cloth."

Several ladies scrabbled in their reticules for fresh handkerchiefs, but Mrs. Carlisle had already extended hers, and Dia, who had put into her mama's purse the spanking clean handkerchief, accepted it, plus another lady's to tie it in place.

By this time Lady Knollton's maid had arrived, to be unneeded.

"I think I will have a bit of sherry," Mrs. Burrell said.

There was some collision of roving guests and servants, but the tartar got her sherry and did not seem out of sorts at all. "Thanks to you, my dear," she said to Dia, "it was no disaster."

The flow of tea party talk resumed, until Mrs. Burrell decided it was time to go home. Her carriage was summoned and her hostess, apologetic for what was Mrs. Burrell's own fault, accompanied her down to the door of the house, which was opened to reveal Lord Knollton on the doorstep, about to sound the knocker.

Of course he, seeing that Mrs. Burrell was determined to depart, turned about and accompanied her to her carriage. Then he returned to the house, where a bevy of females was waiting to tell details of Mrs. Drummond Burrell's very close brush with disaster, and the way Miss Carlisle had heroically handled it.

Francis, astonished to find Dia in his house, looked across several heads to Miss Carlisle's lightly flushed face and to her mama's beyond her. "I see," he said, not quite seeing, but understanding Dia had cared for the Dragon of Almack's in some way. "May I escort you and your mother home, Miss Carlisle?"

Relieved that she and her mama would not have to walk after all, Dia led her mother to say farewell to their hostess, intermixed with responses to ladies who complemented her skill.

"Oh, Dia is very clever," Mrs. Carlisle was heard to say happily in reply several times.

When it was Dia's time to thank her hostess for inviting her mother and herself, Lady Knollton replied she had more reason to thank Dia for helping Mrs. Drummond Burrell. "If you had not been here, I might have had to retreat in shame to Francis's manor."

"But it was Mrs. Burrell who spilled the hot tea," objected Mrs. Carlisle, irrepressibly.

Lady Knollton said perhaps she should thank Mrs. Burrell for spilling the tea on *herself.* "Otherwise, it might have marred the leather top of the table nearest her."

Knollton's curricle was summoned back, and they had a brief wait as grooms had already begun to unhitch the pair.

"May I call tomorrow?" his lordship asked, when he saw they would not sit down to linger in his house.

Dia and her mama both at once said, "Yes," and laughed at each other. They had not intended to sound overanxious, and they were not that, only glad, for they liked Lord Knollton.

Lady Knollton prevented any awkwardness by switching the conversation to something innocuous and asking Dia if she had noticed other trees leafing out like the ones at Kensington Gardens. "We enjoy the ones in Grosvenor Square that we can glimpse from our front windows here. Before long, the Season will be ending and I will go to Francis's manor. Have you made any plans to remove there, Francis?"

His lordship replied, "Not yet. I've often wondered why the Season must occur in springtime, when one wants to enjoy a burst of bloom. However, there are some unsettled matters here that need my attention."

"Pooh!" said her ladyship. "Let your man of business busy himself with them. That is what he is supposed to do." If she was needling her stepson, the Carlisles did not guess it. Actually, she was not, only probing for his personal plans.

The viscount said sweetly, "You are welcome at the manor anytime you wish to go, dear Mother. I always supposed you preferred London."

"Usually I do. More happens here. But it is good for Sara to run about the manor in a way she cannot in the city. What are your plans, Mrs. Carlisle?"

Dia's mother said, "I have always lived at London. All year, we are here. There are no trees or flowers in our court, but Dia and I take little walks in our neighborhood on pleasant days." Where they walked, or what shrubs they might have viewed, she did not say, being more interested in shop windows.

When all had gone and servants had carried away cups and food, Lady Knollton lingered before the crumbling coals of the fire, staring at them, but not seeing them. The family manor was in her thoughts. Dia had been perfect here, poised, not self-conscious. How would she fit there? The servants in town were devoted to her, yet she could not detect any resentment of Unknowns. Certainly the other guests had shown none. All in all, the afternoon had been reassuring.

After Francis returned, Lady Knollton asked no questions, nor did he. What had taken him galloping from town that day was not mentioned. A young unattached gentleman might have had many reasons for going anywhere, and one could expect him to resent being catechized. At least he had come in time to see Dia at ease among his acquaintances.

"Do we have any engagement for tonight?" he asked.

Lydia said, "No."

"Remember that I will be escorting you to Almack's on Wednesday," he said.

"As if I could forget!" she exclaimed. "The young buds will look at me enviously, and I shall enjoy that, even if their mamas are disgruntled."

"Flattery!" Francis protested. "Do you not suppose I enjoy having a beautiful lady on my arm?"

"Yes—but a stepmother," she reminded. "And do not think that I have not suspected that you find me a sort of protection."

He had enough wits to have thought of protection from aggressive damsels, yet he did enjoy her company. There would be none lovelier at Almack's. Other men would envy him, and yet—it was Dia who charmed him—who knew nothing of contemporary dialogue and social give and take. Maybe she was not as lively in discourse as some, and not inclined to gossip like many girls, yet always ready with intelligent response. He was not prepared to explain this to Lydia, even if he could do so.

"Was there a near crisis with hot tea?" he asked.

"Yes. It is almost impossible to entertain ladies with delicate cups and not have something spilled. The thing about our little upset was that the tea was very hot and came nigh to burning Mrs. Burrell, if it had not been for Miss Carlisle's quick action. Only a little dab. And then Miss Carlisle was taking charge of making a bandage in the most competent way."

His lordship said, "I see. Very fortunate." He smiled slightly and said he hated to mention food, but would they be having a bite to eat before retiring to bed?

"Oh, I have had pretty little sandwiches and cakes—Cook's best—and I am not hungry at all," she admitted, chagrined. "I suppose you have been driving recklessly and are starving now.

Very likely Cook is waiting impatiently to assuage your appetite with hearty beef. Ring the bell and let us find out."

But evidently a servant was lurking in the hall, for Francis had hardly heaved himself to his feet, before his butler entered.

"If you would like something to eat, my lord, Cook will have a meal upon the table in ten minutes."

"Splendid," said Lord Knollton, going toward the door. "That will give me time to wash off a bit of dust."

Lady Knollton continued to relax beside the dwindling flame of the fireplace. A near disaster had been avoided. Mrs. Burrell remained well-disposed toward Dia Carlisle. Mrs. Carlisle seemed less featherheaded than before. Francis was safely returned and did not seem lovelorn. Perhaps she had been worrying without need.

One thing she must remember, though, was that no application from her, no Act of Parliament, could secure a voucher for an unknown Miss Carlisle to enter the sacred portals of Almack's.

Good heavens! Did the girl know how to dance? Not likely.

"What am I thinking of?" Lady Knollton asked herself. "Is this girl only Francis's passing fancy, because of being *new?*"

She must remember that Francis was his father's true son. She had always been able to expect perfect behavior from both of them. Now Francis was of an age for romance. Was it possible he was actually considering an *affaire?*

She felt an overpowering need to protect gentle Miss Carlisle from being hurt . . . and herself from disillusionment.

Without following the reasoning of his stepmother, Knollton had developed a similar aim, which obliged him to return to Dia the bracelet that she had so obviously valued. Its age implied a sentimental value above any purchase price. Besides, what would he do with it himself? At the time of buying it he had mentioned "a gift for my sister," yet little Lady Sara was too young for such an object now. Indeed, her tiny wrist would be too small for it.

He would not mention the bracelet to Lydia, for she might

misunderstand. It did not occur to him that Dia herself would leap to unfortunate conclusions.

Miss Carlisle had intimated he was welcome to call on Monday, which allowed him eighteen or twenty hours in which to conceive a way to see her alone, for it was important to keep the transaction private between them.

Meanwhile, Dia and her mama were happily telling their friends at Number 2 how pleasant it had been to be received graciously at a residence of the first stare in Mayfair.

Eighteen

Mr. Pond returned to London on Monday to be told by Miss Docking, who saw him first, that the Carlisle ladies had been received by Lady Knollton for tea at Knollton House.

"No!" he exclaimed. "What can it mean? Are you saying her ladyship invited them herself? Was the viscount there?"

"No, he wasn't. That is, he had gone from town, but arrived home just as the party was ending, so he brought our ladies back to Number 2. Mrs. Carlisle wore the new dress that Miss Dia made."

Pond cared nothing for what Mrs. Carlisle wore. "I've warned her about that fellow," he said single-mindedly.

"So have we all," agreed Miss Docking, "although he seems decent enough. But I am telling you it was a tea party—a number of ladies, with *him* gone out of town."

Mr. Pond, who had set down his luggage, said, "I will have to speak to Dia about this! Are they awake?" Without waiting for an answer from Miss Docking, he crossed the hall and rapped upon the Carlisles' door.

Evidently the ladies were not in their parlor, for there was no voice saying to come in, but after a moment footsteps could be heard, and Dia opened the door.

"Mr. Pond! You're home sooner than we thought. Was it a good trip?"

"Yes. No. I hardly remember," he said gruffly. "What's this I hear of your going to Knollton's place?"

By his saying, "What's this?" she realized that he was cross with her, which was ridiculous. She said pacifically, "It is Lady Knollton's place, too, you know. We were invited by *her,* which you must agree was a kindness."

"Others were there? The viscount wasn't?"

"There were several pleasant ladies, including Mrs. Drummond Burrell, of whom you have read in Society news and whom I had already met. His lordship was not present. But, yes, he did return unexpectedly from an afternoon with friends somewhere. He was kind enough to bring Mama and me home." As Dia spoke, she fervently hoped Lord Knollton would not choose this moment to make his promised call.

He did not.

Mr. Pond, mollified, said, "Oh, well, if your mother was along. . . . But do not forget what I have told you." He picked up his bags from the foot of the stairs and continued to his room.

Dia and Miss Docking exchanged comprehensive looks.

"He cares about you like a papa," the older woman said.

The younger one said, "I know. It is nonsensical." She could not imagine his lordship's ever being ungentlemanly.

Some squares away at this time, Francis Milne, Lord Knollton, was dressing slowly with the assistance of Mr. Shooker. When the valet had gone out with discarded nightclothes, Lord Knollton opened his dresser drawer, took out Dia's gold bracelet, and tucked it deep into a pocket.

Then he descended to a brunch, of which he did not savor much. Only his elderly Cousin Emalie was sipping coffee at the table, Lydia had gone shopping.

His lordship was unsure at what time to call upon Miss Carlisle. He had an idea that her mother was in the habit of taking naps. He also thought breakfast was early at Number 2. It therefore followed that Mrs. Carlisle might be on her bed again by eleven, so that was the time he chose for his call upon the daughter. There was nothing furtive about his plan; it was simply that he thought the girl would prefer that no one should know he was returning her bracelet, for obviously she had not wanted to be seen selling it.

He could call at eleven.

But Mrs. Carlisle had overslept that morning, and consequently was just up and dressed; she had had a late breakfast fetched by Dia. She was alert and ready for conversation, especially as it brought the social world of London to her parlor in the person of Lord Knollton.

So, while the bracelet burned his pocket, his lordship sat down and made polite conversation that was only civil give and take suitable for a morning call and such as Mrs. Carlisle could easily join. It was necessary to resort to weather as a topic, present temperatures continuing pleasant.

"I have always wondered how anyone can predict weather," Mrs. Carlisle remarked.

"So have I," admitted his lordship. "My coachman, Wally, has a way of looking north, east, south, and west, and squeezing his eyes shut—"

"Why does he do that?"

"To feel invisible messages, I presume. Then he tells me when to set out." Knollton laughed. "I would not dare to disagree." He had abandoned all hope of a private word with Miss Carlisle, and would have to try another visit in a day or two. After luncheon, perhaps. Surely he could catch Mrs. Carlisle napping sometime!

They continued to discuss weather repetitively, Knollton being more interested in Miss Carlisle's face, which he imagined to be wan. He thought how delightful for him it would be to bring a sparkle to her hazel eyes. She would enjoy having her heirloom to wear again, he concluded without the least tingle of doubt.

Dia also felt a strange bit of emotion in the air; she sought another topic of conversation. "Poor Mr. Folkes has been unable to find a flat to rent for his wives." She giggled. "He is expecting to wed only one, but he is liable to acquire two."

"Cannot the other sister continue here?" Knollton asked.

Dia shook her head. "I am afraid Jane cannot afford the room alone. Besides, her mother will be fretting about her safety."

"It is only proper for Jane to have a companion," Mrs. Carlisle said. "The people in this house are very kind, but she needs another her own age, if she cannot have a mother."

Evidently, Mrs. Carlisle supposed she was taking care of Dia, instead of the other way around.

At this time they could hear the heavy steps of male feet descending the stairs, which meant either Pond or Whipple. Prudently Lord Knollton decided it was time for him to leave. He bowed smartly to the ladies and stepped into the hall just as Mr. Pond reached the bottom of the flight.

"Good day, Mr. Pond," his lordship said cordially, to which the vendor of fabrics responded gravely, "Good day, my lord."

Both bowed minimally, the viscount departed from the building, and Mr. Pond went into the Carlisles' parlor, shaking his head (which cost Dia a pang), and said to her mother: "I am glad to see you are present."

"Where else would I be?" asked Mrs. Carlisle. "I live here."

"It begins to look like his lordship does, too," he commented.

"Oh, no," Mrs. Carlisle replied. "All the rooms are taken."

At this Dia was obliged to hide a smile, and Pond ground his teeth. "I meant," he amplified, "that His Worship spends all his time at Number 2."

"Not quite all," Dia said innocently. "He spends many days with his stepmother and his small sister, Sara."

Fortunately her mother did not add anything to this.

"Before long, he and his family will be moving to the country for the summer," Mr. Pond consoled himself.

"What are your plans, dear sir," asked Dia. "Another trip, I suppose? First you will take time for a rest, will you not?"

Not immune to her concern for himself, Mr. Pond replied more pleasantly, "A bit, thank you, my dear. And of course I must repack my samples, for folding and unfolding them causes wrinkles. Even samples must look perfect, if I am to hope for orders. Tell me, what news of Mary Ann? Any rooms found?"

"No," Dia replied. "I am progressing with the wedding dress, and Mr. Folkes has spoken with Mr. Lloyd about the ceremony. He and Mary Ann are eager to set a date for the wedding."

"Mr. Folkes, the papa, has offered a room in his flat to them," Mrs. Carlisle reminded.

Dia said, "Yes, but that will leave Jane all alone, and the girls say their mother cannot like that."

"Of course not," replied Pond firmly. "Jane would be lonely. Besides, we cannot be responsible for her—at least, not as your mama and I together can watch over you, Dia."

Dia rewarded him with a slight smile. She wished she could say flatly that sometimes his supervision—his lack of trust—was oppressive.

Mr. Pond, having put on his hat, bade them good-bye and went off on unspecified business. For a while, he roamed the neighborhood, watching for rental signs. Then, having found none, he made his way to a favorite pub, where he could enjoy coffee and scan the news journals. Mr. Lloyd, he thought, would not be party to any hasty nuptials in his church.

No one—not Dia, her mama, Lord Knollton, Pond, Mary Ann Froam, nor Mary Ann's sister—was in the best of spirits. Each had his or her uncertainties, yet they understood the necessity of getting on with their lives as best they could. Mary Ann, at least, had the expectation of happiness, and the viscount was buoyed by the conviction that he could do a benevolent service for the uncomplaining Miss Carlisle.

Meanwhile, Shooker, setting his lordship's dresser in order, had discovered that the mysterious gold bracelet was missing from the drawer where it had been resting, unwanted, for some weeks. What did this mean? Shooker would have liked to consult Adam, yet hesitated to do so; it had been his own secret—his and Lord Knollton's, unless his lordship had merely forgotten it. All the same, it was passing strange.

Neither servant was feeling easy as they sat across from each other at their meal that night. They did not have much to say, though the housekeeper beside them was speaking of Lady Knollton's recent tea party.

"Such a pleasure to have a lady in the house," she remarked. "I wonder when his lordship will settle on a hostess of his own. He cannot expect Lady Lydia to devote herself to him forever, though I am sure we would not like to lose her to another family."

Lord Knollton's two special servants were in perfect accord with this sentiment, even if they considered it inappropriate to discuss such matters with *her*. Their eyes met. Shooker had something to reveal . . . after they were alone . . . and so had Adam.

So often did the two men linger that their doing it this night caused no comment. When they were the last at the table, Shooker spoke. "There has been a lady's bracelet in his lordship's dresser—"

"Yes?" encouraged Adam.

"It has now gone," said the valet sepulchrally.

Adam admitted he did not understand, but added that their amiable employer had not been "himself" this day.

"True," agreed Mr. Shooker, feeling some comfort in sharing anxiety.

"We made a call on Miss Carlisle this midday, and his lordship came away looking glum."

"No!" said Shooker softly but emphatically. "Is it possible he *made an offer and was refused?*"

Adam replied judiciously "It's possible, but I cannot think any lady would refuse him." He went on quickly to admit that he knew Shooker did not think an Unknown was good enough for a viscount, but it was his opinion that Miss C was a very sweet lady, besides being beautiful. "Though she does not seem to realize how beautiful."

"You are not one to judge," Shooker objected.

"I've eyes, haven't I? And ears. She never says an ugly word. Do you want a Society female without a brain in her head?"

Shooker admitted he did not.

Maids came into the dining hall at that point, so the men separated, and Shooker went up to his master's chamber to see that the chambermaids had set all in order, with the bed neatly turned down, although the top drawer of his lordship's dresser seemed slightly askew.

He drew it out and saw the mysterious gold bracelet had been returned to its nest among the cuff buttons.

Time to lay this fact before Adam, Shooker decided, somewhat troubled. Since Lord and Lady Knollton had gone off to Almack's in a closed carriage, with Wally driving, he might catch Adam in his room above the stable. He put on a hat, because he always wore one when venturing out during his free time, and went through a rear door to reach the mews.

Adam was there, perched in an open upper window, chewing on a cold cigar. No sparks were permitted in his lordship's stable.

"Evening, Shooker," he said, having removed the cigar, so as to speak plainly. "Come in. What is on your mind?"

"Same thing as at supper," Mr. Shooker replied, "but a bit of a mystery since we last spoke. The bracelet is back where it was."

They eyed one another.

"For some time," began the valet, "there has been this strange bracelet in his lordship's drawer—not grand enough for Lady Lydia."

"For little Lady Sara?" suggested Adam. "She's having a birthday soon."

Shooker said he had at first thought that, but decided it was too large, too heavy for the child.

"And not grand enough for a—?"

"No," responded the valet. "No jewels, just gold links." They understood each other. "Is it possible he took it to Miss Carlisle and she wouldn't have it? You know her better than I."

Adam could not resist saying that Mr. Shooker did not know her at all. "I haven't had me eye on them every minute—though when I haven't, her mama has, but I can swear to one thing, she's a gentle lady through and through. No 'arrangements' for her, no sir!"

"If—" began the valet. "If his lordship should go so far as to make her an offer of marriage, do you think she would agree?"

Adam leaned back and held up his cold cigar to study it. "If—mind, I say *if*—she thought she was hearing an honest-to-God offer of matrimony—well, it's my opinion she likes him, sure enough. And don't let me see you look down your nose at her, for she's a very special little lady!"

To his surprise, Shooker laughed. "All right, all right," he said. "I respect your opinion. Besides, we both want his lordship to be happy . . . and he's an unhappy man this moment."

"So what do we do?" asked Adam.

"It would help," Shooker said slowly, "if we knew Lady Lydia's view, but I'll get nothing out of her maid. Could Wally know anything?"

Adam chuckled then. "Only that Little Miss made his lordship give up a comfortable seat to him, when he was hurt. I surely do wonder why the girl should have sent Our Gent packing, when he offered a modest bracelet, *if* he did do that. I feel she likes him verra well."

"Do you think," asked Mr. Shooker slowly, "that all is at an end?"

"Naw. The bracelet's back in the drawer, isn't it?"

At this, the valet beamed. "Oh, very good! Very good! Looks as if his lordship hopes to find a particular wrist for it. Even if I should feel nosy (and I *will*) I'll watch that bracelet."

Adam replied that he wished he knew what Lady Knollton knew—and thought.

Nineteen

Lady Knollton did not know what to think. Her stepson seemed oddly unlike himself. Perfectly turned out and splendidly handsome, considerate. Yet he had a serious, distracted mien and did not dance much. They had the first dance together as was planned, and she saw him lead out Mrs. Drummond Burrell later. She could not watch closely, for her own beaux were pestering her for dances, but what she could see was Francis chatting first with one patroness and then another. Young ladies languished in vain; he did not appear to notice them.

She knew nothing of gold bracelets.

But years of being a fond stepmother had taught her to sense his moods. He was unhappy.

In the carriage, when they were going home, and were snug in darkness, she said gently, "Are you going to tell me what is wrong?"

"Wrong? W-what makes you think that?" he responded.

"The flatness in your voice, for one thing. And you scarcely danced all evening."

"Well, if you must know," he said finally, "I have been thinking of Dia Carlisle. She puzzles me. So—evasive."

Catching his interest? Dia sounded clever to Lydia.

"How did you meet this girl?" she demanded.

He began slowly. "Several weeks ago I encountered her in a jeweler's shop, where she was trying to sell a gold bracelet. Hendrick's—and he doesn't buy things, you know."

Lady Knollton did not know Hendrick and whether he did or did not buy, but she nodded.

"Dia, Miss Carlisle, seemed distressed, so then—I offered to buy the bracelet—and paid her fifty pounds."

Lydia murmured, "I see. But how did you become acquainted with her and the people of Langham Court?"

"I sent Adam to follow where she went," he admitted, sheepishly. "To—to see that she and her little maid reached home safely with the money. Then, afterward, well, I called."

"And so did I," said his stepmother.

"You know, then. Pleasant folk—all the tenants of the house."

He paused, and Lydia pointed out regretfully, "But not from whom to choose a bride that would be sure to please your father."

"You mean I must not?"

As they passed a lighted flambeau, Lydia looked seriously into his eyes. "The 'must' is not whom you cannot choose, but whom you cannot be happy without. I have made a point to know this girl, and—yes, Francis, I think she is genuine— though I cannot be sure. I must ask that you allow a little more time in order to be certain. Why this girl?"

"Because she is different."

"Different? In what way?"

He hesitated. "I don't know. And it is hard to find out. I never have a private moment with her."

"Alone? Oh, Francis, surely you know that would be improper!"

He returned wryly, "I do know. What I mean is, never a word not heard by her mother—or the prudish Pond—or others of the house. It would be pleasant to speak only for her ears, to coax a response." His voice became wheedling to his stepmother's ears. "Oh, nothing really improper, Lydia. This in view of someone—anyone—who need not actually hear our conversation. How am I to know this girl, if everyone has an ear cocked, so that we must speak quiet platitudes and cannot become truly acquainted?"

Lydia at first said nothing. *All the world loves a lover,* she thought. *I am as bad as the rest.* And she could not resist this particular lover.

"All I ask," she began, "is one thing. Well, three things. Is she decent? Are you sure about loving her? Will this girl make you happy?"

"I don't *know,*" he reiterated. "She is so serene, enchanting, and not the least aware of her charm. I have to know more, Mama dear!"

Lydia took a deep breath. "Very well. I will have her for a visit to the Hall. Her mother, too, of course. You will not join us until I have formed some opinion of her amiability, her depth, her fitness for being Viscountess Knollton. After that, I will send you word to come. I cannot, of course, promise she will accept you."

"True, true," he admitted soberly. Then he suspected that her eyes were twinkling. "You are a humbug, Mama! You are not doubtful of Dia at all. Pray, introduce her to the Society of Chipping Bend, such as it is. Vicar Holt can spot a fraud, I expect."

"Not if he is as taken by her pretty face and ways as you, are! It will be interesting to see what his wife and Mrs. Quinn think."

In the morning, when Lydia had sent off a note of invitation to the Carlisles, she dressed for walking to Bond Street with her maid.

Francis sat down to a hot breakfast. He was munching thoughtfully when his butler came to say his man of business was asking to see him.

"Put him in my study," his lordship said, "and say I will be along in five minutes."

In those five minutes, he hungrily gulped down most of his breakfast, then went along to startle Mr. Hull with the glory of a brocaded dressing gown.

"Morning, Hull," said his lordship, more cheerful than he had been thirty minutes before. "Have you found a flat for Mr. Folkes?"

"Yes, my lord," said Mr. Hull, glad to have something favorable to report. "A very pleasant flat that is under restoration, so it should be spanking new in three weeks, if Mr. Folkes can wait that long. It is the other side of Oxford Street from Folkes's shop—in Soho, but only a short walk from Wells Street."

"Hum-m," murmured Knollton. "Means the ladies would have to cross Oxford traffic."

"Yes, my lord," admitted Mr. Hull, "but I crossed it twice myself this morning without being trampled by horses."

"Very well. Mr. Folkes is planning to be married as soon as he obtains a home for his wife and her sister. Tell him about this, by all means. Do not mention me, remember!"

"Yes, indeed, my lord," replied Mr. Hull. "I will let you know if Mr. Folkes takes the place."

"And I'll want to hear when the marriage is to be solemnized, and when the family will move into the new accommodations."

If Hull thought it was strange for a viscount to take such interest in a marriage, while knowing so little about the couple and their plans, he kept it to himself. Today was Thursday. If the banns were announced on the coming Sunday and on two successive Sundays, the couple could be wed in nineteen days at the soonest. Perhaps a bit soon to take possession of the flat—time to fit in a wedding journey, if they desired.

Should Lady Knollton have recognized her anguished stepson in this decisive nobleman, she would have been more confident of his future. Mr. Hull, cagey businessman though he was, had no idea of Knollton's turbulent feelings.

In a matter of hours, young Mr. Folkes had examined the flat (two sunny bedchambers, a sitting room, and a private kitchen, just as wanted), had paid a deposit, and rushed to tell his intended bride the good news.

"We will go to Rye," he said to his delighted *fiancée.* "That is the original home of my family, with *such* a view! Have you ever seen the Channel, dearest?"

Dearest had seen nothing but Stoke Poges and London. In any case, she would go anywhere with Mr. Folkes, but what, she asked, about Jane?

"It is only for a few days. We must wheedle your mama to stay until we return."

Mary Ann was dreamy with happiness, and Jane was almost the same, having no jealous feelings, and being thrilled for her sister. If it happened to one of them, why not some day to the other?

As for Folkes Senior, he was delighted to see such enthusiasm and efficiency in his son, who met with Mr. Lloyd to arrange a small morning ceremony, and wrote graciously to Mrs. Froam, urging her to attend the wedding, remain a few days with Jane while the bridal couple was at Rye, and assist in the move to the new building upon their return. Some furniture was to be included in the rental. Bit by bit, Mr. and Mrs. Robert Folkes would add more.

Already the social Season, which was of no concern to the inhabitants of Number 2, was in full swing. It was June—beautiful, sunlit June—and church bells were beginning to ring for *débutantes* who were so fortunate as to have attracted husbands satisfactory to their parents.

Saint Paul's and Saint George's would be the most popular settings for elegant weddings. All Souls, so newly finished—indeed, details were still being completed—was less "smart" and therefore less in demand. Young Mr. Folkes, in the absence of Mary Ann's widowed mother, had called upon Mr. Lloyd and designed their simple service. He and his friend, Mr. Middledore, called often for the Froam girls. Number 2 was awash with romance.

Mr. Pond pronounced Folkes to be a decent chap.

Lord Knollton did not appear, except in Dia's thoughts when she did not suppress them. As Dia completed the bridal dress and refurbished one of Jane's, adding a bit of lace to the bottom of the sleeves, she wondered how Mr. Pond could endorse Mr. Folkes, while denigrating his lordship.

In some ways the wedding was to be a very small one, with only fourteen to take part, including the Reverend Mr. Lloyd. It meant a great deal to everyone at Number 2, except the ash boy who thought it mushy. None supposed that Lord Knollton might have a concern for the matter, as he did. Even Lady Lydia knew nothing of such a minor event, so consequently did not guess that her stepson might be intensely interested. His man of business, Hull, kept him informed, and his lordship—after much argument with himself—decided to attend uninvited.

But first, there was the prospect of ladies visiting at Knoll Hall, and Lydia could not be hurried. There were arrangements to be made; she thought she might invite Julia Collingwood to come, since she already had met Dia and might make Dia feel more comfortable.

"If Julia comes to Knoll Hall," Lydia said to her stepson, "you might consider going to stay with Colly. That way, being closer to our manor, you can reach us sooner, when I send word for you to join us. The two girls seemed to take a fancy to each other."

This sounded good to his lordship. "When should I start from here?"

Lydia considered. "I will have to go ahead to make arrangements. Let me see. . . . Suppose I leave tomorrow and send the carriage back the next day for our visitors. Then allow a day on the road for them, for they will not like reckless speed. You can leave the next day for Colly's place. I will write when you are to come."

Francis said, "I think I understand. Day One you leave town, Day Three the Carlisles leave, and Day Four I leave. How long shall I have to wait with Colly? Weeks? Months?"

"Until I decide the time is right," Lydia responded sternly.

"How intimidating you are, dear Mama." He followed that with a hug, and as Lady Knollton knew nothing of gold bracelets, she foresaw no problems, no anxiety about her own part in this. Was it a mistake to receive this unknown girl (and her slightly befogged mother) at Knoll Hall? Was it encouraging them to spin impractical dreams? So far, she had seen nothing of mannerisms or grammar to give her disgust. The girl did not put herself forward obnoxiously; her mama's conversation was erratic, yet amusing. It was worth a gamble to make Francis take a sober look at what his future might entail. His happiness really mattered to Lydia. If the girl passed all tests that close acquaintance could cause, Lydia did not think she would be failing a duty to the husband with whom she had been so happy herself.

In the morning Lady Knollton sent a cordial note to Dia and her mother, inviting them to spend some time with her at Lord Knollton's manor in Gloucestershire. The number of days being unspecified left an opening for sending them home, if the visit proved unsatisfactory. "There will be no gentlemen," she wrote, "just a few ladies, possibly Julia Collingwood, if her husband can exist without her. No formal dress will be needed."

Dia was enchanted. Neither she nor her mother had spent any time outside London, and it was plain that she need have no embarrassment of confronting Francis Dubois Milne, Lord Knollton. Nor would she give the mortifying impression of *following his lordship* around the country. Truly, Lady Knollton was very considerate. Dia was prepared to love Francis's stepmother. In general, Dia liked most people, and those she liked she soon came to love; it was a quality of her nature that his lordship had sensed and to which he had been attracted. What Dia understood (if her mother did not) was that the invitation was conditional upon her and her mother's fitting smoothly into village society of Chipping Bend, Gloucestershire.

In a very few days Lady Knollton's traveling carriage with four glossy chestnuts had carried the Carlisles on the first lap to Knoll Hall. Five comfortable hours later they had reached their destination.

"Are you exhausted?" asked their hostess, coming out onto the carriage circle to welcome them cordially. She had traveled two days ahead, so she was perfectly relaxed and bright eyed. The guests were overcome by such distinguishing attention.

"Come into my sitting room at once," Lydia urged "Remove your bonnets—so tiresome. Minta will take them and your pelisses—this is Minta—and you must have revitalizing tea or wine, whichever you prefer."

Lydia led them to a cool green room, while two men in pale grey livery carried their luggage to another wing. "Julia Collingwood came yesterday," she told Dia, "but she is walking somewhere in the gardens. We were not sure when to expect you."

Mrs. Carlisle was able to say, "Such a comfortable journey. Fresh horses waiting at every stop . . ." Talking was something she readily did, though frequently on trivial matters. She was happy to accept a light, sweet wine, which had been selected for them by their wise hostess because of its being mild.

Above the mantel, here, was a portrait of a gentleman, stern of face, but mild of eye, and Lady Knollton, seeing Dia's interest in it, said, "That is my husband, fifth Viscount Knollton. Do you think he resembled Francis?" Francis was not in residence, yet evidently he was not to be forgotten.

Dia, a bit breathless, admitted she did think so.

Her mama, less inhibited, said, "Not so amiable as young Knollton."

Lady Lydia's laugh tinkled merrily. "Painted before he married *me*. I swear he was the dearest dear imaginable!"

Her ladyship began to talk then of persons they might expect to see. "My cousin, who lives with me in London, does not like to travel and chose to stay behind. I believe there is a harp recital she wishes to hear. She used to play the harp very well until the joints of her hands became gnarled. So sad. But you will be glad to see Julia Collingwood again, will you not?"

"Oh, yes," said Dia with unfeigned delight. "I enjoyed her so much when you took us to Kensington Gardens."

Lady Lydia said she believed she heard a voice now asking for them in the hall. Sure enough, Julia Collingwood joined them, to clasp Dia's hand in both of hers, saying, "How glad I am to see you again! I have told my husband that we are kindred souls—liking the blooms of Spring after damp early months."

"And the sunshine," agreed Dia warmly, having risen to greet the other girl. This was a friend unlike any she had at Number 2, although she would always be grateful for the generous spirit of the lodging house, which was the only home she had ever known. "Lady Collingwood, may I introduce my mother?"

"How do you do?" managed Mrs. Carlisle faintly, much appreciating the warmth of Julia's smile.

There was no time for more, as little Sara had appeared in the doorway, holding a doll snugly.

"Come in, dearest," said her fond mother. "Make a pretty curtsy for Mrs. Carlisle and my friend, Miss Carlisle."

Recognizing the distinction between "Mrs." and "Miss," Sara curtsied to Dia's mother, then came to Dia, holding out her doll and saying, "This is Suzanne. She came from France and does not speak English yet."

"*Bonjour*, Mademoiselle Suzanne," said Dia promptly. "What a pretty frock you have!"

"Yes, but she fell down and tore her skirt!"

"Dear me," Dia said. "So she did. Would you like me to mend the rip? I have had some experience with things like that."

Lady Sara indicated that she would like that very much, and soon the two were seated upon a sofa discussing fashions, leaving Julia and Lady Lydia to entertain Mrs. Carlisle, though it was Mrs. Carlisle who held their attention by describing at some length how clever Dia was with a needle. Fortunately, she stopped short of saying Dia made most of their clothes, only expatiating on the wedding gown soon to be put to use at All Souls Church.

Here Lady Knollton adroitly took over the conversation by saying the new church was quite unusual and asking Lady Collingwood if she had seen it.

"A pointed cone roof, above a circular porch," she was saying, just as Dia, Sara, and Mademoiselle Suzanne rose from their sofa and disappeared down the hall.

"I believe Sara thinks my visitor belongs to her!" Lady Knollton remarked with a laugh.

Julia Collingwood suggested, "Perhaps they have gone to examine the doll's wardrobe."

Whatever the reason for the departure, Lady Knollton was much struck by Dia's kindness to her daughter. Was it a case of children together? Dia was very young, Lydia knew, yet wonderfully poised in her manner with elders. She was glimpsing some of what had appealed to Francis.

Her ladyship decided it was time to send Mrs. Carlisle for a rest before dinner. Accordingly, she led the two visiting ladies to their chambers, Mrs. Carlisle being impressed by finding a private sitting room between her chamber and Dia's; they could look down into the garden that Julia Collingwood had recently explored. Though Mrs. Carlisle was essentially an urban person, preferring shop windows to bucolic vistas, she could appreciate the restful artistry of this estate.

Lady Knollton said she would find Dia and send her to join her mother. Then she led Julia across the hall to the room in which the young woman had already spent a night.

"Well, Julia, what do you think?" she asked.

"Just what I thought after two minutes walking with Miss Carlisle in Kensington Gardens. A very sweet girl, though not so sweet as to lack common sense."

"Do you mean sense to snap up a prime *parti?*"

Julia shook her head. "I do not mean worldly sense. She knows very well that she is not his social equal, but she is not ashamed of her mother or her circumstances. I like her."

"So do I," admitted Lydia ruefully. "Did you notice her kindness to Sara? I daresay she would be good to Francis."

"Isn't that what we want?"

"Yes, but her mother . . ."

"Harmless," said Julia. "Perfectly adequate manners."

"But what could we do with her? She would be lost without

her daughter to direct her thoughts. I mean, what could Francis do? Would she be a stone about his neck—fearful of Society?"

Julia said, "I am not so sure she would care enough about Society to worry over it." She thought a moment. "Now Dia— well, she seems to have a natural poise. With a diamond necklace and an elegant gown, *Lady Dia* could fit in anywhere. I mean, anywhere that matters socially. As for her mother, why not set her up with a small efficient staff at the dower house here? It is vacant, is it not?"

"Until I have to retire there," muttered Lydia gloomily.

"Oh," Julia averred, "the beaux of the *ton* will never allow that. Introduce Mrs. Carlisle to Mrs. Quinn and the vicar's wife. She will be able to walk everywhere in the village and she will adore village life."

In some surprise, Lydia replied, "I had not thought of that. I believe you are right!"

"Dia is just the sweet, pliable sort to make Francis happy, too, if you are fretting about him."

For a moment Lady Knollton was silent. She had fretted about Francis's happiness. And now she advanced another problem. "Even if we can pass Dia off well in her social life as the wife of a viscount, how can she be presented as his *fiancée?* Quite, quite unknown! He has been in such an unnatural state! It would be cruel to deny him the warm relationship such as his father had with me. But assuming he is determined to have this particular wife, how will we be able to puff her off successfully?"

Julia, who was a very clever young woman, admitted her thoughts had been running ahead. "Do you remember Colly's dear old uncle, Lord Spenlow, who lives quietly at Nottingham? Nearly immobile with gout and other ailments, but sharp mentally. He always claims Francis is the most satisfactory friend Colly has. I think I can wheedle him into lending his name as Dia's 'guardian.' It would please and amuse him to outwit Society."

Lady Knollton clasped her hands. "Just the thing! I will agree to almost anything that will make Francis happy. Let us see how things go, how Dia fits here, even how the vicar's wife and Mrs. Quinn relate to Mrs. Carlisle."

"Yes," added Julia, smiling, "and how you relate to Dia."

"I like her. Truly I do." Her ladyship sighed. "It could all blow over. We do not know Dia's feelings."

"We will see," amended Julia. Even an anxious stepmother might yield to romance.

"I have sent Francis to Collingwood for the present."

"Oh, very good!" approved Julia. "Colly will set him straight. When does he come here?"

"When I give permission."

Lydia could think of no more impediments. If Francis's romance was a true, lasting one, she could not oppose it. Besides, the years of fretting about him would be ended. She thought his father would have said the same—if he were alive to know this girl. Lady Lydia gave Julia a rueful smile and went away to find her wee daughter and the guest.

Just before the dinner hour, Lady Knollton's cousin, Miss Wetherall, arrived from Oxford to augment their number. She acknowledged the Carlisles pleasantly, and asked if Cousin Lydia would permit her to eat "in all her dirt."

Cousin Lydia would; Miss Wetherall looked neat and stylish to everyone. Her addition to the group made a change of focus, for Miss Wetherall had no suspicion of a possible future relationship of Dia to herself. Tensions were eased.

As the good weather promised to hold, the ladies decided the next day should be spent in a stroll though Chipping Bend, which was almost on the doorstep, being across the lane from the entrance to Knoll Hall. In fact, the lane at that point formed one of the two main streets of the village.

Though Mrs. Carlisle was not the energetic walker that others of the house party seemed to be, she was impelled by curiosity to join the expedition the next morning.

Immediately opposite the main gate of Knoll Hall was the village church, and next door to it was the vicar's house, from which Mrs. Holt (who had spied them) came to lead them inside the church. They entered to admire carved stalls and beams. Lady Knollton called their attention to the far end of the sanctuary, where there was a lovely stained glass window depicting a haloed shepherd and his lambs. Francis, she told them, used to think the smallest lamb was himself.

"He is large for a lamb now," she said, "but sweet natured still."

Mrs. Holt was pleased to have met the visitors before her friend and next-door neighbor, Mrs. Quinn, could do so.

Mrs. Quinn was in time to see them coming out and had snatched flowers from her blooming dooryard garden to present to Mrs. Carlisle, the eldest of the visitors.

Mrs. Carlisle was enchanted by this attention.

For a few minutes the group clustered in the garden, but masses of plants did not leave much room for seven to stand. Soon Lady Knollton was marshaling her guests to continue through the village, leaving Mrs. Holt and Mrs. Quinn behind, happy to have been invited to a tea party the next afternoon.

Then came a gentle stroll through Chipping Bend to see quaint cottages interspersed with assorted shops. Even in this small village every necessary vendor was represented, most dwelling above their shops. Other cottages were occupied, Lady Knollton said, by workers at the manor.

It was all so different from London. Dia found it utterly charming. What was best of all, and what she had missed at Langham Court, was the profusion of trees and flowers.

Twenty

As he rode north to Collingwood's estate, Lord Knollton wished he had paid attention to details when friends of his had married. Usually, a chap asked permission to address another gentleman's daughter. In this case there was no gentleman for him to approach; it would have to be Mrs. Carlisle, but how might one be serious with her? He yearned for someone to encourage him and not raise insurmountable objections.

Dia, meanwhile, had no expectations of such an honor. His lordship was quite splendid and she had been gratified by his attention, attracted to his person. Would she alienate his stepmother by encouraging his notice of herself?

Fortunately for the uncertainty of both, Lord Knollton was not too egotistical to consult his friend.

"I have seen the girl I want," he said, as soon as they were settled with mugs of excellent ale in Colly's study.

"Julia's new friend?"

"Yes. Dia. I shall want your opinion of her—though if it is negative, I intend to ignore it!"

Colly said, "Very proper attitude."

"But how do I proceed?"

"For God's sake, you don't need me to tell you! Charm her. Court her. Write a sonnet to her eyes."

"Now there I draw the line," Francis declared. "Daresay you never wrote sonnets. I seem to remember you stepped on the ruffle of Julia's dress and tore it, when you met her."

His friend grinned. "She never let's me forget *that*. But, seriously, Francis, admiration never goes amiss. And little attentions count! Think a bit—warm glances, guiding hand on her elbow, catching her eye across the room."

Francis nodded soberly. "I see. But there is one thing that bothers me." And he told Colly about buying Dia's heirloom bracelet. "I don't feel right keeping it."

"So make her a gift of it. Give it back any old time. Doesn't sound valuable."

"No, I do not suppose it is." What was fifty pounds to him? He frowned and told his friend: "I have met hundreds of girls, but not any like this one."

"In what way is she different?" asked his friend cannily, hoping Francis would reveal the seriousness of his attitude.

"Well-l, her eyes are very clear. I mean, she does not seem to be looking over your shoulder for another man while pretending to listen to you. And her manner is gentle, without being wishy-washy, you know. I think she must be like her father, who they say was a scholar, for her mind is certainly better than her mother's, though she—the mother, I mean— is pleasant in a befuddled sort of way. When I remember how protective the men of Dia's lodging house are—well, it makes me think they see her as I do, a little treasure."

"Lovesick!" declared his friend.

Francis protested, "I am not sick at all. I am saying this girl is special, even if not one of the Ten Thousand."

"And so?"

"What should I do next?"

Glad Francis had never heard him call his wife "Precious Doll" or "Kitten," Collingwood advised, "Take it easy, Knollton. You don't need me to tell you. Spend some time with her. Get to know her better. It will all work out one way or another."

"She's spending time with my stepmama now! I have been ordered to stay away until Lydia sends for me."

Colly nodded. "Yes, Julia is there with them. Seems you and I are stuck with each other. More ale?"

Meanwhile, at Knoll Hall, Lady Knollton was too busy entertaining four houseguests to wonder much how her stepson was filling his days.

The next day, after their exploration of Chipping Bend, Lydia permitted her guests to eat a lazy breakfast. Then she organized them for a tour of the rambling manor house, much enlarged and revised over one hundred and fifty years.

Though Dia was enchanted with the mellow antiquity of the most ancient parts, her parent was more impressed by the luxury added by later viscounts, including Francis's father. Both Carlisles were particularly interested to see the core of the establishment, the kitchens, and here a beaming cook was presented to them, glad of the notice, though expecting it.

"Such delicious things you are giving us!" declared Dia, who sounded convincing because she really meant what she said. "I did so enjoy that *soufflé* last night."

"Well, miss, I do have a light hand with *soufflés,*" Cook responded with entrenched modesty. She then added for her mistress's benefit, "I was a mite shorthanded last night, my lady, because our kitchen maid had to be sent to her room with a nasty cough."

"Oh," said Dia immediately, "a gentleman where I live had a most dreadful cough recently. Have you tried garlic?"

"Garlic, miss? You mean to eat?"

The attention of Lady Knollton and the other ladies was caught.

"Not exactly," said Dia. "A broth of garlic buds, simmered until it mushes up like a smooth gruel, does wonders to loosen a cough."

"Nivver say so!"

"Yes," said Dia, nodding affirmation. "It relieved Mr. Pond wonderfully." She did not say that it made the whole house reek, for she thought that unimportant, since it had done a good work on Mr. Pond's chest—the garlic and rich chicken broth, and other things.

"I'll stew some garlic for the girl," Cook promised, "as soon as the ladies has gone from my kitchen."

Strictly speaking, all her hearers understood it was Lord Knollton's kitchen, but Cook was firmly in command. No French chef here!

Lady Knollton led her four guests from the kitchen by way of a door to the kitchen garden, where they dutifully admired rows of herbs and spice plants. From there they moved to flower gardens, which Julia Collingwood and Dia especially admired.

Little Lady Sara came running from the house to take Dia's hand and lead her to a birdbath.

"See this stone?" the child asked. "This is where Suzanne and I tripped, so she fell and tore her dress."

"A spot to be cautious," Dia said solemnly. "Tomorrow let us see if your Nursie has materials with which I can mend Suzanne's frock. I shall want to visit your nursery—if I may."

"Oh, yes," Sara assured her. "When my brother Francis is here, he comes to play with me."

"Nurse says he is still part boy," explained Lydia, coming up to them. "Sometimes even my dearest husband was part boy. It is a puzzling thing about men."

The afternoon was consumed in sharing tea with the two delighted ladies from the village. Mrs. Carlisle was eager to tell them about the new All Souls Church, which she considered as belonging to herself, and she had so many opinions to exchange with them that the three were happily engrossed and had let their tea grow tepid, when a knock came at the front door and a jovial voice could be heard speaking to Lady Knollton's servant.

"Good afternoon, Lester. Ladies left any tea for me?"

Mr. Holt, the vicar, was received with a joyful welcome by the ladies of his small church and their friends. There ensued a babble of voices, which was overborne by Lady Knollton's dignified voice.

"Mrs. Carlisle, Miss Carlisle, let me make known to you our very dear vicar."

"What a pleasure!" he asserted promptly, taking Mrs. Carlisle's hand and squeezing it. Then he turned his head and saw Dia, to whom he repeated, "What a pleasure! Never saw so many beautiful ladies!" Obviously, he was an unusual clergyman, with no inhibitions.

At this point Sara came running to hurl herself against his knees and receive a hug.

He was not, thought the Carlisle ladies, in the dignified style of Mr. Lloyd of their own All Souls, though they warmed to him immediately.

What, he enquired, had brought her ladyship to Chipping Bend at this time? The Season could not be over, could it?

"Oh, we are taking a few fresh breaths," Lady Lydia said lightly. "London can be fatiguing. My cousin has been to see her mother, who was not feeling well."

"Yes," affirmed Miss Wetherall, "but I am glad to say she is better, so I am on my way back to the city. William Blake is to issue a new poem, and I do not want to miss that."

Mrs. Carlisle and her daughter had never heard of Mr. Blake. They acknowledged the name with polite nods.

"My Sara is as bonny as a poem and does not look in need of mental refreshment," the vicar remarked. It was his custom to claim the children of the village his; Lady Knollton took no offense. Though offered tea, he declined, saying he had come to fetch the superintendent of his own house. Did they know what time it was?

Then time was underscored when Sara's Nursie came to take her away for an early supper, and the three from the village rose to go.

"Our daughter, Ruth, is soon to bring our grandchild, Mary, for a visit," Mrs. Quinn told them happily. "They live so far away that we are not able to see them often."

"I am glad to hear they are coming," responded Lady Lydia graciously. "Mary must come to play with Sara one day." There was no sign of condescension in her manner. Sara would enjoy a playmate and would not be contaminated by the grandchild of a village woman who was herself welcome at Knoll Hall. Nursie would watch over them faithfully.

When the villagers had at last gone, Lady Knollton led her guests upstairs for a rest before dinner. Dia persuaded her mama to lie down. Then she went through their sitting room to her own chamber to meditate on the possibility—and excitement —and danger of seeing Viscount Knollton again.

Twenty-one

Julia Collingwood and Lydia, Lady Knollton, by unspoken agreement, met in her ladyship's boudoir to confer about a future existence for Francis.

"Do you think I must encourage Francis to an unequal marriage with this Carlisle girl?" asked Lydia Knollton in a troubled voice.

"Why not?" challenged Lady Julia. "I think you like her. I certainly do. Has he not had his choice of the *ton?*"

"Yes, but you are not his stepmother. I owe it to his father—who made me so happy—to find a proper match for him."

"Do you not like the girl?" countered Julia.

"Well, yes, I do . . . but would my lord? What do you think?"

"That he would like Dia. And Sara does, too. That counts with you, does it not?" teased Julia.

"Yes, it does. I suppose I must allow Francis to make his own choice. What if she declines the honor? Surely she will not! He is very dear—almost my own son. We are very close, you know. There does not seem to be anything wrong with Dia, except she has no social background . . . until she is known as 'Lady Knollton.' Oh, dear, that will make me a dowager for sure!"

"Not if you wed one of your beaux," Julia reminded.

"Do not force me," Lydia begged.

"Of course not. You can be the youngest and most beautiful dowager in England."

Her ladyship contrived a wan smile. "I truly want Francis to be happy," she said.

"Then let him choose his own wife," responded Julia vigorously. "Shall I write Colly to bring Francis here?"

"Very well. If you must," conceded Lady Lydia.

"After all," Julia said craftily, "Francis may have changed his mind."

"You do not think Dia is expecting him to—?"

"No, I don't. And he may not offer. Heaven knows what Colly has been telling him!"

"Oh," said Lady Lydia with a moue, "there is no doubt that Colly is telling him marriage is an enviable estate!"

Julia admitted that she and her husband had been supremely happy. "So were you with Francis's father. A good marriage is the best sort of life, isn't it?" But not, they understood, if based solely upon worldly considerations, like one's wealth and the other's position of influence, as so often was the case.

The ladies, having made a decision with clear consciences, passed a refreshing night. Next morning a courier was sent off to Mr. Collingwood with instruction from his wife to bring Francis to Knoll Hall.

At breakfast Dia told Lady Lydia that she had talked to Nursie about her idea for repairing Suzanne's frock, but Nursie had no suitable scraps. Would it be permissible for her to take Sara into the village to shop for some bits of fabric?

To Sara's delight, Lady Knollton agreed, so while the other ladies settled to a table of whist, Dia and Sara walked down to the lane, where they met the vicar coming from his house on his way to the church.

"Good morning, good morning," he said in his repetitious way. "Where are you ladies bound?"

"To the Everything Shop to purchase fabric for the repair of Suzanne's frock," Dia said.

"And who is Suzanne?" he asked, not identifying the name as belonging to one of his parishoners.

"Can you not recognize a French name?" teased Dia.

"My French doll," Sara explained seriously. "She fell down and tore her dress, so it has to be mended."

The vicar said solemnly that he understood. "Suzanne must be properly dressed for church services."

"And tea parties," added Sara.

Mr. Holt accompanied them to the door of the Everything Shop and held it open. When they had entered, the two young girls—for Dia was young, also—forgot him in their examination of materials.

"I had intended to mend the skirt," Dia said, "and then to hide the mended place with a pretty ruffled apron or a pinafore that will tie at the back with a fluffy bow. What would you think of that?"

Sara thought it was a splendid plan, for one of her own dresses had a pinafore. So they chose a sheer white muslin sprigged with white. Perhaps it would not be a *French* style, yet they felt sure that Suzanne would not be remembering the country of her birth. The small purchase was made.

On the way home, when they passed the Green Grocer, they encountered Mrs. Quinn, who reminded them that her grandchild was to come anyday now. Pleased at the idea of a playfellow, Sara skipped a bit as they continued their walk toward the manor.

No one except Lady Lydia and Lady Collingwood knew their courier would reach Lord Collingwood about noon, so all remained serene in Chipping Bend. Dia had found Julia easiest to know, easiest to talk with, but she admired the calm graciousness of the youthful dowager very much. Life here was a far cry from the coming and going of Number 2.

When Cook sent word that garlic was easing the kitchen maid considerably, Dia felt even more comfortable at Knoll Hall, unaware that Francis Dubois Milne, Viscount Knollton, would be descending upon her in fewer than twenty-four hours.

As a matter of fact, Lord Collingwood had to restrain him laughingly when the courier from Knoll Hall reached them early in the afternoon.

"Easy, easy, old fellow," Colly said. "Nothing is agreed or settled! Julia says you have Lydia's permission to come, but you must use discretion about approaching the girl. Not pounce on her. Good Lord! Must I go with you?"

"Yes, do!" approved Francis. "You must keep me calm. Were you this nervous when offering for Julia?"

"Indeed I was!" avowed Collingwood. "But you must not rush into an offer. This is an opportunity to see Miss Carlisle in a wholly different setting from London. Will she fit Knoll Hall perfectly?"

Francis said he was more interested in whether he suited her.

Colly, who privately thought a rich and comely young viscount should make any damsel swoon with delight, replied cautiously that "things" might have changed in several weeks. Privately, he would not have liked to see his friend domineered by a froward female. "You must certainly be your engaging self, old fellow, but obvious pursuit might be fatal. Ladies like wooing, you see."

Nodding, Francis said, "Yes, yes." He did not comprehend at all, for he was impatient to see Dia again and be welcomed by her, and he was wondering how it would feel to have such a delicious bundle of femininity belonging to him, though he did not admit that to Collingwood.

They agreed to start early the next morning, so as to reach Knoll Hall soon after lunch time, each taking a curricle. Colly would lead, setting a conservative pace to prevent Francis from exhausting his horses.

Also, as he had made the trip many times, Colly would know where and when to make changes, if they should need them.

"These posting houses of yours," Francis said, "will they have good horses for both of us at once?"

"I swear so," Colly answered. "I am as anxious as you to reach Chipping Bend, for I miss Julia, even though she has been gone only a few days."

Francis chuckled. "We are a sad pair, are we not?"

They fell into bed that night and slept like sheepdogs taking a well-deserved rest after herding sheep on the steep slopes above Windermere. A slight excess of wine facilitated matters.

But both were alert next morning, setting out early, each man with his valet beside him, and Colly in the lead as planned. Shooker was grateful for a gentle trot. The two servants had no idea what was in the wind, and they had long been adjusted to whims of their employers. A mile short of Knoll Hall, Colly halted midway in the road and beckoned Francis to trade places with his groom. "Listen to me, old chap," he said quietly. "Be calm, keep your head. Don't alarm the girl by an emotional approach. Might scare an inexperienced young lady."

"Right," replied Francis. "Casual manner? If you say so. Don't grab her, you mean?"

Colly said, "That's it. Keep calm."

Francis returned to his curricle, and they continued on their way.

Meanwhile, at Knoll Hall, Dia had carefully mended Suzanne's dress and cut pieces for the pinafore, watched by a remarkably patient Sara. The child did not wiggle or ask repetitive questions. Nursie assisted by picking up each scrap of muslin or thread as it fell. So engrossed were they at the rear of the house, they did not hear curricles crunching to a stop on the gravel forecourt.

The hurry of servants to the chief portal of Knoll Hall alerted Lady Knollton to what must be the arrival of his lordship. She rose, shot a significant look at Julia, and went from her green salon, where she had been sitting at cards with her cousin and Mrs. Carlisle.

Julia said a bit breathlessly, "I believe my husband has come. Please excuse me." She, too, sped from the room, leaving the other two ladies, Mrs. Carlisle and Miss Wetherall, to play four-handed whist if they thought they could do so.

"What was all that about?" asked Mrs. Carlisle, confused.

"Oh," replied Miss Wetherall, "I expect it is Julia's husband, sure enough. They have been married only about a year, so it is natural that she should be glad to see him."

It was a long time since Mrs. Carlisle had expected a visit from her husband. She could remember him fondly as a considerate spouse, but as they had never been separated (until he died), she had no understanding of reunion—unless in heaven someday.

As might be expected, Julia flew into her husband's embrace.

Francis said to his stepmother, "Where is she?"

She replied, "In the nursery with Sara. Wait—!"

But he had already started up the stairs, two at a time, and only slowed to a reasonable speed. When he reached the nursery, he scratched upon the open door and strolled in casually.

"Francie!" cried Sara, running to her brother. "Suprise!"

He scooped her up, looking over her head to Dia's astonished face. "Colly and I decided we were missing something," he said. "Good day, Nursie. What are you three ladies doing?"

"M-mending Mademoiselle Suzanne's dress," Dia answered, first pale, then turning pink. She thought she had never seen anyone so splendid as Lord Knollton—tall, in buoyant health, and brimming with good spirits. Her pulse accelerated.

He, for his part, was entranced with the domestic scene in which he found her.

With great presence of mind, Nursie had continued to gather scraps and findings. "You will be wanting to go downstairs, Miss Dia," she said calmly, taking charge of two pins.

"Yes," agreed Francis. "Collingwood is with me, Miss Carlisle. Julia will want you to meet him. Yes, monkey"—to Sara—"you can come, too."

Still holding his half sister, Lord Knollton started for the staircase. "Come along, Miss Carlisle. If you enjoy Julia, you will find her husband the best of fellows. A splendid pair!"

Lord Collingwood proved to be about Francis's size and age, though his hair was a very dark auburn. He had side whiskers of somewhat lighter red. By the time Dia and Francis had reached the lower floor, he was standing at the bottom of the steps with his arm about Julia's waist.

"Dia!" cried Julia. "This is my husband, whom you must admire, if you are to be my true friend. Call him Colly."

"Colly," repeated Dia dutifully. "How do you do? Your wife has been such a joy. Thank you for letting her come here. I am happy to have her company again." Finding her mother had followed Miss Wetherall into the hall, she continued quickly, "Mama, may I make Lord Collingwood known to you?"

Pleased with his bow, though he somehow retained a hold on his wife, Mrs. Carlisle nodded and smiled. This gathering, she thought, was getting to be quite a house party—something to tell about at Langham Court. And she was here because Lady Knollton was so friendly. She had not yet discovered that his lordship's interest in her own daughter was the motivation for Lady Lydia's inviting the Carlisles to visit Knoll Hall.

Afterward, when the Collingwoods were alone in their chamber to dress for dinner, Julia asked, "Well. What do you think?"

"Charming creature," he replied at once. "There's nothing better than to wake up to a pretty face—as I have reason to know."

Julia giggled, but commanded him to be serious. "And I have every reason to believe she is as steadfast as she is lovely."

Collingwood said, "Fine. Can we cease to worry about Francis now?" To which Julia answered seriously, "Tell him not to rush her, dearest."

Francis was telling himself the same thing. Dia had met him again without simpers. He must be very sure that she not misunderstand his intentions. She was the modest little beauty whom he had followed from Hendrick's shop; she was as appealing as ever; and—best of all—she was not repulsing him, or even evading him.

Dinner that night went pleasantly, although as host, Francis had Mrs. Carlisle on his right and Lady Collingwood on his left. Damn protocol!

Sara was not at the dinner table. Before she had been marched away by Nursie, she had begged to visit the stable with her brother in the morning. "There's a baby colt there, Francie. Do you think I—"

"Don't ask for a horse yet, puss," he had interrupted. "You will have to grow more."

After dinner Miss Wetherall displayed her usefulness by playing on a pianoforte with a good deal of skill. Eventually she drifted into familiar tunes, which united the group in song.

There had been nothing like this at Number 2.

In the morning, the viscount and his friend, Collingwood, had the breakfast parlor to themselves and partook of a stout breakfast. They did not talk a great deal, Colly wondering how soon he could take his wife home, and Francis thinking morosely that a colt was nothing to interest a young urban lady, just as a stable was no place to be conducting a courtship.

But Sara, the viscount's small sister, knew he had *promised* and his promises were good. Besides, Colly had warned him to "go slowly," at the same time that Julia had, he hoped, urged Dia to give him a chance to reveal his best nature. Obviously, his half sister, Sara, had already succeeded in making herself a friend of Dia—far more easily than he had done.

A friend?

In the long consultation that he had had with Collingwood, Colly said, more than once, that friendship between a husband and wife was a very comfortable thing.

Lord Knollton had mumbled, "Yes, yes." Instead, he was thinking how splendid it would be to hold such a lovely creature in his arms. Only with difficulty could he remember what he and other young bachelors had considered the advantages of bachelorhood. The unity of Colly and Julia and their obvious affection for each other seemed much more desirable. He forgot the friend whose wife was a nag, the one who paid more attention to his *chère amie* than to his wife, and the one whose wife talked perpetually of her ailments or spent recklessly at the gaming tables. His stepmother was not like any of those! Nor, he concluded, would Dia be.

The problem was to catch her alone.

It was a group of five to make the visit to the stable. Conversation was general, with his bailiff adding himself to the number, and two grooms, though they were better mannered than to talk to their superiors unless asked direct questions.

The newborn horse was a bay colt, all legs. "When you have grown up to a horse, Sara, my love," his lordship said firmly, "you will have a very polite mare. Meanwhile, a pony and cart, or a pony to ride, must do for you."

And Sara, who suspected that she would be able to wheedle the colt from him sooner or later, gave him a saucy grin.

"You will have your hands full with a sister like this," Colly warned. Then he swept Sara, shrieking with delight, to sit on his shoulder.

When they returned to the house, Sara was delivered to her mama in the green parlor, and the Collingwoods went up to see that their luggage was packed.

To stay indoors, Francis knew, would be to submerge Dia in the women's group.

"We have not had much of a walk," he said. "Let us stroll through the gardens." Nothing could be more proper than an open stroll, and he might be able to put a large shrub between them and the house.

Dia agreed with a nod, tongue-tied, but pleased. He did not seem alarming . . . or threatening.

Francis spoke idly of the manor and his love of it, and she admired whatever he pointed out to her. When they had turned past the sweet leaves of a bay laurel, he halted her with a touch upon her arm.

"Dia—while we are private—I wish to give you this—"

Francis reached into a pocket and brought out a bracelet that she recognized immediately. Surely, surely he was not going to offer her something so valuable!

"No, no," she whispered.

"But it is yours," he insisted, reaching for her hand.

"No," she said more loudly, recoiling. "You bought it. It is yours. I cannot accept anything so valuable."

Francis, to whom fifty pounds was a trifling sum, made another mistake, saying, "Only fifty pounds. I never missed it."

"You will not miss the bracelet either, for I will not take it back," she retorted sharply. "What sort of 'lady' do you think I am? You cannot buy me with words or money, sir!"

"Indeed," he protested, "I mean this for a gift. There are no—er—strings."

"No," she croaked because of a lump that had risen in her throat. "No strings, because I *will not* accept such a gift. I had thought—you were a gentleman, my lord, but it is now obvious what you think of me!"

"Adorable," he supplied.

"Something to be purchased?" She dashed a hand across her eyes. "Not a pretty sentiment, sir!"

If she had noticed, his lordship had turned very pale.

"You do not understand—"

"Oh, yes, I do. It is very plain that you do not consider me to be—"

"Something to be cherished? My dear, I *do.*" Had she looked into his eyes, she might have believed him, for his eyes were anxious. But her head was bent, as she tried to control her emotions.

Francis, grappling with his own problems, was becoming hot. "If I," he said forcefully, "have misunderstood you, is it not possible that you have mistaken my intent?"

The bracelet, dangling loosely from his hand, created flashes of gold light to reach her tear-filled eyes.

"Everyone warned me," she lamented in a trembling voice, dodging aside to run, zigzagging left and right, through the garden to reach the kitchen door.

Stunned, his lordship slumped upon a garden bench. How could his good deed have misfired? He had not wanted an emotional brangle, yet that is what he indubitably had got.

Dia had slowed through the herbs to catch her breath. Now she entered the building as quietly as possible and passed the kitchen to take a service hall that would lead her to the main staircase. Here a lackey came forward to offer a letter.

"This came for you, miss," he said, holding it out and wondering at her pale face.

She knew she could stay no longer in Lord Knollton's home. This letter, no matter from whom it came or what its message, could pass as an excuse to return to London.

Fortunately, Lydia suspected no base behavior from her stepson, nor emotional outburst from Dia Carlisle.

"Of course you must go, if you are wanted, my dear," her ladyship said when Dia approached her with the crushed letter in her hand. "You made the bridal gown, did you not? I am sure your friend needs you. It will be no trouble to call for the carriage at once. Ring for the maid, dear, to help you pack. Francis does not know about your letter? He will be disappointed. I do not know where he may be just now."

Francis, in a passion of desperation and impatience, was even then striking his boot with a crop, as he waited for his swiftest hack to be saddled so he could gallop after Colly's curricle, which was running ahead of his own route.

"Tell her ladyship and my valet where I have gone," he said. "I expect to return in a day or two." He would have to do that, as he was not taking even a fresh collar with him.

His lordship mounted up and went off at a gallop.

Twenty-two

As neither Lord Collingwood nor his wife had taken much luggage, they were able to stow it under their feet, and his lordship's valet was obliged to perch behind like a groom, which offended his dignity excessively.

However, the ride was not so rough for any of them, since Colly had Julia beside him (where she belonged) and did not feel speed was essential.

Lord Knollton came upon them when they had gone nearly two-thirds of the way home, so both men pulled into the next inn to refresh their throats.

As none were in a hurry, a pause would rest the horses and save having to change them.

"I have to talk to you urgently, Colly," Francis said. "We need a private room. Julia has no maid with her and would be very uncomfortable in the public room alone. She can listen."

Colly nodded and signaled the proprietor. As soon as they had sent Colly's valet to find a seat in the pub, and were themselves settled in a private room, and had ordered food, Julia said, "There is something wrong about Dia, is there not?"

Francis asked, "How did you know something was wrong?"

"It is obvious—a sweating mount and a long face. Never say—"

A servant came then to take their orders. When he had gone away, Julia said, "Something has happened. Have you hurt that gentle girl someway?"

It was true that something unpleasant had occurred.

"Yes," admitted Francis glumly. "I do not know whether she was more hurt or angry. You see, I tried to give her the gold bracelet. It was preying on my mind, making me feel a thief—or at least a heartless male—though I cannot understand how a trinket could matter so much. I never thought of Dia Carlisle as acquisitive. The damn trinket meant nothing to me!"

"What bracelet?" demanded Julia.

At that point, waiters came with coffee and plates of chicken and hearty hunks of bread. Silence was heavy in the parlor while the servants set them about.

When they had withdrawn, Julia said militantly, "You cannot eat a mouthful until you have finished about this bracelet."

Francis shook his head. "Such a brangle! To be brief, I came upon Dia some weeks ago when she was trying to sell a gold bracelet to Hendrick, the jeweler, who does not buy, only sells. She seemed distressed, so I made an offer of fifty pounds. You know, Colly. I mentioned it to you, and you thought I should return it to her. In short, I bought the damned thing. Then, when I tried to return it today, she flew up in the boughs and accused me of God knows what. It was a very unreasonable interview this morning!"

"Oh, Francis, Francis!" exclaimed Julia. "If you had just asked me, I would have told you what to expect."

Francis shot a glance at his friend. "Speak up, Colly. Tell your wife that you said I should give Dia the damn thing. What use had I for it? And what was fifty pounds to me?"

"Well," said Julia sharply, "I can tell you what it meant to her—an insult at the least—a bribe at the worst."

Her husband said placatingly, "Well now, my dear, Francis was not trying to—er—mislead the girl. The thing was hers. He meant to make a gentlemanly gesture of returning her possession. What do fifty pounds matter?"

"Cork-brained!" Julia retorted. "You should realize they matter very much to someone who lives gallantly—and uncomplaining—in a lodging house on a side street of London!"

"What the devil does Number 2 have to do with this?" objected Francis.

"Yes, what, Julia?" asked Colly in support of Francis.

She looked scathingly at her beloved and at his childhood friend. "Nothing, of course. We are talking of an inexperienced girl who has never had flowery verbal nonsense showered on her. You will find she does not understand the nuances of 'give' and 'accept' in Prince George's circle! Her reaction should make plain her own code of what is proper."

Lord Knollton and Lord Collingwood stared at each other in obvious shock. Francis muttered, "I did not mean—I only meant to give her pleasure. I'm a fool, Colly, and it appears you were—"

"Wrong," his friend admitted. "I did say to give the girl her bracelet. She was sure to be missing it."

Allowing guilt to set in, Julia then let them quaff scorching coffee, which brought out beads of sweat on their brows—although she supposed the cause might be remorse and not heat.

The two friends exchanged looks, and Francis said, "What's to be done?"

Concealing a smile, Julia asked lightly if Francis still intended to make Dia an offer of marriage.

"Yes," he admitted. "But to whom do I apply? Dia never let me say a word. Dammit, she ran away from me! I cannot like to get my head blown off again. If I applied to Mrs. Carlisle, nothing would be clearly understood by her. It would be a worse muddle! And Dia has no father. No brother, either. Who else is there to deal with such a matter?"

Julia smiled mischievously, letting them debate the matter.

Not very hopefully, Colly said, "You don't suppose Lady Lydia could approach the girl—explain the misunderstanding—?"

Francis groaned. "Mama? She would say I must mend my own fences."

"Doesn't she like Dia? Invited her to visit, didn't she? Let's have some ale."

"What has ale to do with your thinking processes?" Francis objected, momentarily distracted.

His friend replied somberly, "Dulls pain."

Julia set them straight. "Dullards need nothing more to lull their wits. It is a simple matter. Approach Mr. Pond."

Fortunately, they had a private parlor, for each man barked, "Pond!" and Francis groaned that Pond hated him. "His interference and cold attitude to me are the beginning of all this trouble," he reminded the others.

Julia said, "But whose advice is Dia more likely to take? She trusts him as she would a father."

"My God!" moaned Francis, though whether in alarm or in disagreement was not clear.

"If the offer is made to *him,*" Julia pointed out, "he must know it is seriously meant."

"Cannot vilify me then? Must agree, you think?"

"Well, he is sure to realize she will never get an offer equally good," Julia asserted with conviction. "This is no reflection on that sweet girl. You must know that single viscounts are not so numerous on the London scene."

Colly cleared his throat. "I do not mean to cause trouble," he mentioned hesitantly, "but is Pond likely to oppose this match on any other grounds—such as your not valuing this girl as much as he wishes to see her valued? Could he view you as merely acquisitive, wanting a fine possession to display to the *ton?*"

"Never fear," Lord Knollton assured him. "I will convince the interfering old marplot. Where can I ask him to meet me? There is no privacy at Langham Court. Would he be willing to come to my house on Upper Brook, or should I suggest my club?"

"You must choose, Francis," Julia told him with a pixie smile. "It is to be the stage for your performance."

"Boodle's then," he said.

That Mr. Pond or Miss Carlisle might refuse an offer from the aristocracy did not occur to Francis's friends. Promising to join the viscount in London before long, Lord and Lady Collingwood resumed their journey, his lordship's valet clinging to the groom's perch in humiliation (though too faithful to plot rebellion).

Francis returned leisurely to Chipping Bend, halting once along the way to rest his mount. Without his friends to encourage him, he began to have doubts about how Mr. Pond would reply to him. And Dia? Had he offended her unforgivably? Had she rejected him forever? At least, as far as he knew, there was no rival on the scene.

Of another thing he was sure: No other young lady that he had met would suit him so well for a lifetime. Tantrums or not.

He returned his weary hack to the stable at Knoll Hall, ordered out his curricle, and shouted in the service door of the house for Shooker to come down in five minutes with his luggage. Orders like these were nothing new to his lordship's servants, who actually thrived on drama.

At almost this same time, Dia and her mother were nearing London, Mrs. Carlisle having dozed off, and Dia slumping in exhaustion from the effort to make trivial conversation that avoided all mention of lords, ladies, manors, and romantic dreams.

Not many hours after this, Francis reached and entered his town house, sending his exhausted valet strictly to bed, dragging off his driving gloves, demanding, "Brandy at once," and striding to his particular sanctum. What did one write to an interfering nonfather?

> *Sir:*
>
> *I will be most appreciative if you will join me at ten on Friday morning at my club, Boodle's, for a quiet conversation regarding one in whom you and I have a mutual interest.*

That should not get the fellow's dander up, Francis thought, reading over the note and sealing it with a wafer. He addressed the missive to Mr. Pond, then called a lackey to deliver it at Number 2 of Langham Court. Would Pond obey the summons? As soon as the note had gone, Francis wondered if he should have been more conciliating or less demanding or more assured—supplying hints of mutual satisfaction. Well, two days later he would know.

And as he had hoped, Mr. Pond made no mention to Dia of this communication. It sounded quite civil to the cloth merchant—almost cordial. He had his opinions of nobility, he did, yet there was nothing in the note to offend him. And if a glittering match could be forged for Dia, he was willing and eager to do his damnedest for the girl. This letter could not mean a slip on the shoulder for Dia. It was too polite. Too open.

But Pond would keep his thoughts secret until he heard what Lord Knollton had to say. Mr. Pond was capable of strong words himself and no one intimidated him.

On Friday the two men met, both being as courteous as was possible in view of the differences in station. His lordship spoke of his "admiration" and "esteem" and desire to honor Miss Carlisle as his wife. The word quite dazzled Pond, who nodded solemnly and waited to hear more.

"It is my intention to settle twenty thousand pounds upon her, and of course I will make arrangements for her in my will," the viscount said. He was speaking to a business man, though one whose best sales had never reached such heights.

"Er," murmured Mr. Pond, "very proper, I believe, though what her sentiments may be, I cannot promise. She arrived home quite—er—distraught."

His lordship nodded and said the misunderstanding was entirely his fault, which he hoped to rectify in a private interview with the young lady, if Mr. Pond would give permission.

Dia's substitute father was pleased to do so. "I cannot promise her response," he warned, though he could not suppose the girl would be able to resist the young noble facing him. His hair was a dark gold, his mouth curved into a beguiling smile, and his eyes met one honestly. His nobility might have been inherited. What Mr. Pond thought even better was an amiable nature. "I will speak seriously to Dia, and will let you know when—if—you may call," he said.

Francis, happily assuming he soon might plead his suit to the adorable creature who had occupied his thoughts for weeks, stretched out his hand to take Mr. Pond's. "Thank you, sir! Indeed, I must call you the best of fellows—"

"I promise nothing," Mr. Pond warned hastily, though in his heart he did not think Dia would be able to resist this handsome gentleman, who spoke so warmly of her and shook hands so genially with himself. "I will send a note to your home, m'lord, when Dia assures me that you are welcome to come."

Lord Knollton offered a glass of celebratory wine, but Mr. Pond declined with a smile and bowed from the room. He could scarcely wait to tell Mr. Whipple the good news; nevertheless, he was obliged to control his pleasure, for it would be Dia's news to relate when she wished to do so.

At Number 2, Pond found Dia alone in the sitting room of the Carlisles' suite; her mother had gone to the cellar to pester Cook with trivial questions about the freshness of eggs.

"My dear girl," he said, seizing the private moment, "will you feel honored to learn that I have had an offer for your hand? What do you say to his lordship, Viscount Knollton?"

Dia stared at him, blanching in alarm. "Oh, surely not!" she exclaimed.

"Truly, my dear. I have had it from his own lips. It would be very fine to be the wife of this young man—but only if you can find room in your heart for him. I see you are quite—dazzled, perhaps? Indeed, to bring this news is exhilarating for me also!"

A searching look at him convinced Dia that Mr. Pond was indeed telling a simple truth. "I do not know what to say," she began. "My parents were so fond—happy together."

He nodded. "I know. You want fondness like that, I suppose. Well, dear girl, no one ever knows what another's marriage may be. You may be equally happy with Knollton, in a different way.

Only say now that I may tell his lordship to come in person tomorrow to receive your answer."

"But Mama—" began Dia.

"Answer Knollton from your heart," Mr. Pond advised. "I have had to alter my own attitude in a hurry, for his lordship has convinced me of his devotion. Indeed, to bring this news is exhilarating for *me* also! Do you like him, dear?' '"

To say no would be a falsehood. "I do not know what to say," she began again.

"Only that I may tell his lordship to come in person tomorrow to receive your answer."

"But Mama—" Dia repeated.

"Answer Knollton first," Mr. Pond advised. "I will undertake to propel your mother on a walk to see a new house being built on Duchess Street, so you will have a short time of privacy with his lordship. He is entitled to that, I think, whatever you may say to him; and if it is yes or no, none need hear or even know."

Dia gave her old friend an enthusiastic hug, the sentiment of which he understood perfectly. He did not doubt that Dia would accept his lordship; the glow of her hazel eyes revealed her heart, he thought.

Dia's mind was in a tumult. To think she had spoken to Francis so horridly! Railed at him more angrily than Pond knew. How could Francis want her, crabby Dia Carlisle, a Nobody?

"Yes, yes," she said turning crimson. "Tell him to come."

"This afternoon," Pond promised. "I will fetch your mother at three. Do urge her to walk out with me. Say you are busy sewing or something."

He patted her cheek lovingly and went away to notify his lordship of an important appointment at exactly ten minutes *past* three.

Dia fled to her little back room to splash water on her cheeks and subdue the heat in them.

Twenty-three

There was barely time for Dia to cool her flushed face with a damp cloth and strip off her dress before her mother had plodded up from the cellar and was calling her.

"I am here, in my room, Mama," she replied, sticking her head around the door. "I felt shabby, so I am putting on another frock, the white that you prefer."

"White is so suitable for young ladies," her mother approved, coming to help with buttons up the back. "I met Mr. Pond in the hall and he wants me to walk to Duchess Street with him to see a new house—though why I cannot imagine. As if I would move from here!"

"Well, it is a fine day for walking," Dia encouraged, "and you will see something other than four walls. Mr. Pond is considerate of everyone. Shall you want to change?"

"Yes," replied her mother, "but I will wash my face before putting on something fresh. It was warm in the kitchen. Cook has the oven heated up for something or other."

Wondering how Mr. Pond was to let his lordship know when to come, but relying on him to do so, Dia brushed her hair violently and then examined herself in the mirror. One should be at her best to receive—oh! was it possible?—a splendid offer! For a moment she thought perhaps she should refuse his addresses, so he would not disgrace his noble name . . . but if he cared deeply, should she not match her wishes to his?

Mr. Pond had solved his problem very easily by sending the

ash boy to run with a note. He was a responsible youngster, not one to loiter. Upper Brook street was well within his range, and his lordship was waiting for a signal.

"I see you are prepared," Dia said to her mother a bit later, upon joining her in their parlor. "It seems a fine day for walking."

Mrs. Carlisle asked, "Why not come with us?"

"Because I was not invited," teased Dia. "He wanted you."

Very promptly at three Mr. Pond knocked at their door, then opened it himself, for it was not locked. "What? What?" he exclaimed archly. "Not keeping me waiting? That is a good beginning. Come along, Mrs. Carlisle. I have an interesting house to show you."

"Do not think you can talk me into moving to a different place," Dia heard her mother say. Good weather and Mr. Pond's jolly spirit had won Mrs. Carlisle completely. She went off with him like a lamb, baaing her pleasure that the dreary days of winter had gone.

Ten minutes later Francis, Lord Knollton, tapped gently, turned the knob, and entered. Dia was twice as enticing as he had remembered! He shut the door, took two steps forward, and held out his arms.

Rosy as a setting sun, Dia walked right into them.

"Darling girl, I never meant to hurt you," he said huskily.

"I was a s-silly girl," she mumbled against his chest.

"Well, then," he continued, with greater assurance, "raise you head so I can—"

But she had done so, and he *could*—that is, could kiss her. Several times, with increasing ardor. They lost track of time for a few minutes, until Knollton lifted his head to catch his breath. "I feel," he said tenderly, "like raising flags and firing off cannons!"

"I think you have done so," she whispered.

Francis eased his hold enough to lean back slightly to have a more complete view of her. "Yes, but there are more to come. Are you going to marry me?"

"You haven't asked me to do so," she countered.

"Shameful! Behaving with so much depravity and *not* bespoke! Well, there is only one thing to do—we must wed. I take it you are willing."

Dia said, "Yes."

"Madam," he declared, "we are betrothed! Propriety and Mr. Pond will not allow me to stay much longer, I fear. Shall I send notices to the journals tomorrow?"

But at this, Dia drew back a trifle. "Please may I have a few more days of privacy? Today is Friday. Only three more days until the wedding of Mary Ann and Mr. Folkes. It would be selfish of me to detract from their wedding by calling attention to my own."

"Your wedding is mine, too," he reminded. "Have I some right to an opinion?"

"Yes, but I think the service for a viscount must be much more grand and glorified than the marriage of Mary Ann and Mr. Folkes, in which only fourteen persons will take part. Your mother will expect more than that for her son," she pointed out as reasonably as she was able, when her inclination was to cast reason to the winds.

His lordship demonstrated that kisses should arrange everything. "You agree with me . . . hum?"

Of course she did agree, not wanting the precious moment to end. Her cheeks were warm and her eyes languorous, melting; yet feeling too much submission might be a mistake in the long run, she managed to say, "Is it not the custom for the bride to set the date? Let us keep our secret until Mary Ann is safely wedded and gone off to Rye. Just four more days. Mary Ann should have her wedding without comparisons."

Francis submitted with a sigh. "As soon as that marriage is performed—" he began.

"As soon as they have gone," Dia corrected, "you can tell whomever you wish."

"But my stepmother?" he asked.

Dia nodded her head against his chest. "Yes," she conceded,

"you will want her to know. But please! No one else. I cannot let Mama know for fear she will tell the world at once."

She could feel laughter rumbling in him. "Our secret only . . . until Mr. and Mrs. Froam drive off!" he agreed.

When he had gone, Dia stood momentarily with her hands to her hot cheeks. From depression she had soared to unimagined heights, and any minute her mother would be returning, so she would have to greet her with her customary calm. That would be difficult enough, but Mr. Pond would be coming, too, and how could she keep him from discerning her rapture?

The thought had scarcely gone through her mind when she heard the outer door wheeze open. Another part of a minute and both had entered the Carlisles' parlor.

"You should have gone with us, Dia," said Mr. Pond outrageously in his normal voice. "We had a pleasant stroll."

Mrs. Carlisle agreed. "Yes, Dia. The sun was just right. The new house looks to be pleasing when finished. It faces on Duchess Street, so it will have more view than we do, but less privacy. Mr. Pond has not convinced me of a need to move."

"Oh, I do not suggest a change," he said mildly. "Number 2 is snug enough. My main purpose in walking there was to provide your mama with fresh air."

What a fib!

"Mr. Pond," Dia declared roundly, "is as wily as a fox! Shall I make tea for us?"

But Pond said he had other matters that needed his attention. "We will meet again for our evening meal, will we not?"

Dia was longing to call him "a wicked manipulator," though he had schemed for her benefit, so she said mildly, "We both have many good deeds of Mr. Pond to thank him for. I am sure Mama enjoyed her walk."

The gentleman inclined his head, winked when Mrs. Carlisle's head was turned, and said ponderously, "My pleasure."

Never had he seemed more of an angel in disguise.

Left to themselves, Mrs. Carlisle settled in her favorite chair to watch the courtyard, while Dia took up a book and sat without seeing a word, though it kept her mama from asking questions. The newly betrothed young lady was scarcely conscious of what was happening around her.

Had Francis gone directly to his stepmama? What was he saying to her now?

There were sounds of the Froam girls entering from outside, and then Mr. Folkes's voice saying, "Why must I leave now?"

To which Mary Ann was heard to reply, "Because we cannot descend on the Carlisle parlor *again*. Besides, Jane and I have dozen of things to do."

"Mercy, yes! Mending and packing and heaven knows what else," Jane said.

There was a pause, while Jane watched young Mr. Folkes kiss her sister's hand and squeeze it. Both girls sighed, though that could not be heard in the Carlisle flat.

"Just three more days—and a fourth to reach Rye." Mr. Folkes reminded them.

In suite A, neither Carlisle lady paid much attention, Mrs. Carlisle being occupied with the empty courtyard, and Dia wondering if Francis was revealing all to Lady Knollton at this moment.

Her ladyship was, indeed, hearing Francis's outpouring of delight. He seemed truly happy, and she hoped she had not been unwise to encourage such a connection.

They laid some plans of introducing Dia to some of their titled friends. Lord Spenlow had to be approached about his imaginary "guardianship" of a girl he had never known existed. Francis was unwilling to take the necessary days to reach his lordship at Nottingham, so declared he would write the gentleman such a letter as to wrench his heart. He did not have Dia's permission for a revelation to Lord Spenlow, yet he was so sure of her as to believe that she would not mind.

Saturday morning Mrs. Carlisle was honored with a note from Lady Knollton, inviting her for an afternoon drive in Hyde Park. A footman was waiting for the response of Mrs. Carlisle, who accepted happily.

Wondering what might or what might not be said between the two mamas, Dia watched her parent go off that afternoon to join the barouche waiting in Langham Street. From this jaunt Mrs. Carlisle returned in good spirits, her visit to Knoll Hall having put her at ease with the elegant lady, whose two additional passengers were perfectly respectable, with minor titles of "honorable," though hardly so elevated as to doubt Mrs. Carlisle's antecedents.

The banns for Miss Froam and Mr. Folkes were read on three Sundays, the one on the morrow being last of all. Their marriage would take place the next day after that. Excitement ran high at Number 2.

Mrs. Froam arrived alone on Saturday, it being understood in the widow's family that her three younger children would have to meet their new brother another time. There were not funds enough for them to travel, nor was there room in Mary Ann's chamber for them to sleep. Miss Docking provided a trundle bed, and no one asked which Froam lady would use it. Their general good spirits made everything seem easy and satisfactory.

Cook kept pots of water boiling constantly for both bathing and tea. Even she expected to attend the great (though small) event, leaving the ash boy in charge of coals.

To accommodate Mr. Lloyd's schedule, as well as to allow the bridal pair daylight for travel to Rye, the hour of half after ten was chosen. James Middledore came at nine to fetch Mary Ann's small trunk; it was his assigned duty to see it set upon the post chaise that would carry the newly wedded couple on their trip.

Then, on a perfect, gilded Monday morning fit for lovers, Mr. Folkes, his son, and the groom's friend, James Middledore, collected everyone from Number 2 for the short walk to All Souls Church. Mr. Folkes, who had abandoned his commercial dignity to rejoice openly, insisted that Mrs. Froam should lead their "parade" with him. They were followed by a radiant Mary Ann, looking like a flower in the flounced pink dress that Dia had made; she was escorted by young Mr. Folkes, seeming alternately besotted with love or tenderly serious. Every now and then, when he bent his head to have a view beneath the brim of her pink-trimmed bonnet, he was rather heedless of his steps. It was unplanned, but James Middledore seized Jane's elbow to draw her into line with utmost gallantry, and Mr. Pond offered am arm to Mrs. Carlisle, which allowed Mr. Whipple the pleasure of escorting Dia.

No particular plan had been made, but it fell out nicely. Miss Docking (without her apron) was quite dignified in a grey gown with white ruches about throat and wrists; she marshaled Cory and Cook, both shy with others of the group, not venturing a word, not even to each other.

When they spilled from the court onto Langham Street, passersby stepped aside with smiles, recognizing a bridal procession, if not one walking down an aisle.

Mary Ann and Robert could have asked no more.

Happily, all entered by a side door with a subdued sort of piety and intense interest to gather before Mr. Lloyd. Only three of the thirteen had ever been wed; it was a poignant time for them, but the obvious glow of the bride and groom set a mood of joy. Only the poor waif, Cory, felt a brief moment of sadness . . . until she reminded herself that there was always hope. And had she not found a safe harbor at Number 2?

Dia, in anticipation of joy to come her way—though probably bought with a greater and more daunting ceremony than this—heard every word, every challenge and promise as if engraved on her own heart. She had not seen Lord Knollton sitting in a far back pew.

The words of the service were familiar and sweet, impelling Miss Docking to wipe her eyes and smile beatifically at the same time.

After speaking of the sanctity of marriage, and after hearing the vows, and pronouncing Robert and Mary Ann to be husband and wife, Mr. Lloyd led the bridal pair into the vestry, which was as yet unfinished—so recently had All Souls been built—

but it held the register, which the couple signed, Mary Ann writing her maiden name for the last time. Then they returned to the sanctuary to be joyfully received and embraced by the small group of friends and family. All participants, even the least emotional ones, were truly touched.

As Mr. Lloyd had ordered the bells to be sounded, it was during this splendid music that the bridal couple led their merry troupe down the main aisle and out the front door of the church, all beginning to chatter joyfully as they clustered on the portico. Nearby the post chaise was ready for the newly wedded pair to use in galloping to Rye.

Dia, one of the last to follow the exodus, discovered Lord Knollton waiting to catch her left hand and draw her aside. The others, trailing the bride, did not notice her edging away from the group. Only Francis saw her adoring smile, returning it with a similar one of his own, while he slipped a ring onto her finger. She gasped with pleasure and dismay, but fortunately the wedding party had left them behind and spilled outdoors. Hastily twisting the ring toward her palm to conceal a confection of diamonds and emeralds, she blushed furiously, yet caressed Francis with her eyes.

He could not have been more gratified. "There!" he whispered fondly. "You cannot back out now! The announcement will appear tomorrow."

"You promised not to—" she began to protest.

His lordship smiled in an irresistible manner, said, "Day Four," tenderly, and touched his finger to his lips in a warning of discretion. Both thought no one would guess their secret, but if anyone had looked when they followed to the portico, their radiant faces gave the matter way.